MARIGOLD

HEATHER MITCHELL MANHEIM

ISBN: 978-1-09835-728-3 (printed)

IABN: 978-1-09835-729-0 (eBook)

TABLE OF CONTENTS

MARCH 28, 2027 - RUBY

Ruby rolled over and moved her head slightly to the left. The muscles on the right side of her neck were so tight and stiff; it was causing her to have another pounding headache that wound its way down her shoulders and back muscles. It was hard to tell where the headache pain ended, and the muscle pain started. All the different soreness was intertwined as one as it wove through her body. Both the little and big knots felt linked together throughout her, from head to toe, connecting dots that caused her constant discomfort and pain. She stretched as much as she could and reached above her head, barely making it the few inches needed to push the alarm clock into view: 2:47 a.m. Her stomach was queasy, and her mouth was parched and dry. She briefly considered getting up to use the restroom but was afraid she would faint if she did. She tried to fall back asleep, but sleep didn't come easily these days. The rest she got was fitful, and it wasn't long before Ruby was looking at the clock again: 3:05 a.m. Nausea or not, she had to go to the restroom. Her stomach cramped intensely. The pain was shooting arrows through her stomach and lower abdomen. It felt as if perhaps an old, knotted oak tree had somehow taken root in her stomach, and it was growing its twisted roots through her intestines. She pulled herself to the edge of the bed and got up slowly, using the side of the wall to steady herself. She took two steps before she collapsed into a balled-up heap on the floor. After a few minutes, she slowly pulled herself up and attempted her early morning trek again, but quickly, her body gave way under her, and she slumped against the wall before sliding down to the floor. On her third try, she decided it was best to crawl to the bathroom, or she would never make it there.

After she used the restroom, Ruby felt slightly better and pulled herself up and over from the toilet to the sink to wash her hands. She noticed the irony of washing her hands when she already had a highly infectious, incurable disease. As she stood before the mirror, she stared at her reflection. Her skin looked ashen and gray. Her complexion, once flawless and creamy, was now pockmarked and swimming with pimples. Her cheeks were gaunt, deep hollows where once she had plump, rosy little apples. The long, full light brown hair that her late husband always said reminded him of sun-kissed honey now hung in short, broken-off straggly thin strands that pasted against the edges of her damp, clammy face. She looked more like a drowned rat than a goddess blessed by the nectar of bees. Her once beautiful brown eyes were sunken in and, underneath, rimmed with dark foreboding circles. It looked as if she hadn't ever slept. They were like big dark pools of oil, and she felt like she could almost see the virus swimming in the cesspools beneath her eyes. That odd thought made her laugh at herself, something she hadn't done in a long time. She immediately wished she hadn't, though; her dry lips cracked open at the tension caused by the slight rise at the corners of her mouth, and a thin stream of crimson blood formed.

It was imminent; the next few months would bring nothing but more pain, more illness, and eventually death. Ruby slowly moved her thin, emaciated hand over her belly. Her only hope was that she'd be able to hold onto the frail, delicate threads of life she clung to until her baby was born. She internally questioned herself why this was her wish since once her baby was out, the poor soul would suffer the same fate. That was unless her daily and most fervent prayer that she and so many others prayed received an answer: that this dreaded plague would have a cure by then. Ruby knew they were working on something; the news and positive stories abounded. She didn't know if the rumors were indeed true, and if they were, how much longer it would take. But, a list of mothers were willing to subject themselves and their unborn babies to test medications, and Ruby's name was near the top of the list.

MAY 18, 2051 – DAVIS

Davis couldn't remember when President Everett took office in May of 2027. It happened twenty-four years ago when she was newly born. She had been the first infant to receive the Marigold Injection, so-called because of the inoculation medicine's golden yellow-orange hue. Depending on a person's skin tone, they took on some variation of that hue themselves. A fair-skinned recipient took on the full color in their skin, from the tips of their toes to the top of their head, for several days as it protected the said recipient from the dreaded Lombardi Plague. Darker-skinned recipients held the color in the sclera of their eyes, their nailbeds, and in some cases, their skin could look gold-flecked. The Marigold Injection was the cure to the Lombardi Plague, named because of the person who brought the pandemic to the masses.

What started as legitimate medical experimentation ended up causing a domino effect of destruction. Dr. D.W. Lombardi and his assistant, Dr. Jack Everett, worked in Dr. Lombardi's lab, experimenting on medicines to alleviate or possibly cure the common cold. However, as Dr. Everett would explain later, Dr. Lombardi's once genuine desire to help people became a mania. Dr. Lombardi started to perform bizarre experiments, and he began injecting patients with different cold viruses to try his developmental and unproven medications. When months passed without any breakthroughs, he started injecting them with several viruses at once, causing the real tragedy. After a one-week vacation, Dr. Everett walked in to find Dr. Lombardi running a series of tests on several people. Dr. Everett started to work through the logs to discover what was happening. He saw that Dr. Lombardi had infected people with things like Ebola, AIDS, and Marburg disease. Then Lombardi started to inject them with dangerous chemical compounds, sometimes mixed with other rare viruses. Dr. Everett tried valiantly to stop Dr. Lombardi, and a fight ensued. Dr. Lombardi pushed Dr. Everett into a rack of chemicals next to a lit Bunsen burner. The accident caused a massive spill and a volatile fire. One by one, like dominos, flames and explosions broke beakers and destroyed testing stations. Toxins, viruses, and noxious chemicals dissipated into the air.

Later, Dr. D.W. Lombardi and all his patients were found deceased. A lucky survivor, Dr. Everett, was located just outside the lab, suffering from smoke inhalation and minor wounds. A thorough investigation declared how overwhelmingly lucky Dr. Everett was. In the analysis of the evidence, they found he had no involvement in the crimes committed. When Dr. Everett was transported to the hospital to recuperate, the lab and surrounding areas were sanitized, cleaned, and disinfected. Burned items and ashes were disposed of properly, thinking at the time was that they had contained the virus and rare diseases. They did not know until later that ash particulates encompassed a new so-called mega virus that worked its way into the city's air and water supply. Once one person was infected, it spread like wildfire until it was a mass pandemic. It did not take long for it to leave the United States' shores and infect other countries. Those who contracted the scourge could expect, as the disease took them on a slow downward spiral in ever-increasing intensities: Extreme muscle stiffness. Insomnia. Acute migraines. Severe nausea and intestinal cramps. Pneumonia. Ulcerated skin. And eventually, as they descended deeper and deeper into the symptoms, they would welcome certain death.

When everything was at its bleakest, Dr. Everett had fully recuperated and was back at home. The young man was brilliant, just twenty-seven-years-old and well into his first year as a Doctor of Chemistry when he had started studying with Dr. D.W. Lombardi to become an expert in infectious diseases. When the trial and investigation began, the one big regret Dr. Everett said he had was not trying to stop Dr. Lombardi sooner. Even before his vacation, Dr. Everett had started to wonder about a few questionable things. However, Dr. Everett had been fond of the old doctor and had looked up to him at that time. Coupled with the fact that he didn't know the extent of Dr. Lombardi's reprehensible trials, he had kept quiet. As a dual alibi, the notebooks showed Dr. Lombardi had conducted his most sinister tests alone while Dr. Everett was on vacation. Dr. Everett was finally proven innocent of any wrongdoing. It took a while for the populace to forgive and trust Dr. Everett; however, everyone eventually realized it wasn't his fault. Helpful to redeeming his innocence was that as soon as he was able, Dr. Everett started to work posthaste to find a cure for the Lombardi Plague. By chance, he had already taken many of Dr. Lombardi's notes and binders home to study. Because of this, the preservation of much of Dr. Lombardi's work and understanding of what went right and, more importantly, what went wrong was available for research. However, nobody knew if Dr. Everett's experiments, to be done under the scrutiny of an eagle-eyed medical ethics committee, would be successful nor how long they would take. Patience wasn't just in short supply because of restlessness, but because there simply wouldn't be time to save humanity if the cure took more than a few months.

When the sitting president, President Bagen, had become infected, the nation watched with fevered anticipation—both in the physical and emotional sense. Dr. Everett was working on his vaccine, but the tests had not gone as well as people had hoped. While some symptoms could be alleviated, people were still dying at an alarming rate. When President Bagen made a speech about how doctors estimated that he only had a few weeks to live, his face was already sunken in and ashen, and his speech was coming out in short bursts between labored breaths. He didn't even make it two weeks, and the decimated nation laid their President to rest. Next in line, the Vice President didn't even make it to her turn to be president as people died out of order of the succession list, creating an odd game of political leapfrog that nobody was winning. When it got down to Mrs.

Shepard, oddly enough, the Secretary of Health and Human Services, it sufficed to say people were more than alarmed and worried about who they might end up with for POTUS. While most people had concerns above and beyond who might be president, this was additional stress added to the United States' unsure future. After Mr. Cooper, the Secretary of Homeland Security went to his final resting place; there were no more options. The United States was sans a president. With the county in flux and so many ill people, nobody knew what would become of the country or the presidential offices.

Then, a ray of sunshine beamed into the world.

Baby Davis was born. All seven pounds, four ounces, and nineteen inches entered the world screaming on April 21, 2027. Her mother had become infected with the plague, and there was an absolute certainty that baby Davis herself would be born with it. And she had been. In the short history scrapbook of her life Davis received at the state care facility she grew up in, it told of a baby girl who had been born that day. Her mother was on a list to find possible cures and happened to be the top name when labor started. Some unsuccessful tests had taken place before Davis's arrival, but a new medicine that previously tested well in lab settings was administered to Davis and her mom. Baby Davis and her mother would be the very first humans to receive the Marigold Injection and possibly be the test subjects that would hopefully show the planet a way out of inevitable extinction. As the collective world—at least what remained of it—held its breath to see if the panacea would work, baby Davis was escorted away into a private care facility and monitored by top health professionals and Dr. Everett. They had attempted to inject baby Davis's mother as well. However, Dr. Everett sadly announced that she had passed because of the virus and a difficult labor and delivery. On the brighter side of things, a week after baby Davis was born, it was reported to the world and told far and wide that the Marigold Injection had been a massive success. Results had been almost immediate in the baby girl. First, she temporarily turned a bright golden-yellow due to the medicine, and then she ceased to have any symptoms of the Lombardi Plague and was indeed found free of the virus in test after test. The world had the first patient ever to survive and be cured of the dreaded Lombardi Plague.

However, with only a handful of senators, congresspeople, and governors left in office, the nation found itself without prominent elected officials. The remaining state and federal representatives organized an emergency election almost immediately after the triumphant vaccination announcement. There were three names to choose from: Mr. Louis, a senator from Wisconsin; Mrs. Chiu, the governor of New York; and Dr. Everett of California. In a monumental election, it was a landslide decision that Dr. Everett would become president, even though at the age of twenty-seven, he was younger than the minimum age to run for president. So many people had elevated him to the role of a savior that it made him unbeatable. The resolution before the election was to return to the system that was used prior to 1804. That system directed that the runner-up in the election was to be the vice president. However, since the vast majority of votes went to President Everett and the other two candidates received so few, they decided no vice president would be appointed. Instead, every remaining politician, totaling thirty-one in total, would form one advisory committee to the president. Another new change was that the new president was elected to an eight-year term. The politicians wagered that after the annihilation that the United States had suffered, it would take a minimum of eight years, or two regular presidential terms, to rectify some of the damage and start to rebuild the country and populace. The last change was to dissolve all state lines and form one United State.

Now, twenty-four years after that historical election, Davis found herself in the audience of this momentous celebration. As the first patient to receive the vaccination that had saved her life and many others, she was included in the celebration. She was looking forward to a speech scheduled to be delivered by President Everett.

Davis shifted nervously in her seat as President Everett took to the podium. She straightened her shoulders, smoothed her glossy golden honey-blonde hair back, and put her best smile on. It wasn't difficult; it was easy. It was natural to love President Everett; he was handsome, with his dark black hair with some gray peppered in and dreamy brown eyes that always looked as if they had a great thought behind them. He was fifty-one now but not weathered and tired looking. Davis wondered if that was the yoga. President Everett was a known yoga fan and had included twenty minutes every morning in the school-aged children's curriculum. Every school day, children would line up in the schoolyard or gym and follow along with President Everett himself as a projected image assisted the children in the daily routine. President Everett also had the friendliest smile and such straight white teeth. He was known to be a good husband and father. Even his mannerisms seemed warm and inviting. He had the uncanny ability to speak to an entire audience yet make everyone feel like they were the most important one there. Davis couldn't be happier to be sitting in the audience to celebrate the anniversary of the end of the epidemic. A beautiful May day for the speech settled on the crowd. It was slightly warm, with the sun shining down and a soft breeze blowing through the trees, rustling the leaves a little as President Everett started to make his inauguration speech on the first day of his fourth unanimous election into the office of president.

"We are the people, and the people are we," said President Everett, opening his speech with the United State traditional slogan. "The anniversary of our freedom from the horrible Lombardi Pandemic has just passed. We dedicate this memorial today to the approximately two hundred and fifty million who succumbed to the virus." He paused after saying this while staff pulled a red cloth off a tall shiny black granite obelisk. Several rows of golden slashes etched into the granite gleamed. President Everett continued. "Each golden mark indicates fifty thousand souls lost. The Lombardi Plague sadly took the lives of those fellow citizens, our family members, and friends. So many lost, no corner was safe, no person left untouched.

Even those who survived thanks to the Marigold Injection had parents, siblings, and friends perish. With great courage and strength, this country picked itself up and fought back the scourge to make the world safe again. We understood we were a united people in one fight, so we erased state borders and became the United State of America, and we remain united as one. When we rebuilt ourselves into the United State, we also managed to erase crimes. Erase homelessness and disease. And advance humankind into the next level of education, health care, and humanity. And now it is my extreme pleasure to be elected for a fourth term, another eight years as not just your president, but your friend, and to again hold the office I hold so dearly and treasure. Thank you for your trust, and I look forward to continuing as the leader of this great country."

MAY 18, 2051 - QUINN

Quinn watched President Everett speak through the big screen posted in the town square as it was not possible to attend it in person. She didn't mind; she didn't even remember when the epidemic took place. Quinn was not even born yet when the United States and the rest of the world underwent the worst plague known in history. The photos she had seen were burned into her mind, though. Gaunt faces looking out with terrified, vacant eyes. Tired and worn-out nurses and doctors with hazmat suits on. There was one picture that she could never forget, one that haunted her specifically: a little boy who had died from the virus; he was maybe all of ten years old. She felt most badly about it when she thought about his small feet sticking up on the edge of his coffin. The crematorium he was taken to had run out of longer coffins. They only had a small one, for babies or tiny kids. So, they placed this little guy in his too-small coffin and just propped his feet up on the bottom edge of it.

Quinn supposed she shouldn't be too judgmental about it; the crematorium only used the coffins for funeral purposes anyhow. The Lombardi Plague victims were placed in their coffins behind a thick, triple-layer glass wall for the remaining family to file by and say their goodbyes. Mortuaries did not take any chances. Cadavers, along with their coffins, were incinerated directly following the funeral. Remotely vacuumed ashes became trapped inside double-thick steel urns. In this way, no toxins or particles from the diseased victims could escape into the air. They took every precaution to contain the pestilence.

Quinn learned all this at school. They had a mandatory class in second grade about it all. Back then, she reminded herself that she loved President Everett. She had thought of him as a hip fatherly type, kind, and of service to the people. Quinn now watched President Everett with cautious admiration, almost because he seemed too good, too perfect. It was like staring at something you didn't want to see. It reminded her of a movie she had seen in one of her school classes. The film showed hungry citizens lined up against cold looking brick walls, waiting for food handouts from the government. Some were falling against the walls, barely able to stand up. It made her sick to look at it, but she also couldn't help but look at it. She had some kind of fascination with it, even though she hated to admit that. She couldn't help but wonder if staring long enough would reveal the demons in President Everett's eyes. *Everybody must have one or two,* she thought. There was no way she could say it in public, but she didn't always like President Everett anymore, even though there was quite a bit that seemed likable. He looked friendly and sounded intelligent and warm. Previously, when listening to his speeches, it gave her a good, safe feeling in the pit of her stomach. Now, that feeling had begun to grow into a twisted knot of fear and anxiety every time she heard him speak. While at one time she had been proud to call herself a loyal resident of the United State, she now had questions. One of the main reasons for her new-found questioning was the compulsory event she had to attend tonight.

When a girl turned fifteen, they were considered a young lady, and they also came of age for purposes of work and as a marriage prospect. Quinn had just turned fifteen, and while not an unattractive girl, she was a bit scrawny, with a tiny body: breasts, hips, waist, and even neck and wrists; she was just a wisp of a girl. She had her mousy brown hair in the standard short bob-length hair everyone else had, but her round face wasn't flattered by it as she wished. Her best feature was her beautiful brown eyes. But eligible men did not care about the eyes. They cared about women who had hips wide enough that it looked like they could repopulate the world on their own. That had been the number one mandate President Everett had given the citizens—to procreate until the United State had millions of citizens again. Admittedly, they were getting there.

A girl couldn't marry until she was sixteen, but at fifteen, girls needed to attend mandatory events hosted by the government to be seen by eligible husbands. Well, "eligible" was decided by the government. These were all men who were higher in the government or business establishments. If Quinn had the bad luck, like her friend Adams, who fell in love with a farmer, chances were, she'd never get to marry them. Men that worked in fields or with machinery married the "leftover" women, those who were not matched by twenty. Quinn struggled with the fact she may have to marry someone she did not love. Events for the "leftovers" were far more casual; you even got to wear your regular tunic and pants. For the fancy Courting Event, girls had to wear a dress. The only time they could do so. A brown, tan, or dark cream dress checked out from the Pods. She hated wearing a dress, but she was required to wear one. These events were obligatory, and if she got caught skipping it, there would be trouble for her. Quinn walked into the ample, open space. By day, a local high school gym, by evening, an overwrought dating ritual.

Quinn, being fifteen, was recently done with school and waiting for a work assignment. Jobs varied depending on if someone was selected to marry and, if she was, to whom. The rumor by men went that most women got assigned to "cushy" jobs in offices. Fetching the inexplicable four-ounce coffee, limited to one a day and sans sugar or cream—that the executives were allowed every day. They set up the VidCom for oh-so-important meetings. In reality, the real job was babysitter/ego-inflator/confidence booster, and sometimes paramour.

Getting her game face on, she looked around the gym when she walked in. Light infiltrated the space, which very much looked like sunlight despite it being evening. The walls were a creamy ivory color but somehow escaped a scuff or even a particle of dust. The decorations, the tablecloths, and cutouts of stars dangling from the ceiling were all black. A beautiful gold ribbon that looked spun from real gold framed and held each star and the remaining ribbon hung down past the bottom of the stars. Adorning the bottom part of the ribbon were several smaller cascading gold stars that sparkled in the light. Beautiful golden birds gracefully circled and lightly chirped overhead. They had long golden tails—similar to a peacock's tail but all golden and wispier and more delicate. They must have been computer-generated because Quinn never saw anything remotely like that in the wild, zoos, or even books she had read about animals. A sleek redwood floor would be their dance floor for the evening. She almost choked when she saw the cardboard cutout you could take a picture with—a victorious looking President Everett holding a syringe filled with shining Marigold Injection elixir.

That was a very much unneeded addition to the party, she thought.

Quinn didn't love the events, to say the least, especially when this particular older man, Namaguchi, would look or rather, it seemed, leer at her. She had only attended one Courting Event before this one. Her first one had yielded no Inquiries of Interest, the official form a man would submit when he was interested in meeting a young lady. In effect, it was a proposal. For high ranking officials, once they turned in an Inquiry of Interest, it went directly to President Everett himself for the stamp of approval. For lesser ranking officials, Security Patrol Guards, and business people, the local officials gave them yay or nay. A no was rarely given to any man on his Inquiry form unless there was a specific reason to give. For instance, when Baxter wanted to marry Olson, he was given a "no". It was because Baxter's father went directly to the city officials and said he wanted to marry Olson himself and that his son had gone above his head. So, the Inquiry was changed, and the comely Ms. Olson became the bride to the elder Baxter, twenty-eight years her senior, and the husband to seven other wives. As more men had perished in the Lombardi Plague, women outnumbered men as much as ten to one in some areas, so men were allowed to take more than one wife.

After the "yes" stamp was on an Inquiry of Interest, the form went to the parents or guardian of the young lady. Then, along with her parents or guardian, the girl would go to the resident Pod counselor. Everyone would discuss with the girl how lucky she was that she had been selected and by whom. The girl would also hear the top three job assignments under consideration for her. She then had twenty-four hours to discuss with anyone she wished if this was a marriage she wanted to enter. But, as Quinn understood, it was a decision in name only. Multiple stories floated around about women who turned down proposals. They went missing or ended up going from a prospective job of an office assistant to someplace like the garbage fields. Even if they somehow managed to acquire a good job, their families and friends would most likely shun them. It was an honor to receive Inquiries and to have them approved by officials. Turning it down was almost tantamount to treason. Quinn knew all of this. She also knew it was early on in her debut, and sometimes it took a few events to get acquainted with the men, especially after the Baxter Olson Debacle, as it was known. Still, she shuddered at the idea of being inquired about by the likes of someone like Namaguchi.

Perhaps, Namaguchi had been handsome when he was younger, but it was hard for Quinn to imagine. She didn't know how old he was, but she figured he was older than her grandparents. All she knew was he intimidated and scared her. He was likely once tall, probably 5'11" if Quinn were to guess. But he was now quite stooped over with a cane to help him walk. His hair was wispy and snow-white, a hoary thin cobweb that always seemed out of sorts. Large, tired-looking bags collected under his expressionless brown eyes. He wore the standard men's uniform, a brown tunic that went slightly past his waist, a slim-legged brown khaki pant, and brown boots, the laced-up tops covering his pants' cuff. Namaguchi was part of President Everett's team and, being so, already had ten wives. Quinn would never trust him with anything. Since she had to attend the dance, she secretly hoped that she would find a suitable and nice husband—or did she? She was never quite sure what she wanted on that front. It was fun to think that there might be a husband of her dreams out there. But she also felt like she wasn't quite ready to get married and start having babies. Quinn tried to stuff it in the back of her mind. Typically, she would socialize with girls around her age at any event or gathering. But, considering what was expected of her tonight, she was in a sour mood, feeling tired and overwhelmed. For some reason, she felt a deep sense of foreboding. So, when she entered the dance floor's central area, she quickly surveyed the room and saw a black and gold decorative curtain held out about five feet from the back wall. Quinn went behind the curtain with a chair that she found on the way, putting it back there as quickly as possible, and then lowered herself into it, making herself as little as she possibly could.

Quinn was deep in thought, so deep that she didn't see the shadow that lurked behind her. She didn't notice until the body moved directly behind her into the little available light that was there and a weathered, veiny hand with knobby knuckles was on her shoulder.

Oh no, she thought, *how could I be so stupid!*

Looking back at her was Namaguchi. Quickly, he pulled his hand back from her shoulder. In his other hand, he was holding out a cup of the so-called "party punch" served at these events. It wasn't like the punch in the history of food books she had read in school. That history told of all the evil things President Everett had removed from the world. One improvement President Everett touted he had made was eliminating almost all artificial ingredients, refined sugars and carbohydrates, and excessive salt from the food supply. Artificial flavorings and colors, along with tons of sugar, no longer tainted all the food. The "party punch" was water with fruit in it, the only fruit you could consume in the United State. And, there Namaguchi was with the cup. Quinn took the cup and focused on the punch for a moment, trying to gather her thoughts and find a way to escape. It was too late, though. The next thing she heard was Namaguchi in his croaky, old-man voice saying, "There you are. I've been looking for you."

AUGUST 18, 2056 - QUINN

Oh damn, thought Quinn, *not again;* she felt herself rising in the air about three inches, and she moved her fingers slowly before they became immobilized. The soft tingling of the pale blue light beams she was in gave her goosebumps, but that was the only sensation she had. Quinn immediately cleared her mind of her original thoughts. She had become an expert at thinking of nothing in particular, exactly what one had to do when being scanned. It didn't matter what she replaced her hatred of President Everett with; it only mattered that she got rid of those thoughts. The Drone Scanner held her in its beam, checking her for negative thoughts on President Everett. Reading her brain, taking her pulse—was she lying? Its job was to discover anything that might be *something.* She decided to think about the President Everett museum, a Palace dedicated to teaching people how amazing their President was—yes, that was an excellent thought to sink into her mind. The outstanding accomplishments of President Everett. Luckily it worked, and next, she was slowly being lowered to the ground, the beam loosening its grip. Her state-issued brown slip-on canvas shoes she wore touched the ground. Taking a deep breath, she slowly stood up as the scanner moved on. Running her fingers through her short brown hair and straightening out her brown tunic that went to her mid-thigh, Quinn could not believe it was five years since she had been in the city and slept in a Pod. She took it in. Everything was brown or gray. Plain. Modest. Government-issued. She looked around for a minute.

Everything was drab. Even the trees looked brown and dry. She shook her head, then started to move; she had to get to a Pod before they closed.

There were Pods spaced evenly over the county. Placed every hundred miles or so, they were large gray buildings that held thousands; in the front, large iron doors slammed shut precisely at nine in the evening to secure the inhabitants. The drawback was it also kept everyone out, whether they were a legitimate resident or not. You could take the transport busses that ran from workplaces to the Pods, but if someone was close to being late, there was no way a bus could get there on time. You just had to hope you were close enough to a Pod to run if need be or be prepared to spend the night outside. Usually, it was not too bad in what was previously known as California; it was often warm enough depending on your exact location. But, finding a secure place, away from wild animals and roaming Security Patrols, was another obstacle all together.

Security Patrols were groups of three to six men. Quinn once read a book about twentieth-century entertainment. People used to watch something called wrestling, and wrestlers, that's what the Security Patrols looked like to her. Large, brawny men with tall and broad shoulders and big meaty hands that looked like they could rip right through your chest, pulling the beating heart from your chest. That was from a movie she remembered reading about from that same book. The only thing different from wrestlers was the outfits. The Security Patrols, of course, did not wear tight spandex outfits in loud colors. They wore the customary muddy brown of the United State, as everyone else did. However, also incorporated was a lighter shade brown that made a camouflage pattern on their bulletproof armor that covered them pretty much from top to bottom. They wore plasticky looking armor instead of the cotton tunics and pants everyone else had. You could see their faces; the plate on their brown bulletproof helmets was transparent; Quinn supposed it was so they could scowl at you. She didn't understand why they had to be bulletproof, though. Nobody had any guns anymore except the government. Regardless, it was essential to avoid the

Security Patrols because they asked few questions, and even when they did, they acknowledged your answer with the large guns they carried.

It was tricky because, technically, it was illegal to sleep on the streets. But the Pods didn't open again until seven in the morning—even then, you couldn't get in. That's when the people who had stayed overnight got forced out to leave for their government-assigned job. If you had a day off from work or didn't have a job due to being elderly, you had to spend your day in one of the city's parks, museums, libraries, or the Everett Center. After the Pods were closed, crews came and cleaned the communal sleeping, showering, and eating areas. People could return between noon and two in the afternoon to get a midday serving of a government-administered nutrition biscuit. If your job was too far from the Pod to go and get your lunch, the work facility had a government-ran luncheon room that provided your biscuit. Besides that, a biscuit at breakfast and dinner were the only food ever received; water was the only thing to drink. However, it wasn't quite the well-oiled system the government claimed it was, Quinn figured. One of the problems was when you got to a Pod; it could already be full for the night. She knew this rarely happened as most people selected a Pod closest to their work and always stayed at that particular one for ease and a sense of routine. But if you went to visit family in another part of the country, or when groups of workers got reassigned, it could happen.

As Quinn passed the stationed Security Patrol outside the Pod, she had to admit everything was always spotless and sterile, very industrial. Nobody had anything different than what anyone else had. At least that was true for those who were able to stay in a Class One Pod. The Pods meant for Class Two or Three citizens were not as nice. At the other end of that spectrum were the Pods exclusively HE Citizens. She was sure those were plusher and comfortable, but she'd never been in one.

As disturbing as the Pods could be, Quinn had to admit they were the only place you could get some food, a shower, and a place to sleep. Personal homes, buildings, and businesses no longer existed as part of the new American order. Naturally, there were still jobs, and the expectation was that each person in the country would do their part. Farmers grew wheat, corn, and a variety of other vegetables for the nutrition biscuits. Factories created biscuits, and there were people needed to repair transport vehicles and Drone Scanners. Droves of people had to clean, sanitize, and keep the Pods running smoothly; there was no end to the work. Upper-class jobs were still available, of course, the government and those who worked at the President Everett Center and President Everett Museum; they had administrators, curators, and tour guides. Doctors and nurses were needed to keep the public up-to-date on inoculations and wellness checks. Business people still made deals, maybe not stock trading or sell-ing anything, but creating computers, music equipment for the classrooms, and everything in between. Then they ran the logistics to get them from one place to another. Quinn knew less about that. She had left before she ever had a job assignment. So, she was aware these things existed, but she didn't have an in-depth knowledge of it.

One thing Quinn did know about was the Pods. She had spent many evenings in them, and she found herself now making her way toward a building that was labeled "Government Pod CA-03-1." A simple enough system, the "CA" meant it was located in the state formerly known as California, the "03" indicated that it was the third one to be built there, and the "1" was to designate that this Pod was only meant for a Class One Citizen. She said a silent wish she could get in with no problems.

AUGUST 18, 2056 – DAVIS

Davis exited the transport bus and walked home to the Pod she went to every day after work. Suddenly, she felt herself starting to rise in the air and becoming immobilized by a soft blue beam of light. *Nothing to worry about*, she thought as the pale blue light beam surrounded her. Relaxing was easy, just floating in the hazy glow. *In reality, it was quite pretty*, thought Davis. It was no trouble clearing her mind and thinking of nothing. She knew she had nothing to fear as the Drone Scanner checked her. As it lowered her and the blue light turned to green, indicating she could go, she heard the alarms go off a few feet away and saw a man caught in red light. *Oh, no, someone didn't pass scanning*, she thought with concern. *Well*, she felt matter-of-factly, *we have ways to take care of that, and he'll be better off for it in the end.*

She smoothed down her simple brown tunic that went down to mid-thigh when she saw a patch of dust on the jodhpurs underneath. *A simple but comfortable outfit*, she thought. And she took pride in the jodhpurs she wore. Only workers of the Everett Center could wear those. She didn't like them getting dusty, though, and there was a large patch of dust on her right leg almost down to her foot. It must have happened when she was in the scanning drone beam. The beams tended to swirl up a little dust around you when they had you immobilized. Davis always wanted to be presentable and clean. She took out the dust cloths she purposely carried in her brown canvas knapsack for such an occasion. She rubbed at the dust until it disappeared, and the jodhpurs became spotless again.

Davis worked her way past the Security Patrol outside and then through the large steel doors marked for that area: "CA-03-1." She was proud to be approaching this Pod. It was a Pod only meant for Class One Citizens who had complied with the land's rules and regulations and the President's decrees. She had the credentials to enter, and she was delighted by it. But it did bother her a little bit that she could not enter a "HE" Pod—a Pod for people who had attained the highest enlightenment. As stated in the constitution scribed by President Everett, the names of highly enlight-ened citizens would come to the President in a dream; only he could speak directly to God and was the messenger for God here on earth. President Everett rarely ever named someone, but when he did, there was great fan-fare and celebration. Davis had not yet come to President Everett in his dreams, but she knew one day she would. She applied all her efforts at being a great citizen, and she loved her country. Everything was orderly, including her. Neat; clean. And of course, she was proud knowing the fact she was the first baby ever to survive the Lombardi Plague thanks to President Everett's Marigold vaccine.

She often wondered if the reason she wasn't a HE yet was maybe, and this was a big maybe in her head, was that President Everett had some kind of higher purpose planned for her. At the age of twenty-nine, the fact she'd not been married yet was odd. Davis hadn't even had any Inquiries of Interest, not one. Not even a farmer on the outskirts, and now she was the only one of her friends that had not been married and had children. She never asked why; she simply trusted it would work out for her. After all, her job worked out for her. She had been assigned a job, a very high-ranking job, without the benefit of having a spouse yet. Davis worked at the Everett Center, the rehabilitation center for those who had strayed off the path of good citizenship. She mostly filed reports but spoke to President Everett on the phone once, when he called to check the center's condition. He cared so much, just another thing she loved about him. She silently laughed at herself now, after her thoughts of husbands and children when she knew better than to wonder about her place in the world. The government not only took care of everything that she would ever need but also all the needs anyone might have: shelter, food, medicine, entertainment. She neither questioned nor challenged anything. Sure, Davis knew some people wondered things. She saw it first hand at The Everett Center. She had even heard a story once that some people didn't believe in the caste system they had, that they didn't think the President was talking to God and getting names for the HEs. "Ridiculous," Davis meant to say to herself, but a delicate whisper escaped her lips and betrayed her inner thought. She quickly looked around, glad to see nobody had noticed her.

When she got to the door of the Pod, she presented her ID Card and greeted the Security Patrol, "We are the people, and the people are we." The patrol guard repeated it back to her and scanned her ID Card.

"Approved," he said. "Also, you are coming up for vaccination in two days. Please report to med bay by 0900 hours on Thursday." Davis didn't love vaccination day. It didn't hurt, and of course, it saved her from all sorts of diseases and viruses. It was an advanced version of the Marigold Injection. Not only did it provide lasting protection from the Lombardi Plague but also the flu and other illnesses. However, like everyone else, after she received it, her skin turned a sickly gold-yellow for about a week. *That is never a good look for anyone,* she thought. This time she was able to keep the thought in her head and not verbally spill out her feelings.

AUGUST 18, 2056 - QUINN

Quinn caught a glance at Davis as they were both making their way into the Pod at the same time. Quinn would not have time to talk to her, but she hoped she could trail her after they entered. Quinn handed her ID Card to a Security Guard, and he scanned it. He scowled as they were wont to do. "It looks like you haven't checked into any Pods for a few days now…four days to be exact?" He made a quiet humph sound and then added, "Nor have you checked into work. What's going on?"

Another Security Patrol guard worked his way over, getting his gun at the ready. "What seems the problem? Trouble maker?"

"Not sure yet, checking."

Come on, Ringo, thought Quinn. *Do your magic.* Ringo had told her that once Clark's card got scanned, he would need a few minutes. He already had access to the ID Card files, but he had to receive Quinn's initial scan to alter the information and quickly swap Clark's photo with Quinn's. She lightly cleared her throat. "I'm sorry for the trouble. I dropped my ID Card on my way here, and it landed in some mud. I tried cleaning it off, but maybe it is not reading correctly now? Can I go to the ID Station and have them rerun it? Maybe type it in manually?"

The first guard handed her the card back, and the second guard roughly took her by the shoulder and said, "This way."

He shrugged his shoulders, indicating Quinn should follow him over to a table; she barely remembered to say, "We are the people, and the people are we" when she approached the guard behind the desk. She realized she had forgotten to say it when she had encountered the first guards. She hoped that saying it now would not raise suspicions.

Quinn handed her card to the guard station at the ID Station, and he grabbed it and scanned it. Another red light. She could barely breathe. She somehow got out the explanation again about dropping the card and asked the guard if they would be so kind as to either clean the ID Card for her or enter the information manually. She figured they would clean it; she knew they were a bunch of clean freaks around here. The guard took out a little spray bottle of cleaning solution and cleaned the entire card, not just the mag strip. Then he took a lint cloth out and ran that over the ID. Finally, he ran it through an ultralight blue light and rescanned it. All the while, never smiling or saying anything to Quinn.

The light finally turned green, and she said a silent prayer of thanks and then walked deeper into the building as the guards waved her on.

Damn, she thought. Since she had taken so long to get cleared, Davis was gone. She scanned the foyer of the Pod several times to no avail.

Quinn decided to focus on the positive. She was thankful she had stumbled upon that corpse a few days ago and pilfered her ID Card, showing her new name of "Clark" and "Class One." She felt terrible for Clark, whoever she was, but it wasn't as if Quinn could do anything for her. She might as well use her ID to benefit the cause. Clark unknowingly set the plan in motion that they had been working so hard on. Part of that plan included Quinn passing herself off as a Class One Citizen. Besides that, she already had two misconduct alerts on her personal ID Card. It was now sitting in a steel case underground. The IDs were pretty indestructible and had GPS locator devices, but between the steel and depth underground, it would not be located. However, if she didn't pass herself off as Clark and they found out who she was, not only could it jeopardize the others, but one more misconduct, and she was toast.

You were only allowed two misconduct alerts. Each time, you went through lengthy and painful "reprogramming." Her first misconduct was sheer stupidity. She was dumb enough to say within earshot of a burly Security Patrol that she wished President Everett would burn in hell since he'd put them all in hell. That got her two months in the reprogramming center—better known as the Everett Center—and knocked her down to a Class Two Citizen—a "Potential Troublemaker" citizen. One of the worst things about being Class Two was the Pods. Much dirtier and more crowded than Class One, and a limited supply of food and water. It was quite common to miss a meal or two and not get a bed for the night when you had to live in the Class Two Pods.

Quinn's second misconduct alert was about a year after she got out of the reprogramming center the first time. A drone scanned her, and Quinn had not yet learned to rid her thoughts of negativity toward the government. She had not yet learned to hide her mistrust for the President. She didn't even remember her specific feeling of disgruntlement that day, but it got her a red light and held her immobilized until a security caravan came and collected her. That got her three months in the Everett Center and demoted to a Class Three Citizen—"Trouble Maker" citizen. Those Pods were even worse. You were lucky to get a blanket in a dirty corner, much less food. Overcrowded with sick people, sometimes with mental illness, which the government always claimed to have eliminated. But mental illness and sickness still existed, all right. It was just hidden in odd corners of the country, where there was less overall population and more security. Being Class Three also came with a strict reprimand: One more misconduct, and it was a death sentence. No lawyers. No trial. No judge or jury. Just an automatic firing squad in your immediate future.

Quinn had heard stories from her friends in the bunker, all the terrible tales. She even heard that just getting sick was enough to get you misconduct alerts because they assumed you didn't get your vaccination when you were supposed to. Ana, one of her friends, told Quinn about her parents, Camila, her mom, and Jose, her father. Jose had some kind of terminal illness—cancer, from what Ana could deduce from the books she had read. It didn't take long for him to become a Class Three Citizen once he got ill. Camila did not want to leave him, especially since she knew the end was near for him. They ran into the woods to try and fend for themselves while Camila attempted to find a way to care for Jose. Because Camila and Ana repeatedly did not check into any Pods, they were automatically knocked down to Class Two and then Three themselves. They had to take the utmost care not to get caught, but they were starving, so one night, Camila tried to break into a storage unit holding nutrition biscuits. Camila was caught and dragged into the city square and shot right through the head. Ana saw the whole thing; she was only ten at the time. Ana never knew what became of her dad; he probably starved to death, she assumed. Since, typically, they did not execute children, Ana got dragged off to the Everett Center for Children. She received, in her words, "all the pro-Everett programming one could want" until she met Namaguchi at a Courting Dance. Ana became his fourth wife at the age of sixteen.

Quinn supposed it was kismet when she and Ana met. She loved that word, "kismet." Almost like they kissed when they met. She knew her forbidden love for Ana would never come to fruition. The Everettisim Church taught against same-sex relationships. Although, one of her friends in the bunker, Audrey, once told her they were not precisely a puritanical country like they had been, many, many years ago. Now, everything was all sort of a mishmash of what struck President Everett's fancy. However, not everything the President decreed was necessarily enforced. Because of the reduced population, there were not enough Security Patrol Guards to go around and watch people get intimate. So really, you could do almost what you pleased with another person of age as long as you did it quietly and discreetly. But the minute it reached the public eye, as it indeed would if one of the people involved was the wife of a Chief Officer, *kiss that kiss goodbye,* Quinn thought to herself. She just wished it was easier to do than say. Her heart was always arguing with her brain on this one, each piece of her like fighters, trying to knock out the other with reason or emotion, whatever the case may be. She wasn't even sure why she felt this way about Ana, another woman. It was not something that was ever shown to her or discussed, so it caused her some confusion and angst. Quinn admired Ana's beauty, who wore her dark brown hair long in defiance of the law about having it in a bob cut. Ana also had smooth brown skin that reminded Quinn of milk chocolate, which Quinn had only tasted once. Namaguchi had brought some chocolates as a gift to Ana when they married. It was contraband, but since he was a top official, it was easy for him to get away with breaking the law. Ana kept the box and ate only one sweet at a time, slowly dwindling the box to the last piece, which she kindly gave to Quinn. It was time to shake that off, though, and forget about that. But one thing Quinn could not forget was the warmth of her hands when she had them around Ana's slim waist. Just once, a hug that lasted a little longer than other hugs, Quinn's hands resting on the curvy divots above Ana's hip bones that Quinn thought were so lovely and inviting. She also could remember her heart pounding so fast against her chest that Quinn was sure Ana could feel it as much as she could feel Ana's heart beating in sync with her own.

Quinn had to remind herself to get back in the game. She was not here to reminisce about warm hugs. She went up to an Information Kiosk and swiped Clark's ID Card. She quickly checked the stats, the most important one being her next vaccination day for Clark's pre-prescribed dose of the Marigold Injection. She had two weeks. Perfect, that was more than enough time. Her next stop was the restroom, and she quickly scurried in. A woman she passed on the way in gave her a sideways glance and a quick mumble of "We are the people, and the people are we." Quinn forgot to say it back, and the lady was out of earshot before she could reply. She took a pause; she could not make mistakes, even if they were simple ones. She used the bathroom, then washed her hands as the guard watched and timed her. However, she surmised it was pointless because she had to enter and exit the bathroom under a wave of blue ultraviolet light that killed all bacteria on those entering and exiting.

Her next stop was the Commissary for her dinner nutrition biscuit and glass of pure distilled and filtered water; her tray also ran under a blue UV light before being handed to her. She ate her meal in silence. While not tasty in any sense of the word, the biscuit would enlarge in her stomach, making her feel full and give her a dose of vitamins and minerals. *All a growing girl needs*, she joked to herself as she bit into the dusty, dry brown biscuit. They were formulated for dietary requirements, not taste, and kept the population at a "healthy weight."

As soon as Quinn finished up, she started up to the eighth floor, the floor for single people. The first and second were for families with more than two children, the third and fourth floors were for families with one or two children, the fifth and sixth for couples with no children, and the seventh and eighth for single people. Children without parents that were under the age of sixteen stayed in separate facilities at The Everett Center. As she climbed the stairs, she took in the clean gray steel all around her. She almost felt as if she could get lost, with everything looking the same. The only time it varied was when she reached a door to a new floor. A red two, three, or four, and on up marked each entrance on the inside and out-side. Quinn noted she didn't see any dust or dirt, no trash or paint chips. Just stark, clean walls, stairs, and doors. They were nothing like the lesser class Pods.

Quinn got to her red-lettered door with "Eighth Floor" on it and opened it up. She hoped she could find an empty bed. She hadn't stayed in this particular Pod in the past, and she knew most people tried to get the same Pod and room every night—call it familiarity. But it didn't mat-ter if you slept in one that had an occupant before you. At least in the Pods for Class One Citizens, every Pod and bed was cleaned, sanitized, and then probably cleaned again. Bed mats that were already bacteria resistant got atomized with antibacterial spray. Sanitized sheets and bedding got replaced daily. They didn't leave any room for bacteria or viruses to thrive in the bedrooms. Overhead lighting was an ultraviolet blue light meant to eliminate germs, and although there was a dimmer "night mode," it was on at all times, so it could keep one awake at night. She kept walking down the hallway, passing thin brown painted plywood doors with a red light on overhead, indicating the room already had an occupant. Finally, about two-thirds of the way down, she saw a door with a green light on above.

Quinn entered and surveyed the area. Not large, maybe one-hundred square feet at most. A small wooden plank was secured to the wall by chains and placed upon it was a mat. Fitted on that was a brown sheet, and on top, an extraordinarily clean brown blanket and small pillow. You could smell the antiseptic in the air. In the corner was a thin brown curtain that hid the toilet, and right outside that, a sink with government-approved anti-bacterial soap and lotion. Next to that, a small brown shelf held clean brown towels. You could also place any possessions you might have. However, most people didn't own many things if they owned anything at all. Since you technically might not be in the same place tomorrow, you carried anything you might have with you in your brown knapsack.

In the Shower Rooms/Laundry Dispensary, you got your clean tunic, pants, socks, and undergarments—turn in the old ones, pick up the new ones. Little changing/shower rooms accommodated your modesty. You simply disrobed in the coffin-sized cubicle behind the brown shower curtain. Then, you put your dirty clothes in an empty nook that was behind another little brown curtain, turned on the lukewarm shower (timed for exactly eight and three-quarters of a minute), and by the time you finished, POOF! New, clean clothes in your size were waiting for you in the nook and warm, high-powered air-jets dried you. The showers came equipped with dispensers filled with your standard government soap, shampoo, and conditioner. Everything smelled of eucalyptus and tea tree, both of which everyone had learned contained antibacterial and antifungal properties. It was a pleasant scent; although the odor was antiseptic, they had managed it so that it wasn't in a sickly way. The aroma was fresh and clean, almost outdoorsy and green-smelling. But, if someone forgot for a moment where they were, their eye caught sight of the ever-lasting blue light that shone overhead, even in the showers.

After her shower, Quinn got back to her room; she lay down on the bed and tried to focus on the day tomorrow; she needed to try and get to sleep; there were so many things to consider and get right. But all she could think of was when she used to be on the third or fourth floors of the Pods, the family Pod rooms, with her mom, dad, and sister. Quinn didn't even know where her family was or what may have happened to them. The last time she saw them was after listening to President Everett's fourth inauguration speech. Then, she left them to go to the Courting Dance, the night Namaguchi took her. People went missing all the time, so it's not like you could file a missing person report. Even if you got a Security Guard to listen to you, they'd likely say she took off, and she was an adult, so they couldn't do anything. The Security Patrol simply did not have enough guards to go chasing every rabbit trail. She lay there in the haze of the blue light, listening to the slight buzz that was ever-present. She took a deep breath and let out a heavy sigh. Her eyes felt tired and heavy, and she rubbed them at the corners, trying to invigorate them. She had bees on the brain, as her mom used to say, so regardless of how tired she was, she knew sleep would not happen any time soon, and even when it did, it would be in fits, as her sleep usually was.

Quinn was also thinking of the lines you found down the middle of the roads. Roadways still existed; even though nobody had personal vehicles, there were transport busses. Quinn wasn't quite sure why she thought of those, but she sometimes did. There was something about them that made her feel the way she felt about herself. She didn't know who she was regarding certain things and tended not to pick either side. She saw herself as a down-the-middle-of-the-road nothing kind of girl. There was only one thing she was sure about, and that was Ana, who was now back in her thoughts. Even though Quinn was positive about her, there was nothing she would ever do about it. And Quinn found herself in the middle of the road once again.

That didn't stop Quinn from thinking about Ana, though. Quinn started reflecting about the one time after Ana had her first baby. Ana had no idea what to do with Russell, her new baby, and now, he was sick. Throwing up like crazy, expelling milk as if his little mouth was a milk waterfall. Russell's brow was hot and sweaty, and he had clammy hands, crying like he was in so much pain. After trying many things—cold compresses, lying down next to him and soothing him throughout the night, and Ana trying to breastfeed in short bursts throughout the duration, the little guy finally settled down and fell asleep. They kept a watch together, for hours, to make sure his breathing was even, and he kept his temperature and milk down. Once he was safe and sleeping well, Ana, tired and sweaty brow herself, looked at Quinn and started cracking up like she heard the funniest joke she had ever heard. "That," she said, "was ridiculous. I have never seen so much vomit!"

Quinn started laughing too and went over to Ana to give her a sleepy hug and reassuring pat on the back. "You did good, mama."

"We both did well, thank you. And I suppose if we can laugh over this abysmal night, we truly are best friends. Thank you again."

The thought made Quinn smile. One thing she liked most was her ability to laugh and have fun with Ana. Yes, she was damn sexy too, but it was also her laugh, her conversation, and their friendship; she valued that all deeply. And despite feeling a certain way, Quinn would never risk that friendship. Just like that, she realized that she'd decided against it after all.

Quinn got up for a stretch and to try to clear her mind a bit. There was a small window on the far wall; she pushed back the little brown curtain and looked out. There were so many stars out there. She had never really understood astronomy; she had tried to learn a bit of it in the library, but it didn't make a lot of sense to her. She didn't understand how things could rotate and move all the time up there in space, but somehow, the constellations always kept their shape. For thousands of years, they had maintained the formation of Orion and Scorpius. *Oh well*, she thought, *you don't need to understand a situation to think it is beautiful.* And at that, she found herself thinking of Ana yet again. She forced those thoughts from her mind and went back to the bed with a laugh, thinking that tomorrow things would also start with a big bang.

Quinn finally fell into a troubled sleep and had such an odd dream. She felt as if she was falling, falling, and as she did, hands reached out to grab her, pulling her one way and another. She kept trying to yell out to make them stop, but although her mouth was opening, no sound would come out. She finally fell onto a gigantic piece of chocolate, and it caved in and trapped her inside the sticky center. Nothing could get her out to the top. She felt as if she couldn't breathe, and she would die soon if something didn't happen. Suddenly, a hand reached down through the top of the chocolate, and she grabbed for it. Quinn quickly saw that her rescue was made possible by Ana. Standing there, somehow, now the chocolate was more stable. They were able to stand there easily without it caving or sinking in. She hugged Ana and got chocolate all over Ana. She tried to apologize, but still, no sound would come out. Ana reached out her finger, taking a swipe of chocolate off Quinn's cheek, and then licked it off her finger seductively. Ana then made a mad, quick leap for Quinn as if she must be with her instantly. Quickly, they were rolling around together, pulling at each other's clothing, but as everything was chocolate covered, their hands simply slipped all over the place. The last thing Quinn remembered before waking was that they were about to fall off the top of the enormous chocolate piece. When she did wake, it was with a start and a pounding heart in her chest.

Quinn looked at the clock that was on the wall. It was only a little after 4:00 a.m. She wished the library was open, but it didn't open until 5:00 a.m. You couldn't get your breakfast biscuit until then, either. She decided to go over the plan in her head. One step at a time. #1: Find Davis. #2: Secure Davis—and that is as far as she got. She must have drifted off until the speaker woke her by announcing it was now 5:00 a.m. and the Pod Services were open for business.

AUGUST 19, 2056 – TAKEN

Now, she had to hurry. Quinn had to find Davis; and hoped she would be in the Commissary. Not that Quinn had time to eat, but she also wouldn't mind grabbing a nutrition biscuit if she were able. She quickly grabbed her knapsack and beat feet down to the Commissary. Quinn ran in through the blue light above and scanned the area. She did not see Davis, and she only had about twenty minutes or so. She was just about to turn around and check the library when Davis went right by her to go into the Commissary. Without thinking or even really remembering her scripted lines, she grabbed Davis's hand. Davis jumped back. "Hey, what are you doing? Who are you?" Davis said in an angry tone, laced with shock and concern.

Quinn coughed. "Oh, I'm sorry. I didn't mean to startle you. I thought you were someone else," she was barely able to get out.

Davis's face and tone softened. "That's okay. Can I help you find someone?"

Quinn had to think quickly and had to come up with a reason to get Davis out of that area and to the front of the Pod. "Maybe you can help me. Your name is Davis, right? I think you work at the Everett Center? I mean, you must, because of the uh, jodhpurs, right?"

"Um, yes, but I don't know how I can help you?"

"I just wanted to see if you could come outside and see this person. They're going mad. I think they may need to go to the center. For education. For reeducation."

"I think that is a bit out of my realm. If a citizen needs help, a Security Patrol or Drone Scanner should pick them up."

"I know, yes, that is true, but they were screaming your name."

"Well, I certainly won't go then; it could be dangerous."

"No! They were blaming you. They said you put them up to it. They said you were against Everett. You have to stop them!"

Call it frustration with Quinn or self-preservation (or a little bit of both), but that was enough, and Davis ran to the door with Quinn. As they stepped out of the door, a deafening explosion rocked into the side of Pod CA-03-1. The last thing Davis remembered hearing was a repeating announcement over the loudspeaker: "All Security Patrol to the south side of the Pod. All Security Patrol to the south side of the Pod. All Security Patrol to the south…" then somebody put a hood over Davis's head before they shoved her into a vehicle.

AUGUST 20, 2056 - CAPTIVITY

Davis awoke with a start; she was cold, clammy and her head pounded with a pain worse than anything she had ever known before. Davis tried to reach up to her head to wipe some of the sweat away. However, she was unable, quickly seeing her hands tied down to the bed. She moved her legs a little bit and found her legs were tied down as well. Davis tried to strain her eyes; in the middle of the ceiling, a dull bulb emitted a pale yellowish light, but it wasn't enough to see much. Confusion swirled around her—*where was she? What was this?* It took a few seconds for her to remember, and then she gasped as she remembered and simultaneously realized there was no blue light. Nothing to kill the germs, nothing to protect her from whatever was in this room she found herself in.

Quinn walked into the room. "Are you okay? How are you feeling?"

Davis scoffed. "Am I *okay*! How am I *feeling*?" she yelled, even though it made her head pound even worse. "Are you kidding me? You're crazy! You kidnapped me! And now, I am in extreme danger. Just let me go, let me go now, and I won't turn you in for anything. You should, however, consider turning yourself in for your betterment."

Quinn gave Davis a minute to get out what she needed to get out; she knew how this felt, the confusion and being so scared. "I promise you; you're all right. You are not in danger at all. I brought you some water. I can help you drink—"

Davis stepped over Quinn's words. "You are insane. I will not have anything to do with anything you give me," Davis said with angry indignancy.

Quinn patiently waited. "I know this is scary. I again promise you, you're okay. I'll come to check on you in a little bit, but you should think about having some water."

Davis snorted and glared; if she could only throw daggers with her eyes, she would kill that hateful girl.

Davis eventually drifted into sleep, of sorts. She kept waking up and would try her arms and legs for movement, hoping that what was happening was a nightmare and not reality. She did notice that her throat was dry and scratchy, but it wasn't just her throat. It felt as if a vile fire was smoldering at the bottom of her lungs, the smoke rising up her throat, irritating it, drying it out, and leaving an acrid taste. Poisoned or not, that water was sounding better and better. She imagined it being ice cold, refreshing, and soothing. She thought she might start crying, something she never did. She had never been in so much pain or had been so confused. Her pleasantly laid out life was, in her opinion, well-appointed. And she never had any concerns before now. However, thinking and deducing hadn't exactly been a part of her daily life. Sure, she had to occasionally figure things out, for example, at work, decide what room to put people in, but her computer would always show her what spaces were vacant, so even that wasn't a deep thought. She decided to stop thinking; that was much easier. But thoughts kept creeping in, and one was that the girl didn't return as she had promised. It gave her enough time to figure out that the water was probably safe; if that insufferable girl were going to kill her, it wouldn't likely be by poisoning her water.

Finally, after what seemed like hours to Davis, Quinn came back in the room and quietly spoke. "Hello, Davis. I'm just checking on you and wanted to see if you felt like any water now."

Anger had dwindled in Davis as her thirst had increased. She simply had no energy to growl and fight. She let out a big sigh, and even that made the fire in her throat flame up with scratch and burn. "Yes, I would like some water," she got out in a dry voice. She purposely left off the please, and that gave her a bit of self-satisfaction.

Quinn walked over to the bed and tipped the cup to Davis's lips. Davis noticed that her lips felt dehydrated and parched. She rolled her eyes at the thought of being given this water by this horrible girl, being taken care of like a child, and the water was room temperature.

It was as if Quinn read her mind. "My name is Quinn, by the way. I know this must seem scary and weird to you, and for that, I'm sorry. I promise it will all make sense soon."

Davis just simply had nothing else in her to fight this, to argue anything. She did manage to ask if it was possible to get colder water, though.

Quinn replied, "Honestly, room temperature is better right now. The cold will upset your stomach. And, I hate to say it, but you are about to get sick. Very, very sick. You will not die; remember that. But you will feel like you are dying. Every comfort we can give you, you will need it. I'm going to bring you some food in a minute. We do not have nutrition biscuits here, so we'll start with simple foods that will be easier on your system."

Quinn left the room but came back after a few minutes. She sat next to the bed and very patiently fed Davis some dry crackers that were not that far different from nutrition biscuits and a few spoons of rice and applesauce and, in between, sips of room temperature water. At first, Davis hesitated to eat anything, but hunger took over, and she relented after a small protest because she was feeling famished. Davis figured it would be unlikely to be killed through poisoned food and water. And, she wasn't sure what time of day it was, or when she has last eaten.

Quinn spoke again, "I know it wasn't much food, but it's best not to overdo it right now. I'm going to leave a large pitcher of water with a straw.

I'll release one of your hands from the restraint so you can grab it. Do you prefer your left or your right?"

Davis was surprised at this question. Most people assumed she was right-handed, but she was indeed left-handed. There were two tables next to the bed, one on each side. After Davis told Quinn her preference, Quinn placed the pitcher on the table to the left and undid the restraint on her left wrist. Quinn then sat with Davis until she started to yawn and drift off. Quinn knew that she would sleep often and become weakened to such an extent that over the next few days, escape wouldn't be a concern.

AUGUST 22, 2056 –
DETOXIFICATION EXPLAINED

Quinn came into the room and saw Davis at the start of the process. She felt terrible about what she knew was going to happen to Davis, but she knew it was all part of the plan and that in the end, it would all be for the better. "How are you feeling, Davis?"

"I'm okay, I think. I have no strength, though, and am very tired, but I feel as if I've slept for days. I'm also confused; I know other people have been in here to feed me and refill my water. How many people are here?"

"We have several people here, but there's nothing to worry about. Everyone is friendly, and you'll get to know them in time. Don't worry about anyone who comes in here; nobody will harm you. You have been asleep for two days off and on but have been mostly sleeping, and I hesitate to tell you, as a reminder, you are about to get very sick."

"How can you possibly know that?"

"You are going to be detoxing from not having your vaccination."

Davis had forgotten entirely about the vaccination. She forgot she was due for it. And now, she tried to calculate in her head if she was already overdue or if today, she was due. "You're past due, if you're wondering. It's why we took you when we did. In the first steps of the detox, you will be exhausted and weak. You have noticed that already. I will be honest with you, and I'm sorry about this part of it. You are going to feel very, very ill. Your head will hurt—"

"My head already hurts. It hurts since I've been here," Davis said grumpily. She then got a weird look on her face. "Also, this is embarrassing, but what about using the restroom?"

"Don't be embarrassed. It's fine; we've all been there, and everyone needs help once in a while. You haven't eaten much, really, and although you've been drinking water, you're also dehydrated. So, don't worry. But we have ways to deal with anything. And in a few days, you'll be strong enough to get up and use the restroom by yourself."

"Great. All my dreams are coming true," Davis said with sarcasm. "Okay, while we have this pleasant little chat, why are you forcing me to get sick? Why are you neglecting to give me my vaccine?"

"Because it's not to keep the Lombardi Plague away. It administers a mind-control drug."

AUGUST 22, 2056 – DETOXIFICATION

Davis could vaguely remember wanting to argue with Quinn. She knew Quinn had said something absurd, but Davis felt so over-fatigued and ill that she simply didn't have it in her power to say or do anything. And now, she lay there, barely able to move and feeling more afflicted; it was beyond belief. She'd never really been sick in the past. At least Davis didn't remember ever having any type of real malaise. President Everett and his vaccinations had kept her well all these years. *Why change anything? Blast Quinn and her damn withdrawing*, she thought. But she kept drifting off into a sweaty, fidgety sleep, and after a while, she forgot the ridiculous things Quinn had even said to her.

Davis was aware that people were coming in and out of the room, occasionally giving her fresh water to sip and, sometimes, refreshing ice chips. Every so often, she got a spoonful of a clear broth, a cracker, or a small scoop of rice. It didn't seem to matter what they fed her, though; she threw it all up. She hated the acrid, burning taste at the back of her throat. Davis felt as if a thick black tar was burning up her esophagus, licking the back of her throat, and coating her tongue in a foul taste. She was sore and ached all over; her body was covered in red, itchy welts. Her head pounded, and there was so much pressure and pain as if a massive concrete block was somehow simultaneously tied around her neck, dragging her down, and slamming against both temples at once. From what little awareness she had, the people that came into the room seemed kind. They helped her with the food, water and gave her a fan to try and give her direct cooling, the only thing that remotely gave her any relief. They put cold cloths on her head and cleaned up anything that needed cleaning up. Nothing mattered, though; the only thing that mattered to her was getting out of this misery.

"Kill me," Davis remembered saying one day after Quinn walked in to see her. Davis just needed it to stop, and she didn't know how long she had been in this hell but knew it had been too long. She was finished with this agony.

"It's okay," Quinn softly cooed. "It's almost over." She came over and sat with Davis next to the bed and placed her hand on Davis's forehead. "It seems like your fever may be breaking. That's a good sign."

"How long…how long…" Davis couldn't get the words out; she felt depleted of all her energy and strength.

"Three days," said Quinn, knowing what Davis wanted to hear. "You'll have two or three more rough days, but not as rough as they have been. It will gradually get better. I bet you're going to get very hungry soon. You've barely had any food. I'm going to bring you some water; I'm sure you're parched. Other than that, do you want anything specific? Applesauce, broth, crackers—"

"What I want…can you tell me why I'm here? I just want to know what I'm doing here and why you're doing this to me. What is the reason for this? I've never hurt anyone."

"Honestly, can you tell me, have you never really hurt anyone? Were you blameless at the Everett Center?" Quinn raised her voice more than Davis had ever heard from her, and her face got red, her frustration showing. "You know what? I'm sorry. Never mind, this isn't about that. You are here for a reason. In a few days, you can ask any questions you want. Everything will become clear then." What she said next was done so quietly, Davis almost couldn't hear it. Davis thought she said, "I'm sorry."

"No," said Davis after a short pause. "No, in regards to the food you asked about before. Maybe just some water. I'm tired; I think I want to sleep." She then sadly turned away, even though the aches and pains all over her body made her cringe with pain and discomfort. She wasn't thinking about that, though. She was just hoping that Quinn couldn't see the tears starting to fall from her eyes and making a hot streak down her face.

All night, Davis tossed, turned, fell asleep into rough nightmares, and then would wake up, sweat making her clothing stick to her and giving her a cold, clammy feeling. She noticed her body didn't ache and hurt, and her head wasn't pounding as much as it had before. The welts that had irritated her so severely were gone. However, she was still hurting. Both inside and outside hurt now, but she would keep it to herself. She would keep it a secret that the sick feeling in her stomach now mainly had to do with the young boy and what she had done to him.

AUGUST 29, 2056 –
THE FOG BEGINS TO LIFT

The next time Davis awoke, she realized she felt remarkably better, although that sinking feeling about the boy remained. She rolled over on her side, a massive sad feeling surrounding her, making her want to sleep more. But she couldn't deny she was feeling some restlessness and energy. At the same time, Davis felt a bit hazy with her thoughts. It was as if she couldn't decipher reality from dreams and wasn't sure what had happened in the last few weeks. It seemed as if she was trying to look at her life and figure out exactly who she was and what had happened, but somebody had thrown mud right in her eye, and she wasn't seeing or thinking clearly. It was an odd, odd feeling, and words and thoughts kept swirling through her mind at an alarming speed, way too quick for her to snag them and decipher their meaning.

At that moment, a man Davis remembered seeing during her illness walked into her room. He was tall and slim—lanky—and although a long torso held his long arms, legs, and feet, they still seemed as if they were too long for him. It was as if he were not quite put together right, a man in a scarecrow's body. He was maybe sixty-five years old, with thinning light brown hair in a scrawny ponytail at the nape of his neck. He had thin wire glasses that did not hide his large brown eyes—the bridge of the glasses perched on his aquiline nose. Davis had read a book once, *The Legend of Sleepy Hollow*, and she imagined that the protagonist from that book, Ichabod Crane, would have looked precisely as this man did. He had a gentle demeanor about him, and it didn't seem as if he would be mean. However, Davis, being unfamiliar with who he was, made sure the blankets covered her properly. She was wearing clothing, but she wasn't willing to take chances. When he spoke, he spoke softly and kindly. "Hi...how are you, Davis? I'm sorry, I didn't mean to startle you. I hope you're feeling better. I'm not sure if you remember meeting me, but my name is Ringo. Can I do anything for you? Get you anything?"

Since being kidnapped, Davis didn't feel overwhelmingly comfortable with anyone she had come in contact with, but she knew Quinn best, at least. She asked Ringo if he wouldn't mind getting Quinn for her. Ringo nodded his head slowly, bobbing it a few times in rapid succession. "Of course," he said, "I'll send her right in."

When Quinn came in, she parroted Ringo's earlier thoughts, asking how Davis was doing and if she needed anything. "I'm feeling better, thank you. But I would like to have more information, please. About why I'm here, where I'm at, and what is going on," Davis said smugly.

"Honestly, a lot of the information you will receive will be...overwhelming, to say the least. I know that sounds scary, but I want to remind you nobody here wants to do you any harm, and you're safe." Quinn took a deep breath before continuing, "I can tell you where you are. You're in a bunker. Ringo, you met him; he built this years ago. It was his doomsday bunker." She waited a beat for Davis to respond. But Davis just looked down at her hands, nervously twiddling her thumbs for a few seconds, so Quinn continued, "Do you feel like you can get up and use the restroom and shower yourself?"

"No, I'm not sure, I mean. Maybe, but I'm feeling a bit unstable still."

"I'll bring you some food. After you eat and maybe have a nap, we'll see then. I promise you, when you're feeling up to it, we will all sit together at a table and go over exactly what is going on. We'll answer your questions."

Davis replied, sounding sad, "Yes, that sounds okay." And as Quinn had almost exited the room, Davis said, "Oh, Quinn?"

"Yes?"

"Thank you," replied Davis with a shy smile.

Quinn left the room, but she returned shortly with some water, vegetable broth, and crackers. She brought them over on a tray and set it on the table next to Davis. "Do you think you can feed yourself? I can tell you some things while you eat if you like."

"Yes, thank you. I think that will work fine."

"Great…okay, let's just start at where you are. I mentioned before that you're in Ringo's doomsday bunker. When President Everett started aggressively taking over—"

"Aggressively taking over?" Davis scoffed, interrupting.

Quinn paused a second before continuing. She had to remember that Davis was still coming off the last of the mind control drugs, and not only that, it would take some time. Davis had known one thing her whole life, and suddenly, a group of people unknown to her was trying to convince her that something else entirely different was the truth. "I'm sorry. I shouldn't have used that language. Some of us here have had less than pleasant experiences with the government, and I let that cloud my language. Again, I apologize if I offended you."

Quinn's frankness surprised Davis. At the same time, something was nagging in her brain to retort in a rude and insulting way. Without really thinking of what she was saying, she answered delicately, "That's okay, don't worry. You can continue, please?"

"Sure. So, Ringo was a doomsday prepper. Maybe you have heard of them at some point?"

"Yes, I've heard some but don't know a lot about them."

"That's okay. You don't need to. Ringo and some others he was friends with built these underground bunkers. They stocked them with food, clean water, first aid kits, medical supplies, you name it, any basic human need, and Ringo stocked it. His bunker is enough for twelve people comfortably, and up to fifteen if need be. We only have eight full-time residents and between four and six part-time, depending on circumstances. Underground tunnels connect us to three other doomsday bunkers that family and friends of Ringo built. They are all set up similarly to us. We have water and some frozen food; that food will last at least another year, maybe two, if we're careful. But we also have a hydroponic garden that grows lettuce, spinach, peppers, tomatoes; we grow potatoes too."

"What is a hydroponic garden? And wait, what? No nutrition biscuits? How do you get all the nutrition you need?"

"To answer the question—food gives us all the nutrition we need. Once upon a time, there were no nutrition biscuits."

"But I thought there were excess sugar and salt in all those things."

"Yes, in some of the processed stuff we have, that is true. But in the stuff we grow, it's natural sugar—the nutrition biscuits have sugar and salt too because you need some in your diet. They just forget to mention that part when they're telling you about how healthy they are, but I think we're getting off track," said Quinn as she sensed Davis was getting frustrated with the quasi-negative talk about the government. "Let me tell you a little about hydroponic gardening since you asked. Let me go grab a pot first so I can show you what it looks like."

A little bit later, Quinn came back into the room with a small clear pot. A green sprout was growing out of a beaker of water suspended in the middle. "So, this is one of our small pots. Most of the ones we have are a lot larger. But Ringo has these little ones for people to have in their room if they want. These small ones are flowers that bring a little color into our world. Anyhow, hydroponics is a method of growing plants without soil. They work pretty much anywhere as long as you have access to clean water—we have an intricate filtering system as we have to reuse much of our water. Nutrients are added into the water, and also, you need airflow. We have a filtered air recycling system for the air we breathe and for the plants. Ringo is the expert; there are some other items I'm not as familiar with, coconut fibers and small clay rocks; he knows when and where to place them in the plants."

"Wow, that's quite a lot," said Davis. "I'm still not sure about eating other things besides biscuits."

"But you have! You are sipping broth and eating crackers right now!"

Davis looked down and realized she had indeed been eating something other than the nutrition biscuits. It was another odd feeling for her; another piece of her brain was floating up above her head and not making sense. She realized, previously, as she ate, her mind mechanically tricked her into thinking she was eating nutrition biscuits. But it had turned out that wasn't what she was eating at all. *Very odd*, she thought to herself, *extraordinary indeed*. She was feeling overwhelmed again, and fatigue was starting to put weight on her eyelids. "Yes, you are right. I feel silly. I wasn't even thinking about it."

"I understand; I know confusing things are going on right now."

"Thank you. I think if it's okay, let's finish talking tonight; I want to get some sleep."

"Yes, of course. That's perfectly fine. If you want to freshen up at all, there is a bathroom around the corner from your room. Just walk out, turn right, walk about five feet past the 'Bathroom Supplies' closet, then another few feet, and the bathroom will be on the left. It is a full bathroom with a shower. I brought you towels if you want to freshen up. We have two other full bathrooms and then two with a toilet and sink only, but the one I told you about is the closest to you."

"Thank you; you've been most helpful. I think I just need to sleep right now."

Davis felt as if she was already drifting off as she said the words. She was aware of Quinn leaving the room but felt detached as if she was floating above her body and was not hundred percent aware of what was going on.

Quinn wished her a good night as she departed, not sure if Davis had even heard her. She felt terrible; she honestly did because Quinn knew what was coming, and she knew it wouldn't be pleasant. As the physical discomfort waned, the emotional distress would intensify.

AUGUST 30, 2056 – THE LONGEST DAY

Davis slept for what felt like many hours, maybe a whole other day, it seemed, but she didn't have a clue what time she even went to sleep. But she did know she felt pretty good, almost like she was on the brink of being back to her old self. There were still some nagging bits; it felt as if little bugs were crawling around her brain and occasionally biting off a piece. It didn't exactly hurt, but it didn't feel right, either. It was a weird sensation, just like pretty much everything else had been since she got to the bunker. Bizarre, odd feelings that led her not to be fully aware, not entirely sure what was real and what wasn't. She felt very vague and ambiguous about herself and life itself.

Suddenly feeling very awake and—she hated to say it—but she felt gross, Davis decided it was time to head to the restroom. She didn't know when the last time she had taken a shower. Davis remembered Quinn telling her where the bathroom was but was still feeling a bit nervous about just getting over her illness. She had never been ill like that and did not know what the after-effects might be. The last thing she wanted to do was throw up or faint. She very slowly and methodically pulled herself into a sitting position. When she felt okay with that, she stood up but kept one hand on the edge of the bed headboard to make sure she was stable. Although Davis felt a bit lightheaded, it passed after a moment. She slowly worked her way over to where Quinn had set the pink, fluffy towels down and went to pick them up. All of that seemed to go fine, so she opened the door and stepped out.

After Davis found the restroom, she took her time taking a leisurely shower. She wasn't sure why she took her time; she was used to timed showers. But, something about it felt so invigorating and refreshing, so peaceful and calming; the steaming water carried away some of her stress and worries. She also got a kick out of trying some of the different soaps and shampoos they had. Other scents, unlike the eucalyptus and tea tree scent she was accustomed to using. She found she was quite fond of the hyacinth scented bath soap. *Hyacinth*, she played with the word in her mind. She wasn't quite sure how to say it, really, but it smelled amazing. It was a sweet, delicate floral scent, with a mildly spicy undertone that was intoxicating. She looked at the picture on the soap bottle; she had never seen them in person. The little blooms grew up the stem, creating columns of flowers in blue, pink, and white on their stems, verdant with thick, broad leaves. Davis thought they looked like mini flower fireworks. *Flowerworks*. She laughed to herself at her corny joke.

After her shower, she continued primping herself with the beauty products they had in the bathroom. There were different lotions and hair care products. She knew she was somewhat wasteful, and for that, would apologize to everyone. By nature, Davis wasn't usually an extravagant person. Although again, she had never really had the opportunity to be. But it felt so good to find pleasure in these little things and pamper herself; something never experienced before. And, quite honestly, she wasn't sure if she would ever be able to do this again. She regretted putting on her dirty clothing; the handy little window cutout she was used to retrieving her fresh clothing from was missing.

After she had finished in the restroom, Davis made her way back to what she supposed was "her" bedroom. She didn't feel it was indeed hers; she belonged at the Pods, getting ready to work at the Everett Center. *Didn't she?* she thought. She felt confident about residing in the Pods and working at the Everett Center. But then there was another bite on her brain, another annoying wisp of something chewed off and spat out, and she had to admit she wasn't even sure where she belonged. Davis walked in and noticed a small closet to her right. There were some hooks on the door, where the damp towels could hang.

Davis looked around the room. It was the first time she had been aware enough to survey her surroundings. She couldn't believe it: color. She was so used to only seeing white, gray, brown, and maybe some black. The world was various shades of those colors. Naturally, the sky was blue, and the grass green, and you could find wildflowers now and then in all shades of colors. But painted things or those manufactured, and fabrics that were dyed colors, were always in lackluster hues or were without pigment altogether. Davis had never seen anything like this room. The carpet was a bright blue, dotted with little yellow flowers. Still not made, her messy bed was covered with off-white sheets, a gray blanket, and a quilt on top of that. The quilt was a series of blue and green triangles, sewn together to form boxes. The triangle squares had white borders. In the center was a yellow diamond. There was even a little white table and dresser, yellow flowers with green leaves painted in the corners. The same pattern decorated the bed frame, white with cheery flowers and leaves marching along the head-board. The wall pattern alternated between thick and thin stripes in navy blue, shamrock green, and white. A blue shelf on the wall held two large yellow pots that had artificial red flowers. Placed at opposite edges on each end, in between the flower pots, were books, and—she had to admit—a pretty creepy looking clown doll right smack in the middle between the books. Davis got up to take a closer look at the books, clown, and flowers. She loved books and spent a lot of time in the libraries in all Pods and at the Everett Center. Davis read the titles, running her finger over the weath-ered spines. *To Kill a Mockingbird, Catcher in the Rye, Little Women*—she had read all those and thought very highly of them. There were also a few magazines, different fashion and cooking magazines, but nothing specific she recognized. There was one book lying on its side, *Frankenstein*. She had never read that one and pulled it off the shelf. Then something caught Davis's eye, and she walked over a little further with the book still in her hand. A metal chain was hanging down from a metal plate on the wall. She pulled the chain with her free hand, and the metal plate pulled open, and *whoosh*, a cool breeze came out into the room.

"You're lucky." Quinn walked into the room, startling Davis, making her jump back and drop her book. "I'm sorry, I didn't mean to spook you. I was just going to say you have one of the few rooms with a vent. Ringo fixed up some of the rooms with some kind of weird exchange vents—I'm not quite sure how he did it. But it's pretty genius. A fan somehow sucks air from outside; then, several filters remove any impurities and toxins, and then another fan blows a fresh breeze out. They were pretty intricate to make, though, so only a few rooms have them. And this is one of them."

"Oh, what about the creepy clown? Is there a reason for that?" Davis said with a slight smile.

Quinn couldn't tell if Davis was sincere or being ornery. Quinn took a bet on genuine and politely answered that it had been Ringo's when he was a child. He had kept some books, magazines, trinkets, and mementos in the bunker and allocated them among the rooms for decoration.

"Oh, does that explain that too?" laughed Davis as she nodded her head toward a very bizarre framed poster. It was on the far side of the bed, between the nightstand and the wall. It was directly across from the closet, so earlier, when she turned around after hanging up her towels, she had first seen this poster featuring multi-colored rainbow cartoon bears that were dancing around a rainbow spiral.

"Ah…yes…that gem," replied Quinn. "Well, you *did* get the air vent. Therefore, you also get the bears."

Davis got a solemn look on her face and then looked downward. She felt uncomfortable and awkward. Her head was buzzing again, and she started to get worried if she didn't sit down soon, falling over may become inevitable. She got herself over to the bed, sitting lightly on the edge of the mattress.

"I'm sorry if that was too much." Quinn was looking concerned, and Davis noticed something in her eyes. Quinn looked compassionate. Davis felt like she hadn't seen that in a long time, or even that she'd ever seen it or even had compassion herself. Perhaps she did. Davis hoped that it was in her all the time, a deep-rooted feeling waiting to become unearthed. Like a dull dream fading, she felt something in her brain awakening. She nodded her head in a way that let Quinn know it was okay.

"Anyhow, I brought you some clean clothes. Sorry I didn't bring them in sooner." Quinn walked over and placed the clothes on the edge of the bed. "I think these should fit. I had to guess. After you get dressed, if you're up to it, I can show you around, where the food and water are and the garden. Also, where you can find other clothes and do laundry, that kind of thing. And if you want, you can meet the others." After a short pause, she added, "But, take your time. No rush. We can even do it tomorrow or later in the week."

Before Quinn left, Davis noticed another look in her eye. A look that told her the meeting actually could not wait.

~

Although it was clear she should, Davis couldn't get herself to go out right away. Her mind was floating again, and she felt ill. Laying her head down and not meaning to fall asleep, Davis drifted off as if being coerced by sleep. The next thing she realized was that an enormous cat was sitting on her bed looking at her. *That wasn't there before*, Davis thought. She looked at the cat and blinked her eyes several times to make sure it was genuinely there. The cat blinked back. She looked over at the door, seeing it was ajar and how the furry interloper got in. Davis had seen cats in person, feral ones walking in the streets, but she had never been near one. Realizing she'd never been this close, she couldn't be positive that the cat was extra-large, but it seemed that way to her. Humungous but not overweight, the cat was long and lean—looming, like a king looking at his subject, from the edge of the bed. The cat had great large green eyes that seemed to be calling her an idiot. The cat was handsome, a mix of dark and light gray stripes and some cream and white stripes and markings mixed in. The cat's long, slinky tail was slapping the bed softly: *pat, pat, pat*. Davis sat there, not sure what to do. She kind of scrunched back up against the headboard and surveyed the area to see if she could slip out of bed and not go near the cat. *"Meow!"*

It sounded so loud and angry that she let out a little yelp and leaped out of bed. The cat gave her a look of contempt, jumped down from his assumed throne, and sauntered toward Davis. She gave another yelp and backed up against the wall. The cat stopped and took a good long stretch; it seemed to go from his shoulders, down his back, and out each side as the cat shook each leg out individually after stretching. The cat then walked over to Davis, looked up at her in her supposed disdain, rubbed against her legs once, and promptly left the room.

Davis immediately felt silly. She couldn't believe she was afraid of that cat. It had been kind of cute when it gave her a leg rub. The cat gave her a warm, cozy feeling. Especially since she hadn't been sure what to expect, and what had happened was pleasant. She hoped that would happen more and more. She felt the last few days of her life had been so crazy; it had been full of illness, uncertainty, and fear. A pleasant surprise at this point was a welcome surprise, albeit a small event.

Davis realized she was famished and thirsty and that people were waiting on her. She sighed and closed the door until it clicked and then turned back to the bed to dress in the clean clothes Quinn had brought her. She was happy to put some fresh-smelling clothing on, at least. *Another small pleasure to hold onto*, she thought as she pulled on the clean white underwear and clipped on the bra and then the pants, which were weird to her; they were a thick dark blue material that was slightly stiff. The shirt was red and a little too big but soft and comfortable. Lastly, she donned a pair of white socks. Overall, she felt that Quinn had guessed her sizes pretty well; the bra might be a tad loose, but nothing was uncomfortable. She pulled at the edge of her shirt nervously and then walked out the door, scared but eager to find out what was about to happen. She found herself wishing that the cat was there to escort her out.

Alas, the cat was not there, so Davis made her way out of her room solo. She went down the hallway, opposite the way she went for the bathroom. She didn't know which direction she should go but felt like she could hear some sounds coming from that way. She walked slow and steady, peeking around corners and into doors very carefully, unsure what to look for or what she would find. The sounds were getting louder, so there was a certainty she was going the right way. Davis got to a doorway and peeped around a corner, seeing Quinn and another woman in what appeared to be a kitchen. She couldn't hear what Quinn said, who was whispering something to the woman next to her. The other woman started laughing, and she lightly placed her hand on Quinn's shoulder. As she did this, the woman turned her head slightly and saw Davis. "Oh!" she said, "I'm sorry. I didn't see you there." She quickly jerked her hand away from Quinn's shoulder at the same time she spoke.

"Davis, so glad to see you!" said Quinn with a broad smile. "This is Ana. She also lives here with her two children, her little boy Russell W., who turned four in February, and her little girl Mae has just turned two. She's Namaguchi's fourth wife."

Ana walked over and stuck out her hand to shake with Davis. Davis took her warm hand in hers and shook it gingerly. Davis was surprised by the length of her hair; it was longer than any hair she'd seen—and it was shiny, bouncy, and pretty. It was very individualistic, too; something she was not used to seeing, whether it was a hairstyle or anything else. "So, um, how are you feeling?" Ana asked tentatively.

"Better, I think," said Davis. "A lot of confusion still. About why I'm here and such. And I feel like, oh, I don't know; it doesn't matter. It's hard to explain anyhow."

"I'm sure it is confusing, and maybe like you don't know what is real and what is fake, true, or false?"

"That about sums it up, I suppose."

"Well, that is normal. Because it isn't normal to hear everything you've ever known is not true. But believe me, it will even out. It'll all come out in the wash."

"What does that mean, 'it'll all come out in the wash'?"

"Oh, it was just something my mom said to me when I was troubled. It just means that everything will get worked out eventually and that things will be okay in the end. So, don't worry because we can't control when or where it will get figured out, but it will get figured out."

"Your mom sounds wise; does she live here too?"

At this point, Quinn seemed to leap forward, and she piped in, "Are you hungry? Do you need something to eat or drink? We were just getting some lunch together."

"Yes, actually," answered Davis, shyly, quietly. "That's why I came in here in the first place. I hope it is okay."

"Let's see," said Quinn. "What can we feed you? Your stomach is still getting used to regular food, so I don't think we should go crazy. Do you want to try some plain oatmeal, maybe a small salad with no dressing?"

"Well, I don't know really what any of those things are or how they taste. You're the expert. I'll leave it up to you, but is there anything I can do to help you get things ready?"

"No, we're making salads anyhow, and the oatmeal, you just add hot water...it's a good idea. We'll make some for everybody. You can go sit down, and we'll bring everything shortly." Quinn said, pointing out toward a door that connected to the kitchen. "The dining room is in there; some other people are at the table, already."

Quinn turned around and started busying herself with the food. Davis nervously waved to Ana, who was still looking at her, and she made her way out the door Quinn had indicated. Davis walked into a large room, painted a pale yellow. Taking a deep breath, she tentatively crossed the threshold into the unknown.

A group of people sat at a long dark brown wooden table. They all looked at her as if she had antlers growing from her head. Finally, Ringo seemed to remember his manners. "Welcome!" he said in a booming voice that didn't match his stick-thin frame. "Sit down; please come join us."

Davis found an empty spot at the long table; there were white plates and glasses at each, along with a sunny bright yellow napkin and silver utensils.

Nobody said anything for a minute. There was a lot of staring. A lot of questions were asked with eyes as uncertainty and tension hung in the air. There was a bowl of nuts in the middle of the table; Davis absentmindedly took one from the bowl and tentatively chewed it as she chewed over thoughts in her brain. "So, I'm Davis," she ventured.

"You met me, Ringo, this is my wife Audrey, and our twins Oliver and Olivia," he said, gesturing to a lady and two children sitting right of him. "You're eating almonds, you know? They might be difficult to digest since you've never had them. They are great nutrition for you. I like to call nuts 'nature's vitamins'"—Ringo inserted a pause and slight smile, seemingly amused by his wit—"but you might want to take it easy since you're not used to eating them."

Davis looked down at the nuts and then at Ringo's family. Audrey was striking, with clear, ivory skin and large brown eyes, prominent cheekbones, and a shapely chin. Davis immediately coveted that chin. Her own had a narrowness to it and was a cleft chin. When Audrey spoke, Davis was even more surprised. She had an accent. "We are glad to have you here with us, Davis. I know it has been a difficult few days, but please count us as friends. We're here to help you with anything you might want or need."

"Thank you, but really, can someone please tell me why I am here? What is this all about?"

Ringo answered, slowly and calmly, as if he was explaining to a child. "I know you must be very confused, and a lot is going on for you. But, please, believe me, it will be better for you if we start slow. We'll have a real sit-down after dinner tonight, and..." Ringo trailed off, and Davis seemed to know that she wouldn't find any answers in the immediate future. She decided to try something else, try to at least open conversation and get to know these people who were her captors yet seemed to mean her no harm.

"You know, I might be digressing a bit, but thoughts have been floating in and out of my mind, and I want to ask before I forget. But how do you get all this food?"

"We grow some of it," Audrey answered. "Some items were vacuum-sealed and stored in our deep freezers when we realized we would have to come down here. Like the almonds, actually. We have hidden solar panels up top for electricity, and the fans Ringo made create some additional electricity. They keep us running: freezer, fridge, lights, oven, we even have heating for winter, but we do keep it cold in here, at sixty-three, to conserve. But it takes the edge of winter off. And—" Audrey was nervously rambling; Davis decided to cut in and changed the topic.

"Oh, thank you. That's interesting. Can I digress again and ask about your accent? I've never met anyone with an accent."

"Yes, I'm from Annecy, France. It's a small town, a little less than an hour out of Geneva, Switzerland."

"How did you get here? I mean, we haven't had legal immigration for so long."

"I moved here for work and then was married to Ringo about a year before the borders were closed. Then I went to France to visit my family.

I knew things were getting touchy here once they cured the Lombardi Plague, and policies were changing." She looked at Davis to make sure she was following without discrimination and not getting upset by what she said. She saw Davis was just listening intently, so she continued. "As I was saying, I knew things were uneasy, but I didn't expect them to close the borders. Especially for dual citizens! But, when they closed the borders overnight, I had to fight my way back in. Thankfully, being married to an American helped. It was still a lot of hoops to jump through and not at all easy. But I made it back, we made our way down here, and we had these two great kiddos."

Davis was shocked. She knew the borders had been closed, but she had no idea they had locked out those even with dual citizenship. She wondered how many people this could have affected, people stuck in another country when their homes and families were here. Just because they possibly didn't have a spouse. It made her realize that this would also affect Audrey's ability to see her family in France. She then looked over at the kids. The kids that had never met their maternal grandparents, aunts, uncles, cousins. Previously, she knew the borders being closed meant families kept apart, but she never really thought about it. Suddenly, it seemed as if a fog had lifted from her brain to show her just how devastating this must have been to people. She mindlessly took another almond and thoughtlessly chewed it. She snapped back and realized she had been staring at the kids. They had got their looks from their mom. Cheery, happy, plump apples for cheeks. Lovely, shiny chestnut brown hair. And adorable round non-cleft chins. They both smiled at her but didn't speak. After a moment, Davis asked another question she had been pondering.

"So, there is another thing that I've been thinking about. Why do some people have the names regulated by the government, like myself and Quinn? The government prohibits any first names and allows only certain surnames, but you guys have first names," said Davis, remembering the day she turned fifteen, and they showed her the list of approved surnames. The government assigned children without parents their names, and she, like many others, simply chose to keep the name they gave her when she was born. There were only about a hundred to pick from as President Everett said it fostered community spirit and togetherness for people to have similar names. But since there had been so many orphans with assigned names that had little to do with actual ancestry or familial relation, a Davis could easily marry another Davis. The government kept pretty extensive records, and genetic testing before marriage ensured you were not too closely related.

Audrey answered, "Well, here, we pick our names. Some people have decided to keep their government names, like Quinn. Others, like Ringo and myself, picked our own and chose names for our kids. The important thing here is people have that choice. And actually, our kids did too. Ana named her son 'Russell,' but on his own, he decided he liked the sound of Russell W. So, he added the *W*, and we all call him by the full name that he picked, Russell W."

"What does your name mean, Ringo?" asked Davis. "Ringo? I've never heard anything like that."

"I picked my name from someone who was a famous drummer at one time, a long time ago. A lot of people didn't consider him a great drummer. I do, but regardless, what you can't deny is that he was revolutionary. Different, creative, but not a show-off or pretentious. He played meticulously and tinkered endlessly." Davis noticed that Ringo had started drumming his long slender fingers on the table as he talked about this man. "But, while I drum a little for fun, it's not why I picked the name. It's because I strive to work my computers, inventions, and electronics the way he played drums." Ringo had a shy little laugh, seeming to be a bit embarrassed talking so highly of a man he had never met, or maybe he was ashamed to compare himself to a person he obviously admired.

Davis wasn't entirely sure she understood what Ringo meant by playing his computers and inventions like drums. Audrey saw the confusion on her face. "Before we moved down here, Ringo brought computers, monitors, different components, circuit boards, wires—you name it. Boxes and boxes of wires, tools, programming software. All his things to tinker with and repair any computer program or electronic. But they're getting old, getting worn down, and we don't always have enough power. Sometimes he has to get very creative to get things done, coax results out. But, no matter what amazing things he does or what records he accesses to help us, you'll never hear him brag. He's beyond humble."

The whole time, Ringo was looking down, obviously very shy and modest about the words that his wife was speaking about him. He didn't have to think about it long because soon Quinn was coming out with Ana, bringing in food.

Following behind Ana was someone Davis knew. In fact, she would recognize his face anywhere. He had the same sandy blonde hair that was just a little sticky-up. His eyes were still expressive and green, and they told you he could figure out your deepest, darkest secret with a wink. She remembered everything from his still-boyish, slightly lopsided grin to the birthmark above his right eye and to the scar he had on his left wrist, a mark that somewhat resembled an arrow and pointed to his middle finger. Davis felt her heart quicken, and her temperature rise. "This is Brookshire," started Quinn when she recognized a look. "Oh, do you guys know each other?"

"Yes," replied Brookshire before Davis could utter a word. "We went to school together. We were…well, we were best friends," he finished with that lopsided smile and a shy glance downward.

Davis blushed and took a step back, and with a more devilish grin than Quinn thought possible of her, and replied, "Yes, close friends."

~

Brookshire spoke first. "I can barely believe you are here, Davis. I mean, I heard, of course, but I couldn't believe it until I saw you. And I was out until this morning."

"It's nice to see you again, too. To be honest, I wasn't sure if I ever would. Where were you this morning? I didn't even realize people left here."

Quinn piped in. "Yes, well, this might be a little too much for right now, but we have people who are on, uh, both sides?" she said it like a question. She was also looking at Ringo and Audrey and making eye contact, clearly unsure if she should be saying anything. Ringo gave a slight nod, an indication to continue. "So, Namaguchi, who you met briefly, and Brookshire here are double agents, for lack of a better word. Both work for President Everett, but both are also members of our secret group." Quinn paused for a moment and took a breath. She had been speaking very fast like she still wasn't sure if she should be talking about this. "Duffy and Hernandez, who you haven't met yet, are too. Hernandez is a nurse, and Duffy is a doctor. They both checked in on you several times when you were sick, but you probably were asleep or not aware."

Davis was not quite sure what to think. It was a lot to process; she started to trust and like these people she was meeting, but there were still many questions about why she was here. She felt a reserved apprehension about everything she was hearing. *If everyone here was honorable, why should they have to hide things? Live underground? Have secret double agents*, she thought.

Davis rested her head against her hand and closed her eyes. She was feeling overwhelmed and tired. Suddenly, Brookshire sat next to her and patted her other hand that was still on the table. "I know you've had a lot to think about and process. I want to let you know I'm here for you if you want to talk at all."

"Thank you. You always were a good friend," Davis said with a smile.

"Here, try some food," Brookshire said, spooning her out a portion of oatmeal from the tureen in the center of the table. He took the steaming bowl and placed it on Davis's placemat.

Davis took a small spoonful and held the spoon up, pausing and watching the steam rise off before she took a tentative first bite. "It's good, thanks..." said Davis. "Hot." She mostly added that because she couldn't think of anything else to say, and everyone was staring at her. One thing she hated was people staring at her. However, her remark regarding temperature did nothing to quell the stares she was receiving.

Davis kept eating little bites hoping that someone would also eat or start a different conversation which had nothing to do with Brookshire, her, or Brookshire's dimples. She realized, in all fairness, those dimples had only been brought up in her imagination so far, but she couldn't envision they went unnoticed by everyone else.

After what felt like an eternity, the people at the table remembered their manners and started eating their food. Quinn piled a little lettuce with some shredded carrot on a plate and handed it to Davis. Taking it, she gave Quinn a silent smile of thanks. Davis couldn't believe foods she had only seen in books and on television were on her plate. So far, the foods she tried had been okay, nothing awful, but sort of on the bland side. She suddenly desired this crisp looking lettuce and bright orange carrots. She took in the colors and the freshness of everything before taking a small bite. Cool. Refreshing. She had trouble thinking of adjectives to describe the food, having had nothing like it before. The lettuce didn't have a lot of flavor, but she liked how crisp it was and the mildly sweet taste. The carrots confused her tongue further. Harder in texture with a slightly sweeter flavor than the lettuce but maybe moderately bitter and earthy.

As she was pondering, Quinn piped in and asked her what she thought of the salad. "It's good, thank you," replied Davis. "Interesting. I haven't had anything like this before, but I enjoy it."

"Maybe when you're up to eating more foods, we can add a few tomatoes, cucumbers, toss it with a little olive oil and vinegar. Almost nothing better... Oh! You'll have to try bell peppers in it too! That's one of my favorite things in a salad..." And then Quinn was rambling on with her words just as Audrey had been minutes ago.

Davis realized that everyone was trying but that nobody knew what to say. There was an odd tension that hung in the air. They were trying to get to know each other without being too excited or, possibly worse, too blasé. She decided she wasn't even that hungry anymore, and she decided to put everyone out of their misery. "I am sorry I can't finish. I think I'll just lie down; I'm not feeling too great. Thank you for everything." She paused for a moment and looked around the table. "Ringo, I would very much appreciate it if we can have a real conversation tonight about why I'm here. I don't care anymore how heavy or overwhelming it is. I need to know."

"Of course," Ringo said. "We will make time for that. Do you want Quinn or someone like Brookshire you know a little better here when we talk?"

"Yes, both would be great, thank you." Davis made her way to the door when the large gray tabby walked in and once again considered her. "Oh, by the way, what is it with the cat?"

"That is Buster," Quinn replied. "I found him outside one day, all straggly, dirty, and hungry. I didn't think he would make it, but he somehow has. He's a scrapper. He looks like a beast; he's big and has such a loud, grumpy meow. But he's so sweet. So friendly. He'll sleep with you if you take him with you and put him on the bed."

"Oh…wow. No, thank you. I'm not quite ready for a bedmate yet," and then, to her embarrassment, she caught herself looking up to Brookshire and giving him a slight grin. She caught herself quickly and followed with, "I'm just so tired, and I've never slept with an animal." She again caught her words in her throat and tried desperately not to look at Brookshire. She excused herself quickly before she said anything else dumb.

Davis made her way back to her room and lay down on her bed in the quiet dark. For the second time in a short period, she was desperate. She was desperate to calm her mind and get some rest. Desperate not to think of Brookshire. And desperate to explain to herself why she hadn't tried to escape once.

~

Davis tried to clear her mind. But she could only think about what she needed to ask and what details she needed to clear up. Her mind kept wandering, and her heartbeat was racing. Even though she tried not to, she also kept thinking of Brookshire. They had started as friends in school. Many people thought he would eventually submit a request for marriage to Davis, but that never happened. They held hands once. It was at a Courting Dance. They had found a dark corner away from everyone else and just talked for almost the entire time. They never danced, never kissed, just held hands. Davis remembered looking down at their intertwined hands and seeing that scar on his wrist. She had wished the "arrow" pointed to her heart instead of his finger.

As she fidgeted in bed and tried to calm her mind, she remembered another thing from Brookshire. He had told her if she ever had trouble falling asleep, she should start with *A* in the alphabet and name something she was grateful for that also began with an *A*. Then onto *B* and *C* until she fell asleep, usually a cinch to happen by the more complicated letters like *K*. She tried to relax her body and breathed deeply in and out a few times. She struggled for a few minutes to come up with her first word until she remembered Alvarez, a kind teacher she had in school. Then, her mind quickly shifted as she remembered Alvarez was also a strict follower of President Everett. *Could she trust that anymore?* Davis no longer knew. Eventually, she decided it didn't change the fact Alvarez was a kind person and a great teacher. After a moment, she realized she wasn't going to solve this conundrum tonight, so she tried to push it from her mind and focus on her next letter: *B*. That was easy, Brookshire, of course. *C. Cats*, she thought with a little giggle. She never thought that would be what she'd pick; she wasn't even wholly comfortable with Buster yet. But he was cute and did rub her legs, so she was grateful for the random kindness if nothing else. She got to *D* and couldn't think of anything. Her mind went blank.

She sunk into her thoughts, her brain filing through the different people and places in her life as she drifted off to sleep.

Her sleep came in restless fits. Even though Davis was exhausted, she surmised that she had trouble sleeping because of her anxiety. She was also afraid to sleep through the night and miss her meeting with Ringo. After tossing and turning for a while, she got up and started pacing in the room, trying to organize her thoughts and questions. She went over to the door to crack it open to see if she could hear anything, but she couldn't. After a few minutes, Buster came into the room and started pacing right beside her. As she reached the end of the room and before she would turn around, Buster would look up at her as if saying, *Are we doing this again?* Buster would then turn around a few seconds after her, do a little trot to catch up with her, and then repeat the scenario at the next turn. Davis found great amusement in it at first. Then she started to worry that maybe she was teasing the cat, which wasn't very nice. She knew nothing about animals and didn't know what they might and might not like. For a reason unbeknownst to her, she wanted to try to pick the cat up. Leaning down and putting her hands around the cat from a few different angles, she attempted to figure out what the best way to pick him up would be. Losing all her confidence after Buster gave her a tough-sounding "Meow!" Davis walked over to the bed and sat down instead, to see if he would follow her. He did, jumping up on the bed, sitting next to her, waiting for her to make the next move.

She mindlessly started petting Buster's head and listening to the soft, rumbling purr that came from him. Buster kept bumping his head against her hand with gentle force. His tail held high and slightly twitchy. She leaned back down against the pillows, and Buster curled up next to her, nestled into her side. Before Davis could even think about anything, she drifted off, lulled to sleep by Buster's soft purrs.

It wasn't a deep sleep, but it never was for Davis when the recurring nightmare started. She told herself to wake up—she was always somehow aware when this dream started again, and the last thing she wanted to do was relive this traumatizing nightmare. However, as usual, she stayed asleep. It was the same as always. Darkness and shadows were encompassing everything. Then, out of the dark, a boy's face appeared, he was dirty, and his face was streaked with tears and paralyzed with fear. As he's dragged away from her, he starts begging, reaching out to her for help as she backs away. Screams and shouts are coming from below. As she continued to step back, getting further apart from the boy, the fear and the darkness, she trips backward. Looking down at what tripped her, she sees a black, bloody beating heart. As she screamed in her dream, her brain started to yell at her *wake up, Wake up, WAKE UP!!!* She finally woke up, sitting straight up with a gasp and scaring Buster straight off the bed. Feeling pain, she looked at her palm, where three crescent-shaped marks bled. She had clenched her fist so hard she dug her nails into her hand, making cuts into her palm. She was familiar; this had happened before, too.

Davis rolled over on her side and saw Buster on the floor, giving her a look to let her know she had greatly inconvenienced him; then he left the room. She was glad. Anxiety choked her throat, and sweat beaded her forehead. She wished she knew why this dream haunted her. It always made her wake up depressed, tensed, and full of anxiety. She supposed she had simplified the problem to herself. After all, she knew the reason she had the dream. What she was really after was how she could forget it and make it all go away.

Since Quinn had brought her some more clean clothes and fresh towels, Davis slowly got off the bed and gathered a few things so she could go shower. She wanted to go clean the cuts in her hand and get ready for dinner tonight. She wished she could wash away the wound in her soul, too.

~

After her shower, Davis dressed and, after putting her items back in her room, worked her way back to the dining room. She was also keeping her eyes open for Quinn. Davis spotted Quinn in the kitchen, prepping for dinner. "Hi, Quinn. Do you have any kind of first aid kit, bandages? I somehow cut myself," said Davis, hoping that Quinn would hand over the needed supplies with no questions asked. Luckily, Quinn nodded and walked her down the hallway a bit to a very white and sterile-looking room smelling of antiseptic. "This is the medical room. We have basic supplies in this unlocked cabinet, and then more advanced things Duffy and Hernandez, our medical team, have to be here for." She opened the first cupboard as she was speaking and reached in to pull out a first aid kit. She handed it to Davis and told her that it would have ample supplies.

"Do you need any help? You're okay?"

"Yes, fine, thank you. Just a small cut on my palm." Davis said a quiet word of thanks to herself when Quinn just nodded as she walked out and told her she'd be fixing dinner if she needed anything else.

Davis went about cleaning her hand again in the sink in the room and then pressed some towels on it to dry up the water. Luckily, the bleeding had stopped, and she found some wound cleaner and ointment in the kit and some gauze to wrap around. She tried to do as inconspicuous as job as possible, but she realized that would be impossible. No way anyone would miss this. Trying to think about what she could say about what happened, but she had no idea. Replacing the first aid kit, she decided to stick with not knowing how it happened. Then Davis worked her way back to the kitchen to speak with Quinn.

When she walked in, she saw Quinn cutting food for dinner. Quinn turned and faced her, cheerfully saying, "You okay? Can I get you anything?"

"No, thank you. Do you need any help?"

"I'm almost done. By the way, you'll meet Hernandez and Duffy tonight. And Namaguchi is back too. Just didn't want you to be surprised by the new faces."

"Great, thanks. Should I just go wait in the dining room?"

"Sure, I'll be in there in a few minutes."

Davis walked into the room, but there was nobody there yet. She sat down and sipped the water that was already sitting there for her. Feeling tired, she put her hands on the table, elbows out to the side, and then rested her head atop her hands. Her head was still spinning and pounding in intermittent bursts; she also felt random different throbs and aches. After she relaxed a few moments, she felt a hard bump on her extended elbow. She opened her eyes and peeked out under her arm. Buster, the large gray cat, was bumping her arm with his forehead. He would tilt his head, give her elbow a substantial bump, then turn around in a circle, almost prancing on his velvety feet. A slight hump in his back and his tail held high. Then, he came around again for another bump. Davis lifted her head and started petting the cat, who got his purr motor going in low, grumbly satisfaction.

Quinn walked into the dining room with a large salad bowl. Davis stood up as if in embarrassment that she was petting Buster. Quinn just smiled a friendly grin, sat the salad bowl down, and then took a smaller bowl filled with something to the corner. Buster immediately forgot all about Davis and shot over to that corner without hesitation. He stuck his broad head into the bowl and started chowing down vigorously. Quinn quipped to Davis as Buster ran to the dish, "I see you're making friends with Buster," she said. "He's a sweet cat. I saved him when he was a kitten. He was roaming around the solar panels we have."

"Solar panels. Yes, I think Audrey mentioned those. How do you keep those hidden from troops and such?" asked Davis.

"Well, first, we're pretty far out from anywhere. We are not near any Pods or government centers, factories, or schools. Second, they are some-what hidden. Most look like rocks and boulders. Ringo had an ingenious idea with those. But we do have to go out occasionally and dust them off, clean them a bit. That's where I found Buster, chasing after a lizard or some-thing near the panels. I couldn't find his mom, so I brought him back here."

"I see Buster beat feet—or I guess beat paws—to that dish. What does Buster eat, by the way? Or, do I want to know?" said Davis with a nervous smile.

"Well, honestly, I don't love to think about it, but we are under a bit of a hillside. Mice and moles, little lizards, and things do get in here occasionally." At this comment, it was Quinn's turn to look nervous and seem unsure of herself. She brushed the bit of hair that fell over her eye and twisted her lips up and gave a sort of *what can you do* puff of breath. "On the less gruesome side of things, we also have some freeze-dried eggs, chicken, and fish. We give him a little bit of that when we have our dinner."

"Oh, that's interesting..." Davis's words trailed off as her thoughts wandered; her eyes stared off into space.

Quinn could tell that Davis was slightly uncomfortable. Not sure of herself or what to say. "Well," said Quinn, "I'm going to get the rest of the plates. The rest of the crew should be here in a few moments. We have a dinner bell." At this, Quinn looked like she had a genius thought. A huge mischievous smile flashed across her face, and she added, with what seemed like much spontaneity, "Do you want to ring it?"

Why not, thought Davis. At this point, after all that happened the last few days and today, the longest day of her life—why not ring a damn dinner bell for people she didn't even know?

~

Quinn led Davis to a corner of the kitchen with a box-type object on the wall, sort of a silver pyramid, a little bit bigger than her hand with a metal clapper in the middle of it. "That's the cowbell," said Quinn. "Give it a few smacks with this mallet. 'More cowbell!!!!'" said Quinn, very enthusiastically.

Davis looked at her with a blank stare as she slowly took the mallet from her. Confusion clouded her face. "It's an old joke...from an old show," stammered Quinn in somewhat of a slight laugh/slight quizzical tone. She then added as an explanation, "When I used to be in the Pods, every night I loved watching old TV shows and movies at the library. I found it so interesting; things people said and did and even the clothes they wore. The cowbell thing is from an old TV show. It was quite the joke once upon a time."

"Ah!" exclaimed Davis. "I loved doing that too, watching old movies and television shows. Very interesting. I didn't know that one, though."

"Never mind…sorry. So, go ahead and smack the cowbell."

Clank, clank, clank.

"No, smack it good, fast a few times in a row."

A very tinny, loud clank-a, clank-a, clank-a, CLANK-a!! rang out.

"That'll do it, dinner is served," Quinn said as she carried out a big plate of white filets and handed a plate mounded high with fluffy white piles of some type of food to Davis. Quinn saw the confusion on her face and shot her a short explanation of "potatoes."

~

When Davis came in, she was surprised to see that Ringo, Audrey, and the kids were already settling in. Ana and her children followed soon after and quickly sat. Quinn put the platter on the table and then took a seat next to Ana, delicately placing her hand on Ana's shoulder but quickly removing it. Davis sat in the same spot she had been in earlier, and Brookshire came in shortly after and promptly settled in next to her, causing her to feel suddenly very warm. Davis hoped to herself that the heat in her cheeks was not showing as redness on her face. Then, before she knew it, Namaguchi came in with two people she did not recognize. "This is," Namaguchi said in an exhausted voice, "Hernandez."

Hernandez was a very friendly-looking man, with skin a deep reddish-brown, the color of a sepia photo that Davis had once seen. His small brown eyes squinted with a smile, and with a toothy grin, he stuck out his hand. "I'm the nurse here," said Hernandez.

"Nice to meet you," said Davis quietly. She took Hernandez in with a quizzical stare before realizing it might be rude, so she quickly looked down and away. Davis hadn't meant to be offensive, but she had never seen someone overweight. Not that Hernandez was obese, but he had a small stomach bump that extended over the top of his pants, and his shirt pulled taut over it. He also had a slight padding of pudgy, plump skin under his chin. She was doubly surprised because someone who worked for President Everett would most certainly have to be healthy. President Everett had proclaimed being overweight extinct, claimed he "cured" it by providing people with nutrition biscuits only. Davis saw the posters in her mind. President Everett held a plate of biscuits in one hand, a glass of clear water in the other. The caption read, *Proper nutrition for healthy people!* She had learned her whole life in school that each biscuit contains the exact amount of calories, fat, fiber, and vitamins you need to function. They included macronutrients, minerals, and antioxidants too. She realized she didn't even know what a lot of that meant. She had just learned her whole life that it was true.

Hernandez seemed to read her mind, or Davis was more obvious than she realized. "I know, my weight. Even though I'm only considered about twenty pounds overweight in most historical medical books, you don't see it nowadays. But, because I'm a good nurse, I keep my head down and do my assignments; in short, I know how to play the game, so nobody bothers me."

Davis wondered what he meant by "play the game."

Hernandez, patting his stomach and chuckling, added, "You don't get this for free!" He continued, "I have a weakness for something. These processed cakes they started out calling them '2025 Cakes' because they introduced them that year. But the name changed to 'Canoe Cakes' because of the shape. They were long, about six inches. And they dipped in the middle, which was cream-filled, then…" at that point, Hernandez seemed to get a little excited, "They're covered in *chocolate*. They're not healthy for you, that's for sure. Full of preservatives and with an airtight factory wrapper, they seemingly will last forever. Plus, we place them in vacuum-sealed containers, and those are in our deep freeze. They thaw out pretty nicely and make a treat I can't resist! In the next bunker over, which is run by Romo, they saved many boxes. Romo's father loved them, but he passed two years ago. Nobody else likes them. Nobody but me, that is."

Davis felt quite overwhelmed by this new information and wasn't sure she followed everything. She was grateful when a small older lady came forward. Even though she was probably in her seventies, she seemed perky and lively, with an infectious spirit of happiness that seemed to surround her. In the customary bob, her amber-colored hair had a bit of a curl and wild wave to it, and her warm brown eyes exuded friendliness.

"Oh, stop talking, Hernandez!" she said in a friendly but firm tone. She then looked at Davis and added, "He never stops talking!" and a huge smile spread across her kind face as she extended her hand to Davis. "I'm Duffy, the doctor."

"Nice to meet you, Duffy." Davis was taken a bit aback by how warm and soft her hand was.

"Well, let's eat, shall we?" interjected a tired-sounding Ringo.

Davis was glad; she didn't have anything more to say, and her head started throbbing again. Just as she was about to ask about the food in front of her, two more people came in.

Everybody looked up from the table concurrently with looks of mixed confusion and happy surprise on their faces. "Hi, Romo!" exclaimed Ringo, all the tiredness in his voice evaporated. He then looked over at Davis and, as a way of explanation, introduced them and added that Romo lived in the bunkers that tunneled out to the left of them.

"Who is this with you?" Ringo said, looking back at Romo, who was both tall and slim. Davis noted that the person Ringo was asking Romo about had her black hair, not in a bob but, in a messy, cascading tousle, slightly parted and pinned back in the middle with a bright blue clasp. Davis also saw that Quinn nervously and suddenly stood up, looking past Romo, noticing the girl with the long black hair.

There wasn't a chance for Romo to answer Ringo. Before anyone could say anything else, the girl bounded forward, like a bunny. Spread across her face was a broad grin. Quinn had never seen someone who seemed so naturally bubbly and jubilant. She was all of five feet tall but somehow had the presence of someone ten feet tall, with large blue eyes that looked like liquid pools. A cute, albeit somewhat large and distracting, beauty mark sat above her right eye. She delicately extended her hand toward Quinn and said hello, informing all those present in a cheery voice that her name was Cricket. Quinn greeted her back, then took all of her in—and Cricket was a lot. She had inexplicably short white shorts on that were cut very high on her thigh, the shortest shorts Quinn had ever seen. Cricket had a too small T-shirt stretched across her too large chest; the shirt said in faded pink writing, "Girls Kick Ass." Quinn didn't know what to say, so she just asked her where she found the unique clothing. Cricket laughed long and hard. *Longer and harder than someone should for something that wasn't even that funny*, Quinn thought. But she also thought Cricket was a pretty little thing. Cricket answered back in a chirpy, happy voice, sounding almost as if she was part bird. "I don't know, rummaging around here and there, different boxes that somebody stuck in one of these bunkers! And who cares!" she exclaimed, and as she did, she threw her arms out to the side, making herself into a T-shape.

Quinn couldn't understand the excitement in which Cricket delivered this statement. She acted as if it were the most exciting information ever told. And honestly, it wasn't much information. Quinn was dumbfounded yet fascinated; she had never met anyone like Cricket; she seemed to be such a boundless ball of energy.

Romo piped in, "This is Cricket, everyone, as you have figured out by now." Romo seemed tired, just making this statement. Ana thought it sounded similar to how she felt after a day of chasing the kids around. "Cricket was a runner. We were out doing surveillance, and we saw her caught in a Drone Scanner beam, and we disrupted the signal before we took her. She's been with us a few days; she's a Natural Immune, so there was no recovery."

"What's a Natural Immune?" asked Davis.

Nobody answered her question, but Romo walked over to Davis and put her hand on her shoulder. "You must be Davis. It's nice to meet you; we've heard a lot about you."

"Nice to meet you too," said Davis, for what felt like the seven hundredth time that evening.

"Well, we just wanted to say hi and make introductions. I see you're ready for dinner, and we don't want to interrupt. We wanted to introduce Cricket. She's actually staying over at Bhatt and Lyon's bunker. See you guys later. Enjoy your meal."

"Bye, Romo and Cricket, it was nice to meet you!" said Quinn with a big smile.

"See ya L-A-T-E-R alligators!" said Cricket, spelling out the letters in "later."

She is an oddball, but a cool, cute oddball, thought Quinn.

~

Dinner passed somewhat quickly and unceremoniously after that. The conversation hit a lull, and people enjoyed their salad, tilapia, and potatoes in mostly a satisfied silence. At least everyone seemed satisfied; Davis had never had any of these things before and did not have a lot of food history for comparison. An occasional break in the quiet was just to ask someone if they were enjoying their dinner or not or if they had a good day or not, and other small pleasantries. Davis was both comforted and annoyed by the silence. She felt like these people should be getting to know her, and as she was stuck there, it would be good to learn more about who her captors were. Simultaneously, feeling tired and overwhelmed, Davis was not even sure what to say, so sitting quietly and chewing were happily her only chores at the moment. She was also distracted as Brookshire kept making sideways glances and small smiles toward her, making Davis feel so nervous that just as she decided it would be best not to talk, Ringo spoke up. "Well, with dinner done, maybe we should clean up and have a conversation?" He was looking directly at Davis, and she felt a hot lump in her throat that made it hard to swallow. Ringo stood up, and Audrey quickly told all the kids that they should go and play together—no fighting! Audrey also told Quinn she would clean up the dishes. Then Ringo asked Brookshire to wait while he and Namaguchi went to grab some files. Quinn and Davis helped carry the plates and platters into the kitchen. When Davis walked through the door, she realized that everything was about to change. She didn't know precisely what was changing, but she knew she would never be the same again.

~

Davis gulped as she sat on one side of the table, Brookshire to the right of her, lightly holding her hand. She stared at Ringo, Namaguchi, and Quinn on the other side of the table. Ringo spoke up first. "I know this will be hard to hear, but I promise we'll go through everything and answer all your questions, and there is no need to worry. You're safe here. No matter what happens, I promise we're on your side." Davis felt and looked terrified but nodded in the hopes that Ringo would take this as an indication he should continue. Luckily, he did. "Well, I think the first thing we should start with is the brain control chemical the government injects into you and others regularly. The Marigold Injection."

He paused, and Davis piped in, "I thought that was to keep us safe from illness, the Lombardi Plague?"

"Yes, that is true, in one way. Almost all your vaccinations just have some helpful vitamins and minerals. Once a year, you get protection against the Lombardi Plague, antigens that your immune system recognizes as hostile invaders. You then produce antibodies in response that your body remembers for the future. If the virus reappears, your immune system recognizes the antigen and attacks it immediately before it can spread and cause sickness. Also, once a year, you get a flu shot; it's different than the regular one you usually get every month, but they don't tell you that." Davis nodded again, although she wasn't quite sure she completely understood what Ringo was saying. He continued, "It's not that important. What is important is all of them also have a chemical in there; it alters how your brain works. It makes you susceptible to suggestions, influences. It's pretty powerful brain control. They use this to regulate, curb, and discipline the population according to their needs and wants. If you think about it, you'll now likely remember some things you've done in the past that you would not do now."

Davis had a flash of a young boy, screaming. Tears streaked down his face. "How can they do that?"

"Well, they want the ultimate control, right?" He paused and then added as if further clarification was needed, "I mean, they don't want you thinking for yourselves because that could be dangerous for them." Ringo took a deep breath and held it, pausing for a second, his eyes looking up toward the ceiling as if in deep thought over what to say next. "Davis, for instance, do you think that President Everett eliminated *all* illnesses? That people no longer get, say, cancer? Or have heart attacks? Or strokes? Even on a much lesser train of thought, a common cold or flu? You've been sick before; I know you have because everybody has. You were likely put on a "special assignment," so you were not at work. They convince you it's because you did something wrong. You didn't get your last injection on time. Or you didn't eat or shower properly. And then, you start to believe it. Because as far as you know, they've never lied to you before. And they provide you with a home, job, and food. And your brain processes all those things very fast, and being under their control, you just believe it. You have no choice in it." Here Ringo took a deep breath. "The sad part is—well, it's all tragically sad—the terminally sick people, the people I mentioned who have something like cancer, a stroke, or severe heart attack, they're put away. They're either shoved into a Class Three Pod or a hospital. But, it's a hospital in name only. Nobody takes care of them. They're lucky if they get clean bathrooms, much less any kind of medicine or nutrition."

Davis felt tense and hot all over. She looked down and saw she was squeezing Brookshire's hand very tightly. "Sorry," she said as she wrestled her hand from the firm grip he was returning.

Brookshire stood up. "I think I'll get some water. Does anyone else want any?"

"Yes, please. Would you mind bringing some in for everyone?" said Namaguchi, answering for everyone at the table.

Ringo continued as Brookshire left. "Now, there are people who have a natural immunity to the brain control drug. Quinn is one of those, as is Ana. None of Namaguchi's other wives have it, though. That is why Ana is here, and they are not. The other girl you met tonight, you heard Romo say Cricket was naturally immune as well."

"Did I have natural immunity?" asked Davis.

"No, you didn't. That's why you had such a rough time detoxing from it, sorry to say."

At this point, Brookshire walked back in with a tray full of water glasses. Davis almost leaped out of her seat to grab one and gulped it down as Ringo continued. "Duffy and Hernandez, like other doctors and nurses, have access to patient records. Remember, they take your blood a few times a year too. That's not just to ferret out possible serious illness in the population, but because they want to check for your immunity. They'll red-flag someone showing immunity. Well, Duffy and Hernandez don't, but other medical staff does. It can mean death, or depending on your status; they'll attempt to brainwash you at the Everett Center…"

Here, Davis cut in with a vehement reply, "No, that's not true. I worked at the Everett Center! There is nothing like that at the Everett Center! There is nothing like that going on there!"

"Well, they don't advertise it, dear. It's not on the public tour. They keep it quiet."

Davis shrunk back and closed her eyes. She was trying to think for a minute. Rack her brain to see if any of this made any sense or rang any bells. Nothing did. Nothing made any sense anymore. And then the flash again. The young boy. Fear plastered on his face. Davis shook the thought out of her head, which Ringo mistook as a sign to continue.

"To be perfectly honest, sometimes we take other people like you because you can help us reach other goals." Here, Ringo firmed up his voice and looked Davis right in the eye. "It's still your decision to help us or not. I promise. We don't force you to work with us. We hope you will, naturally, but we don't make you. If you tell me after you hear everything I have to say that you want to leave, we'll make it happen and never bother you again."

Davis slammed down her hand hard on the table. "Okay, I want to leave then!" she said with firm conviction and anger in her voice.

Quinn got a look of shock on her face. "Oh…Davis, I know that seems easiest. But please, just listen to all Ringo has to say. There is a lot more." Brookshire gently placed his hand over Davis's, settling her a bit. But it felt like an uneasy settle. Davis felt as if any minute, the little stability she felt could come tumbling down like a house of cards on her head.

"Okay," Davis said, drawing out the "k" with a long, tired breath ending in a sigh. "You can continue; I'll listen, at least." Her wavering voice and face did not hold the same conviction as her words.

"Look," Ringo continued. "I know this is a lot. Overwhelming." He put his fingers to his temple and rubbed. "This next part will be a little easier to believe; we have some proof." He slid a folder over to Davis. "It's in here. You don't have to look at it now. Just when you get back to your room, and you are feeling up to it. The other thing I want you to understand is there is no rush to figure this out or decide."

Davis put her hand on top of the folder and slid it over to herself. She was trying to feel the weight underneath the cover and tether herself to something that had a physical reality. Even though she fought it, tears started to slide out of her eyes and down her cheeks. Quinn got up from the table and walked to the other side, sitting next to Davis, opposite the side from where Brookshire was, and lightly placed her hand on Davis's back, between her shoulders. Quinn gave a few light rubs trying to convey hope and warmth in a few soft strokes. Davis was surprised to realize she flinched at this kind gesture.

"If you're ready to proceed, we'll go ahead." Davis barely heard the words Ringo spoke to her but took another sip of water and nodded her head slowly. "This part is more Namaguchi's doing. If he would like to take over?"

"Yes," said Namaguchi. "As you know, I'm a close confidant and aide for President Everett. And as it turns out, I was not a Natural Immune to the Marigold Injection but part of a third group that Ringo forgot to mention—I developed immunity over time."

"Were you and Audrey naturally immune, or did it develop?" Davis interrupted, looking at Ringo.

"Neither," he replied. "When we saw what was happening to the country, I came down here with my family. We've never even had the vaccine. Same with Romo and a few others, like Bhatt and Lyon, who are in another bunker. We're in the middle bunker section. We were doomsday preppers, prepping for the end of the world, but we didn't like what the government was doing, so we started slowly transitioning down here, a little bit at a time. When it became clear that we'd have to move to the bunkers permanently, we did so. We were pretty isolated, to begin with; we weren't living in a crowded city. Therefore, the spotlight from the government wasn't on us anyhow. Not to digress too much, sorry."

"No problem," Namaguchi nodded in silent agreement to what Ringo had said. "It may be hard to believe, but everything you've ever learned about the Lombardi Plague is a lie. President Everett was the one to create the Lombardi Plague…"

"Oh, I just can't believe this!" Davis yelled. She was incensed. "Why do you guys hate President Everett this much? Why? Are you jealous of him? The idea of that is so ridiculous!" Davis got up from the table and started pacing around. "And you say you have proof? I can't wait to hear this 'proof you speak of.'" She walked back over to the table and flipped the front cover open, looking at the first document. At the top, it said, "From the Desk of Dr. Jack Everett." Under it were various handwritten notes. There was nothing too specific, the words "Marburg Disease," "Lombardi," and "Plague" with a question mark after it was all there was. "This is your proof? This is nothing!" Davis scoffed with disbelief.

"I know it doesn't look like much," Quinn said reassuringly. "But, please, look at the date at the top."

The date was February 2, 2025. It was almost a full year before the plague began.

AUGUST 31, 2056 – ILLUMINATION

Davis woke up in her room; she had walked away from the table, not looking back after seeing the date on top of the document. She just couldn't believe what she was seeing. Nothing made any sense to her. All night, she lay in her bed, trying to figure out if this was a mistake. She finally realized it must be a fake, a forgery, created to enhance the cause of the people who currently surrounded her. Naturally, Namaguchi would easily be able to get his hand on the letterhead to create the document. She had drifted off to an uneasy sleep, all night dreaming of a young boy screaming and crying as he is dragged off to an unknown doom by unseen hands.

A soft knock came on Davis's door. "Davis?" It was Quinn. "Are you okay? I just want to check on you. Are you hungry or thirsty? It's already late afternoon; you missed breakfast and lunch."

Davis took her time going to the door. She wasn't sure she even wanted to open it; it felt as if fury boiled beneath her brain. But she couldn't deny she was hungry and thirsty. Davis got to the door just as Quinn had given up and started to walk away. Quinn turned around and returned. "You okay?" she said as she handed her a tray with some water and crackers on it and a bowl of fruit that Quinn told Davis was strawberries.

"Um, no, Quinn, not really," Davis said in such a sarcastic way that she surprised even herself. "Let's see," she continued, the sarcasm dripping off every word, "I've been kidnapped. Forced to miss my vaccines and made ill. It's also been promised to me many times I could depart, yet I have not been able to leave." At this, she even stomped her foot like a child who got denied her favorite toy. "I mean, Quinn, you seem to be a smart girl. Do you buy this? What makes what they're doing any different than what they're accusing President Everett of doing?"

Quinn took a deep breath. "I do believe them, yes. Be it my natural immunity or just being here so long, I don't know. I can tell you that before Namaguchi even took me, I was starting to doubt some things. I had a lot of questions in my mind, things that didn't seem right. I was having a hard time trusting President Everett. Then, I got here, and what they said made sense, and they were so kind to me by contrast, I almost immediately trusted them. Maybe foolish, but I've felt comfortable and happy here, although I miss my family."

At this, Davis looked genuinely concerned and calmed down a little bit. "Your family? What happened to them?"

"I don't know. Namaguchi told me they were not naturally immune. And I know from before I came here, they were very staunch supporters of President Everett, just like every other person we knew. I never discussed my feelings about Everett with my family because I didn't want to disappoint them. So, Ringo and Namaguchi told me they brought me here in secrecy as I was in danger because of my natural immunity, which in turn, could put my family in danger. I'm not sure the danger went away, though, as the government knew I was immune, and now all of a sudden, I was gone? They could have interrogated my family, perhaps even hurt or killed them." Davis's eyes got bigger and bigger as Quinn told her story. Davis felt for this young girl, although she didn't believe what Quinn was saying. Davis felt Quinn had been lied to and manipulated by Ringo and Namaguchi. She felt very deeply for her and reached out for her hand to let her know she could continue.

"When Ringo and Namaguchi told me their side of the story, including the fact my family could be in danger, naturally I was inclined to stay because I wanted to protect them. Namaguchi told me he pulled some strings and had their last name changed and reassigned them to a different area of the country. In a small area that gets overlooked frequently. He said my family didn't question it because if the government reassigns you and says your name is going to be different, that happens without question."

"Oh, you poor girl! I think they've lied and manipulated you. I will find a way to get us both out of here. And we'll find someone in President Everett's cabinet we can trust and tell them your whole story, find your family, and you'll all be free." Davis talked so fast and passionately; she hadn't even noticed Quinn shaking her head no.

"Davis, I understand you don't want to be here. But I do. Thank you for your concern, though. There is something else. You didn't look at all the papers last night, and there are more. I brought them. I will leave them with you to look over when and if you want. They're medical records. They show Ana and me as Natural Immunes. And Namaguchi's records show him building immunity over time."

Quinn walked over and placed the papers on Davis's bed. She gave Davis a kind look and asked her if she could do anything else for her. Davis shook her head no and muttered out a half-hearted thanks as Quinn walked toward the door. "I'll let you be then. But, please don't hesitate to let me know if you need anything."

After Quinn left, Davis stood still for a few minutes. She felt numb and less sure of herself than she had before. It made her feel dizzy and crazy. When she felt a little more stable, she walked over and sat on the bed, looking at the folder like it was the Lombardi Plague itself. After mindlessly drinking some water and nibbling on crackers and strawberries, Davis realized she wanted to shower. She wanted the warm water to renew and refresh her. She felt that perhaps a physical transformation could also help her emotional and mental clarity. She could only hope that the water would carry her troubles and pain away with the dirt and sickening sheen of oil she felt on her face.

After Davis cleaned up, she came back into her room ravenous, quickly eating the rest of the food and water, wishing there was more. *Well, these people said I am welcome here*, she thought, so she decided to go to the kitchen and see what food she could find.

In the kitchen, Davis first got another cup of water, downing it. She filled it up again to take back to the room. She opened the fridge and saw the nuts she had the night before and more strawberries. She took some of both and also what looked like some leftover fish. After she pulled the fish out, it seemed as if a beacon had sent out a signal for Buster because only seconds later, he came running into the kitchen, meowing like crazy. "Oh, you dumb cat, go away." Davis lightly kicked at him but immediately felt terrible, wishing she hadn't. She wondered if Buster would take food from her and held out a piece of fish out to him. At first, it seemed Buster didn't trust her, but his want of the fish overcame him, and he slinked over to Davis, weaving in between her legs before gingerly taking the fish from her. Davis decided to leave the cat in the kitchen before all her lunch would be gone.

When Davis got back to her room, she decided to peek at those documents while she ate. Her confidence had returned somewhat, and she had little doubt examining the papers would prove them to be forgeries. She pulled up the first one and looked at it. Her first glance made her heart stop a beat. It appeared to be a legitimate hospital record; there was an embossed watermark in deep blue indelible ink. Davis quickly skimmed all the documents, seeing the watermark on all of them. It looked just like the ones she'd seen all her life when going into the medical center to get her checkups and immunizations. The process was easy: You walked in, let them scan your ID Card, and then were shown into an exam room, maybe after a short wait. The doctor came in with your medical file, which you confirmed was yours by checking the name, ID number, and class status.

Then you initialed the top form with a red pen. Davis spotted all the red marks down each of the papers. *Q*, *A*, or *N*, depending on which one she was reading. And then there was the doctor's signature, also in red. Davis held up the paper to light and looked at the backside to see if the red ink had seeped through the back or if it was just on the top. It had bled through, increasing the legitimacy. Not that she was ready to roll over quite yet. She would examine each line if it took all night, looking for any inconsistencies.

Davis started with Quinn's file as it seemed the shortest. Everything on the top information page lined up with what standard checks would be. But she noticed, when she got to the doctor's notes page that Quinn would not have seen, new notes started appearing when Quinn was twelve: "Possibly immune." Right down the right side—one after another, like little red soldiers marching down the paper. She wondered why it started at twelve and made a mental note to ask the others about that. The next page brought a surprise and one she hadn't seen before. It was another note page. It, too, had the embossed watermark and doctor's signature. The notes went on about how Quinn, now at age fifteen, was confirmed to be a Natural Immune and had shown "slight tendencies of rebellion." The doctor recommended reeducation at the Everett Center.

Ana's forms were similar. At age twelve, "Possibly immune" started showing up, and then at fifteen, she had the rebellion note page. Hers was different, though, after the note indicating "slight tendencies of rebellion." Ana's doctor had noted that Namaguchi had submitted an Inquiry of Interest, and the doctor advised the match and marriage go forward. Dr. Mazella surmised that perhaps being married to Namaguchi, an official in President Everett's cabinet, would positively influence Ana. For almost two years, it seemed to work. Then, the notes continued onto another page, showing Ana's rebellious tendencies had become more vigorous, and she was also showing anger at her appointments. It also included a note that mentioned Namaguchi had started showing immunity in his latest tests. Then, in big red letters at the bottom of the page, the words "Eliminate the pair" were circled.

~

Davis set the files aside and leaned back, her head against the wall. She had no idea what to make of all of this. Her head felt woozy, and fatigue overcame her. Hours later, she awoke with a start. It took her a few moments to realize where she was and what had been going on. She rubbed the sleep from her eyes and took a look around; the files had fallen on the floor and were askew. Davis grabbed the glass of water she had set on the table beside the bed and was happy there was a drink left. She then looked at the clock: 8:07 p.m. She wondered if she had missed dinner. Probably. Not that it mattered to her, she didn't feel like having company. She did feel hungry, though. Before going out, she decided to look at the last papers in the file, Namaguchi's medical report. It seemed the same as the others, except his was much longer, him being quite a bit older. As she suspected by this point, at the end of his report, for two consecutive appointments, it had noted that he had potentially developed immunity and that his wife Ana was a known Natural Immune. After the two notes about potential immunity, a third quickly scrawled note in red saying, "Confirmed, eliminate the pair."

Davis hit her palm against her head in frustrated thought. *They gave him three appointments to see if he was immune or not? That was it? How was that even possible?* Namaguchi was a high-level official. It didn't seem to make any sense that they would decide to eliminate him so quickly. Davis wondered how much of this she could believe.

As Davis pondered the dilemma in her mind, she had a hard time believing that President Everett or anyone in the cabinet could do such a thing. She also realized Namaguchi being in the cabinet made it even more unlikely. But there it was in black and red ink, respectively. Davis decided to set these reports aside for a while. She felt what she needed was some food and a break from looking at these things. Before leaving, she steeled herself to be brave, just in case she encountered anyone outside her room.

Davis made her way to the kitchen and opened the fridge. She didn't know what she wanted and closed the door. She thought about it a second and opened the door to analyze again and see if anything caught her attention. There was nothing that appealed. Davis was not even aware of half of what the items were. She closed the door again and thought for a minute. Davis opened the fridge again and took a quick peek. Nothing. Finally, she walked over to the pantry and found the cracker container. She pulled it out and then got herself some water. She intended to pull out a handful of crackers, go back to her room, and eat there. But, feeling unmotivated, she simply set the container of crackers on the counter, mindlessly eating them. She was halfway through the box, her mind zoned out, and her eyes just focused on the dinner bell in the kitchen. Her spaced-out stare was interrupted by Quinn. "Hey, you okay, Davis?" she asked as she walked in.

Davis shook her head as if trying to remove the cobwebs from her head. "Yeah, I'm fine...okay. I think. I'm sorry. I don't know how to answer that. I am baffled. Quinn, how did you process it all, coming here? Learning this information?"

"I know it is a lot. It is overwhelming. But I benefited from being a Natural Immune, so the facts were more believable for me. I was terrified when Namaguchi took me, though."

"What? He took you?" Davis exclaimed, shock and surprise overtaking her voice.

Quinn continued with her story, "Yes, I was at a Courting Dance. I didn't want to be there, so I tried to be by myself, away from the crowds. He surprised me out of nowhere; he brought some punch and said he wanted to dance with me. I didn't want to, but as you know, you can't refuse. So, we drank our punch—I remember trying to make it quick to finish the interaction. He seemed to be in a hurry too. Then, he took me by the hand, presumably to lead me onto the dance floor. But, quickly, he grabbed me and pulled me out a side door. I had no idea what was going on or what to do. I was pulled into a vehicle by Ringo—although I didn't know who he was then. They put a hood over my head. They kept talking to me, trying to reassure me, calm me down because I couldn't stop crying. Once we got to the bunker, they let me go to my room and calm down a bit, and then Ana came in to talk to me. But, those first few days were very uneasy and scary. I'm sorry you have to go through this."

Davis couldn't believe what she was hearing. It all seemed so, well, unbelievable to her. She decided to change her questioning while her mind tried to process this new information from Quinn. "Do you ever get out of here, get to walk around, or see anything besides these walls? I'm going stir-crazy already, and I haven't been here nearly as long as you. I can't imagine…" Davis's words trailed off into empty air.

"Yes, every once in a while. Maybe the solar panels need cleaning, or sometimes just general things need to be checked on, survey the area. Plus, everyone needs fresh air now and then. I'll pop out for a few minutes every few days. Even if I'm not doing anything in particular, just get fresh air, see the sun, blue sky."

Again, Davis was surprised, a minute-by-minute exercise for her lately. "Do you worry about Drone Scanners or Security Patrols?"

"Well, a little. But, we're pretty isolated here, and we have a scope; we can see above the ground before going up. And the Drone Scanners are easy to fool."

"Really?" inquired Davis, sounding doubtful.

"Yeah, you just clear your mind and then think of something great about President Everett. It doesn't need to be a real thought, just real enough."

"I can't clear my mind, especially lately, although for me, I do not think it would be difficult to have positive thoughts about President Everett."

"Well," said Quinn, thinking about it a minute, "I guess some people need practice at clearing their minds; I did, especially in the beginning. What gets harder is the positive thinking on Everett."

"I wish I could do that now. I'm not feeling very patient about anything these days. Even *thinking* of trying to clear my mind makes me feel exhausted."

"Well, luckily," said Quinn with a momentary pause, "it's not something you have to worry about."

"Why is that?" said Davis, sounding doubtful again.

"Well, if we get our way, the current government will get overthrown. That happens, and the Drone Scanners and Security Patrols go away. If we don't, you either decide to stay here and live life as we do, or you go back and live life as you always have." Quinn looked like she didn't want that third option to happen. She sighed with a bit of hopelessness at the end of her sentence, betraying the cavalier sound to her words.

"Oh!" exclaimed Davis, secretly hoping to get off this topic as quickly as possible. "Sorry to digress, but before I forget…do you know why your medical reports, yours and Ana's, start marking you as Potential Immunes at twelve?"

Quinn scratched her head. "Essentially, I know. There are some details I'm unsure about, but in general, they don't worry too much about kids causing many problems. A little kid can say anything; for instance, the sky is purple, and fish fly in it. People will just laugh and say the kid has a great imagination. Plus, if they're still under mind control, the parents won't believe what the kid says anyhow. If the kid starts getting older and is still saying these things, people might start to wonder or ask more questions about them. And when they start becoming of age, that's when they start to pay their full attention because those kids are going to go off, get married, and have kids of their own. Ringo once said that if one parent is a Natural Immune, the children will likely be. If both parents are, the kids will certainly be. The government can't risk them getting into the population pool like that, so they nip it in the bud before they can have their children."

"I see," said Davis, not feeling at all like she understood. "Well, I think I'm going to try to turn in, try and get some sleep. Goodnight, Quinn."

"Goodnight, sleep well."

As Davis walked to the door, she paused suddenly and turned around, a look of worry and anxiety written on her face. "Oh, Quinn. I'm not sure if I'll be down for breakfast tomorrow. Please don't tell everyone about our conversation. Or that you saw me. I'm just not ready to feel um, well, exposed for lack of a better word."

"Sure thing, no problem," said Quinn with a smile that let Davis knew that she meant it.

"Great, thank you then. And goodnight."

With that, Davis walked out the door and down to her room. As she lay down on her bed, she tried to clear her mind of everything else and focus on something she genuinely wanted to think about. Her mind floated. It landed on Brookshire. *Hmmm*, she thought. *Quinn was right; it was easy if you had the right thing to think about, the right thought could make your soul soar instead of plunge.*

SEPTEMBER 1, 2056 – CILANTRO AND MORE ANSWERS

When Davis awoke, she felt like she had the first good night's sleep she'd had in a long time. No nightmares or screaming boys. No darkness. No confusion. She quickly realized that wasn't entirely true. There was still the complete bewilderment. It felt nice, though, to have the fog lift, for even the half-second it had done so after she awoke. Davis had been in the web between the dream and the waking world for a few precious seconds when everything seemed okay and before reality caught up.

Davis was trying to decide if she would go and eat breakfast with everybody else. She felt a little more comfortable with Quinn and thought perhaps these people knew a bit about what they were saying. Even though she didn't feel like she trusted them completely, she had to admit there was some compelling evidence. It was difficult to imagine that all these papers, signatures, and watermarks were forgeries, especially when some were so specific.

Davis looked at the clock and saw it was only a little after 5 a.m. She didn't think they would have breakfast this early, and she wasn't all that hungry. If anything, her stomach felt a little upset, queasy. She decided she would take a shower first, then figure out breakfast. One thing she had undoubtedly become accustomed to very quickly was the warm, untimed showers. The several pleasant-smelling soaps and shampoos available, and afterward, wrapping herself in a comfy towel that wasn't brown and too little and scratchy like the ones in the Pods was a welcome change also. These were big and soft and a lovely sage green color.

After her shower, Davis decided she would go back to her room, look over the paperwork again, and then meet the group for breakfast. She intended to scour over the paperwork, line by line, to find any inconsistencies, anything that could be a lie or forgery. She looked and looked, every page three times over, almost in a frenzy toward the end of her search. Nothing seemed out of place; it was as it should be. Every *i* dotted and every *t* crossed.

When Davis walked into the breakfast room, she could tell that everyone was sort of surprised to see her. Luckily, they all quickly looked down, although Audrey had to give Oliver a soft slap on his little hand for him to look away from Davis. Even Buster was there and had the decency to turn toward his food bowl when Davis sat down.

"So, what are we having?" asked Ringo in a matter-of-fact way, making Davis think he knew what they were eating and had only asked to break the tension a little bit.

"Eggs and oatmeal, and some nice strawberries from the garden," replied Quinn.

"So," Davis replied, looking at Ringo, "Sorry that I walked out the other night. It was all overwhelming."

"Not a problem at all…not at all!" Ringo said. Even Audrey looked up and gave Davis a friendly smile and added,

"We know. Nobody expects you to feel completely comfortable right away, although, of course, we wish we could bring you that comfort. We all know it isn't that easy, though."

"Thank you," Davis felt choked with emotion as she said it. She didn't know where this emotion was coming from, but it burned hot in her throat as she tried to keep the tears from falling. Brookshire, who sat next to her, put his arm around her shoulder and gave her a warm half hug. That did it—no more stopping the tears. They spilled out, right in front of everybody. Embarrassed, she got up to leave. Brookshire lightly tugged on her hand and indicated with a nod of his head that she should sit back down. Brookshire spoke directly to her, looking into her eyes.

"It's okay, Davis. We all understand. We've all had some ups and downs here. Nobody is going to judge you for feeling sad or questioning things." He then handed her his napkin, but he pulled his hand back at the last minute so that she couldn't take it. Instead, he reached up and dried her tears for her. It helped her feel a little more at peace, although "peaceful" would be the last word she would describe herself as feeling.

Then, as she commonly did, Davis decided to deflect the emotional situation, and she cleared her throat and then looked at Ringo. "So, do you think we can finish the conversation we started, maybe after breakfast?"

"Yes, of course, that is fine," replied Ringo. "Of course," he added as if he needed to certify his earlier affirmation.

Davis chewed mindlessly and silently, as did her tablemates. Nobody made one noise until Buster came over to weave himself in between the legs of everyone at the table. When he got to Namaguchi, he looked up at him and gave him a loud "mew." Davis was surprised this was the target Buster had picked for a tidbit, but more to her amazement, Namaguchi plucked a bit of egg off his plate and held it down for Buster. Namaguchi did not strike Davis as someone who was overly sensitive. Then there were several minutes of silence, only broken by Buster's *mews* as he went from person to person, begging for food. Davis felt like she couldn't stand the silence one more second when a thought popped into her head that made her feel like she had just stumbled upon the key to everything. "So," she blurted out, "How do Namaguchi, Duffy, and Hernandez pass medical checks now? If they're now 'immune'? Because when they go into the city to be double agents for you, they must get their ID Cards scanned and have to go to medical checkups. And they gave an execution order for Namaguchi. How did he escape that?" She gave a huff of satisfaction before lightly slapping her hand down on the table as if she had just solved every mystery since the dawn of time.

"Maybe not in front of the children…" Ringo started to say.

"It's okay," said Duffy, who was at the end of the table. "One of the benefits of being in the medical field is that we can make sure certain documents get certified for all of us. It's not hard to write what they want to see, especially since we've written it so many times for so many others."

"Oh, so you lie?" Davis lifted her eyebrow in skepticism as she said this.

"We don't think of it like that," interjected Hernandez. "Sometimes, we need to bend the truth to make sure people don't get hurt or killed." He sounded a little angry at having to defend himself, which surprised Davis. He had been so amicable before this. She then realized how accusatory what she had said probably sounded.

"I'm sorry," she said. "I don't mean to offend, I'm just trying to get everything sorted out in my mind still, and so many things still don't make any sense." She added a slight smile and nodded toward Hernandez.

"No problem, sorry if I got a little in a huff about it myself. I just really feel like I'm helping people, and having that called into question…" Hernandez trailed his sentence off and looked down, shaking his head as if there could be no question about his actions.

Ringo spoke up once more, "Again; maybe we should set this aside until the children go off to their lessons with Ana."

"Oh!" said Davis, seeing an opportunity to both change the subject and smooth things over. "What are you guys learning?"

Oliver answered, "Well, we're all different ages. So, my sister and I, we're ten, and we do mostly big kid stuff, like math with letters. Did you know you can do math problems with letters like x and y but get number answers?" Oliver seemed very proud of himself as he gave this fact, and Olivia beamed with self-satisfaction herself before butting in.

"Yes, but *I'm better* at the math!" Olivia very excitedly exclaimed.

"Olivia," her mom reprimanded, "You're both very good with your math. And your brother was talking, you interrupted."

"Sorry, bro!" Olivia did not seem too put out having to apologize.

"It's okay, sis. So, we do big kid stuff. But, the little kids, Russell W. and Mae, mostly work on things like letters, numbers, colors. Sometimes we all make music together, or Ana will let us help the little kids; we'll read to them or help them learn how to write," he said, and at this, Oliver got a massive smile on his face, a toothy grin that was missing a few teeth. He very excitedly added, "We get to watch a movie together sometimes. We've seen it a few times. We normally like different stuff 'cause they're so little. But it's a math cartoon Ms. Ana plays for us, *Owl in the Numbers*, and we all like that. Olivia and I like the math problems, the little kids like the owls and their animal friends. Have you ever seen that cartoon? Ms. Davis."

Davis had never been called "Ms." in her life, and she found it tickled her to no end. "No," she replied. "I've never seen that one. It sounds like it might be fun."

Olivia looked to her mom and her brother as if she wanted to make sure neither talked first. "What is your favorite movie, Ms. Davis?"

"Hmmm…" Davis had to think a bit. "I have to think about that a second. I like to read; I go to the library a lot." Davis was getting lost in her thoughts. "I saw one movie once. It was pretty old. It even had a famous Davis in it. It's so old; people had first names still. Her name was Bette Davis, and the movie was called *All About Eve*." Here she paused and tried to sound as if she was relaying some grand, secret information. "The movie is *so old*; it's in black and white! There was no color!"

Both Olivia and Oliver looked stunned and had great big wide eyes. "WHAT!" Olivia and Oliver said together at the same time, which started a round of giggling. "No color!" again, in unison, and another round of giggling.

"That's right. Some movies are so old; not only are they in black and white only, the ones older than that don't have any sound either," said Davis with a nod of assurance.

"Wow," Oliver looked like he couldn't believe it. "Ms. Ana, can we see one of those movies?"

"Well, maybe one day," said Ana. "But, unfortunately, we don't have any of those movies here. I don't think. I'll double-check, but we only have a few movies here. As you know from seeing *Owl in the Numbers* about seventy-three times." Ana said the last part with a smile, indicating she wasn't all that upset the kids had watched a movie they enjoyed so many times.

The kids continued to chit-chat throughout breakfast, and Davis picked at her breakfast. She wasn't too crazy about those eggs. Spongy. Slightly chewy. An odd, off yellowish color. Weird green flecks. "So," Davis asked in a moment of silence, "You just add water to most of this dehydrated stuff? Then it becomes eggs?" her nose betrayed her thoughts about the eggs and scrunched up as if she had smelled something terrible.

"Not a fan of them?" Quinn cut in, smiling. "Honestly, not my favorite either. But, good protein and some other vitamins and minerals. Oh, you know, there is a tiny bit of cilantro in them too. It's a herb. Also good for you. I shouldn't have used it, though. It's very potent, and not everybody likes it. Here, wait." At that, Quinn got up and walked to the kitchen. When she came back, she had a vibrant green leaf on the plate. "Try this; it's just a cilantro leaf."

Davis picked up the sprig and examined the look of it for a moment. She twirled the delicate stem in her fingers before biting it. Quinn felt terrible about Davis's look after she tasted it, but it also cracked her up. Davis looked like she had licked a dirty shoe, spitting out the cilantro into her napkin and grabbing her water glass, drinking fast. She also picked up a strawberry with her free hand and popped it into her mouth the second she finished with the water. After, as if she needed to explain, looking at Quinn, she said, "I did *NOT* like that!!!!"

"I'm sorry; I'm sorry..." Quinn said, trying not to laugh. "I didn't think you'd hate it that much." Everyone else at the table was trying to stifle their laughs, but the kids laughed hysterically and with abandon.

"No, it's okay," Davis picked the chewed leaf out of her napkin and inexplicably smelled it; it seemed like she couldn't believe the flavor existed. Her nose scrunched up again in disgust. "*That*," she said in a very accusing way, "is *very* pungent." As if to clear any confusion that could still exist, she reiterated, "I *really* didn't like that. But it's weird, I didn't love the eggs, but they weren't that bad! There is no way I could imagine eating that cilantro stuff in any way again, though."

"Well," said Quinn, "There is also onion powder, salt, pepper, and a bit of garlic and chives in the eggs. Those are also strong flavors, and I didn't use much cilantro."

"Ah...well, if it's all the same to you, I think I'll skip the rest of my eggs," Davis said while she scraped the eggs to the side of the plate as if she was trying to distance herself from them.

After everyone calmed down a bit from the cilantro excitement and finished their breakfast, Ana helped Quinn and Brookshire clear the table. Duffy and Hernandez took a few items and declared they'd get the dishes done before heading out for the day. Audrey said she would help them and then drive them out. Namaguchi got up and went into the kitchen, oddly, without carrying anything in. However, after a few minutes, he returned out with a tray of water glasses and a full pitcher. He also had two wet rags, one of which he handed to Ringo and one he kept to wipe down opposite sides of the table. Ana busied herself and sent each child to the bathroom individually to brush their teeth, wash up, and get ready for school lessons. As they came back in, she lined them up against the wall and then escorted Mae to the restroom, little Mae toddling next to her, Ana lightly holding her hand. When Ana returned with Mae, she gathered the used wet cloths and asked if they needed anything else before school started. Everyone declined, and Ana said very kindly, "Okay, kids! School time—March!" Off they went, Mae still holding her mom's hand as they made their way through the kitchen door.

"Wow," Davis looked as if she was trying to find something to say. "It seems like everyone pitches in around here and does something."

Ringo answered her as he started passing out the cups and filling them with water. "We try to split up the chores; it's only fair and right. And it's the only way a community like this can survive and thrive. But some people do specific things; Ana is the only one who teaches. I'm the only one who putzes around with the computers and hydroponics, although others sometimes help harvest the garden. Quinn likes to cook, and she's quite good at it. So, we leave her to that for the most part."

Davis nodded her head in silent agreement. She also looked as if she was thinking about something. "Oh, I see, that's pretty nice... By the way, Duffy and Hernandez said they were leaving for the day, and Audrey said she'd take them. Why does she have to take them?"

Ringo's response was light and tentative. He explained to Davis how they had to maintain a secure location and trusted everyone there. Still, if someone were to get caught, imprisoned, and given the brain controlling drugs, they might become persuaded to tell the location. Even if they were immune, they could get tortured to show where the location was. To protect the bunker and especially the children, only Audrey and Ringo knew the exact location. He also reiterated they were somewhat isolated and had a lot of protection as the hills surrounded them. Ringo continued with the description even though Davis felt satisfied with the answer already. "All our solar panels are camouflaged as boulders or by plenty of bushes, trees, and the like. We're tough to locate if you don't know exactly where to look. But, still, it's got to be a complete secret. So, this next part might seem scary, but we ask you to wear a blackout hood in and out. You are perfectly safe the entire time. We have a few electric transport vehicles here, and we have three meeting areas. One is about a mile and a half walk to the Pod you were staying at, and the two others are about a mile from a spot where you can get on a government-owned transport vehicle and go into one of the two town centers."

Davis was mostly familiar with Town Center One. Right in its middle was the Everett Center, where she reported to her job. Town Center Two was where the factories and labs were. They were all located there whether they made those familiar brown sheets or the nutrition biscuits or the Marigold Inoculation formula. Davis was thinking of these things for a moment; Ringo noticed her staring off, her eyes focused on the wall as she picked at some dry skin around her nails. "Davis?" inquired Ringo. "You okay?"

"Yes, sorry, just thinking. About nothing, really. My mind wanders a lot more than it used to. I don't know why." Davis suddenly looked so tired and overwhelmed; the older man felt for her. Ringo explained to her that it was natural. Her brain was still adjusting to life without brain control chemicals. Namaguchi then added that Brookshire and Quinn could come in, and they could discuss anything that Davis had on her mind.

"Well, I guess we might as well add a cherry on top of this sundae of a day. I've been wondering a few things anyhow," Davis said, "if we want to get to that before they come in. It's basic things, I guess. Not about me or anything specific like that."

"Sure," said Ringo and Namaguchi at almost the same time, but they were a little out of sync. Part of the "sure" started before the other, and it gave a weird drawn-out sound to the word. Still, Davis was able to get the idea it was okay to proceed. She asked them how Namaguchi, Duffy, and Hernandez had ever found Ringo and the rest of the people in the bunker. With all the security Ringo and his family had taken, she wasn't sure how they all met.

Ringo took the lead on answering. "I knew Namaguchi, at one time, right before the Lombardi Plague started. We were friendly neighbors.

Audrey and I had already started building the bunkers and moving things down here. We didn't know a virus was coming or even *when* something would happen. We just believed something would eventually threaten our way of life. I told Namaguchi about it, and I said if his family and himself ever needed protection, to come to a certain place—I had a doorbell system set up in a hollowed-out rock. All he had to do was ring it, and it would alert me to pick him up. I told a few people about it; Namaguchi is the only one I ever heard from."

Here Namaguchi interjected, "I had forgotten about it for a long time. It was only after Duffy and Hernandez came to me; we were friendly, and they had been monitoring the medical files and saw my immunity status." At this, Namaguchi paused, looking concerned and sympathetic. "You know, Davis, I went through quite a time believing everything too, even though I had become 'immune.' You're still grasping with learning that everything you ever were told by your government is a lie and done for ultimate control."

Davis didn't know if she fully believed that but nodded her head in agreement because it was easier. She also resumed picking at her nails. "So, you brought Duffy and Hernandez in too, is that right?"

"Yes, that's right. Because of them, we learned of Ana and Quinn."

"Ringo," Davis asked. "You said there were a few people you gave the doorbell location to, but Namaguchi is the only one who ever used it. Are you missing anyone important? Can Duffy and Hernandez check on them?"

"All the people I gave it to, I wish they had shown up, naturally. I've had them all checked upon, and none have any records. I hold out hope that they ran to Canada or Mexico as I know many people did." Ringo looked sad at this, then added, "You always have to have hope," sounding like he had anything but hope.

"Well, how did you know that these people you told the doorbell about that they wouldn't double-cross you?"

"These were my friends that I trusted. It didn't occur to me that they could double-cross me. I also told them about it before things were as bleak as they are now. Even after time passed, I always hoped that they would only use it if need be, not for nefarious purposes. We do have our safety protocols in place, as well. We make sure there are no Scanner Drones or Security Patrols around when we make a pickup or following us when we leave."

Davis felt saddened by the look on Ringo's face and how sad and tired he sounded. Then she started thinking about all the families that became torn apart. If someone were a Natural Immune, they would likely be eliminated or sent to reprogramming. Even if they somehow escaped one of those fates, they would certainly never be able to talk to their families anymore. They would be at odds and believe such different things. *How far does just love protect you?* she wondered.

After a few moments of thought, Davis didn't know if or how she should proceed with questions, especially since most of what she said seemed like banal and vapid general inquiries. But Ringo nodded her on, asking if she had any more questions.

"Well," Davis felt stupid for bringing it up. "It's a silly thing, but I'm just curious. Once Namaguchi and Ana got scheduled to be, er…'eliminated' as I believe the notation said, how did they avoid it?"

Namaguchi took this question. "Luckily for us, Ringo is quite skilled with computers. And he can get into a part of the main system when he wants. He fixed my overall records, saying it was a clerical error that my name got crossed with Ana's. Then, Duffy and Hernandez gave me a full workup and 'free and clear,' and said everything was in order with my physical. It was reported they eliminated Ana, but she was secretly brought here. Plus, I learned to go along with things, even when it bothered me—"

"What types of things bothered you?" interrupted Davis.

"I'd rather not go into that, I'm sorry. I just try to do my work, keep my head down, and know that the unpleasant things will end one day. I also need to protect Ana and the kids. My other wives are not immune, so they are safe at our apartment at the Palace. When I'm here, they think I'm working. I plan most of my days off to be here, but not all. Just in case Everett came by the apartment or my family wondered why I never had a day off. None of the wives ever asks questions, though, and Everett is in control, so he doesn't need to ask questions."

Brookshire had recently come in with Quinn, and Davis looked his way as she asked, "Is it a similar situation for you, Brookshire? With work and your spouses at an apartment at the Everett Palace?" Davis lifted her eyebrow so that her face asked what her voice could not.

"I don't need to schedule days here at any particular time. My work with President Everett causes me to be out of his office often. I'm Head of Security and Surveillance, so frequently, I take trips to different Pods, analyzing data at the medical centers. And, well, I never married. I, uh, wasn't able to marry who I wanted, so I just didn't. I get questions about it sometimes. Sometimes, President Everett sends some of his servants to go back to my apartment with me in the evening for, as he puts it, 'amusement.' But I just play cards with them, or we read in the library. I'm not interested in that, but you don't say 'no' to President Everett."

Davis had no more questions at the moment. She couldn't think of anything else that could be lies or potential pitfalls in the story that Ringo, Namaguchi, Quinn, and Brookshire told her. At the same time, Davis did not feel fully convinced.

"Do you have any more questions, Davis?" asked Namaguchi.

Davis paused and looked at each man and Quinn, staring at them for a few seconds before looking to the next one. She was trying to look stern and severe. Davis wanted them to know she was serious and meant business.

Sensing Davis was starting to get angry and fed up, Brookshire and Quinn decided to calm and comfort her. Brookshire slid a little closer over to Davis, and Quinn took her hand. Instead of calming down, Davis's heart started thumping, and it felt as if her stomach dropped out on the floor.

Feeling a nervous tension in the air, Davis got hot and sweaty and incredibly thirsty all of a sudden. She asked Quinn if she wouldn't mind getting her more water, to which she shook her head no and stood up to refill the glasses from the pitcher that was still on the table.

"Let me just say, Davis, I know this will be a shocking thing to hear. I want to remind you that you're safe, we're here for you, and you can say no." Ringo nodded his head as he said this as if to affirm his words.

"We are here for you; that's number one," Namaguchi included.

"Yes," said Quinn as she sat back down and put her arm back around Davis's shoulder. "Nothing you can do or say will upset us."

Brookshire squeezed even closer, and as Davis already felt as if she were baking in a hot, humid oven, she felt both comforted and claustrophobic packed in like this. She wished they would just get to the crux of the matter.

"Well…let's see…" Ringo seemed to be searching for the right words. "The thing is, when you are set free, you can claim you got kidnapped."

"Right, kidnapped," said Namaguchi.

As Davis tried to comprehend what they were saying, she had to push back on Brookshire slightly and ask Quinn to scoot down for a bit of room. Davis felt like she was being rude but feared passing out if the great squeeze-in continued. As Ringo spoke on, Davis tried to comprehend everything. He was going on about how it would be news if she got kidnapped. That Davis was already newsworthy, considering who she was. The next thing Ringo said made Davis choke back; she felt she must have misunderstood him.

"So, President Everett, he'll want to marry you. As you know, you can't turn that down." One reason Davis wasn't sure she had heard him right was that Ringo rushed that part a lot quicker than he had the other parts of his speech. It was almost as if he said it fast enough, he thought maybe Davis would miss it and agree without fully understanding what

Ringo said. For her part, Davis sat there with eyes large and round, pupils dilated, and mouth agape. She also didn't realize how hard she was squeezing Brookshire's hand. Ringo continued after a pause that felt ten hours long. "And…well…we want you to marry him. When you get close enough to him, say, your wedding night, you assassinate him."

Davis sat there and blankly stared for at least ten minutes. Many things were going through her mind, and she wasn't sure she had heard Ringo correctly. She couldn't believe she heard him right, because it was so absurd. Davis certainly didn't know what to say, but murdering someone was not something she would or could do. For sure, she knew now, helping these people was not a part of her future. Finally, Davis spoke, "I can't do what you're asking. And while you have given me some compelling information, you're also asking me to murder someone: The President! A very popular and much-loved President. I can't. There is no way I can murder anyone! You guys are truly insane for even asking it. I just…I just, the idea of it makes me sick. I can't help even a little bit. I need to go back to my old life now."

"Okay, we understand," said Ringo. "But, honestly, nobody would know you did it. We know that it is asking a lot to take a life, even a vile one; it is a huge ask. Beyond any request we should ask of you. But nobody would know it was you. The President is highly allergic to bee venom. All you have to do is slip it into his food or drink. He'll go into anaphylactic shock quickly. They're not prepared for it because they've eliminated the possibility of bees even being at the Palace. There are no flowers; they fumigate regularly; they won't be able to handle it. Even if someone figures out you slipped him the venom, the Security Patrol would not want it publicized that they failed to protect him. The news headlines the next day will blame a rogue bee, or they'll come up with a complete lie, but it *won't* be that you murdered him."

"Still no," Davis said flatly and curtly before an exasperated chuckle, "No, never in a million years can I or will I murder President Everett for you guys or anyone."

"One last thing," Namaguchi said as he slid a folder across to Davis. "You need to know, Davis, that your mom is alive. Ruby is alive."

SEPTEMBER 2, 2056 - DEPRESSION

Davis found herself back in her room, lying on her bed. She wasn't even quite sure how she got there, not knowing if she had passed out. She didn't even know what day it was or if any time had passed at all. Her stomach was knotted and twisted; between hearing her mom was alive and being asked to murder someone, she felt tormented and disgusted. Her head pounded, she thought, even worse than when she was getting the brain control drugs out of her system. The folder was on her bedside table. She opened it quickly to make sure the words Namaguchi had said about her mom were not just in her head. Inside was a photo showing a woman older than Davis. Yes, she was older, but she thought, *She looks so much like me.* Davis traced her finger along this lady's jawline as hot tears streaked down her face. She couldn't read the report right now; she couldn't even keep looking at the picture. She laid her head back down and fell into a troubled slumber.

The nightmares she was accustomed to haunting her dreams returned. But instead of the boy screaming and being dragged into the blackness, Davis herself snatched the boy and laughed maniacally. She awoke many times in the night, and she would blink, realize where she was, and then turn over as if in denial of her life, only to fall asleep and have the dream again.

Several days passed. Davis refused to look at the file. She only left the room to wash her face in the morning and go to the restroom a few times a day. She had even ceased to shower or change her clothes. Nobody seemed to be around or bothering her. If they saw her in the hallway, they would give her a small, shy smile and then look away. A few times a day, Quinn would knock lightly and speak through the door, asking her how she was doing. Davis never answered. She would open the door and find a tray. There would be a pitcher of water, a glass, a plate of food, a napkin, and utensils. She never ate the food, except maybe a bite or two, and she had a few glasses of water a day, but she mostly took the plate and scraped the leftovers into her trash can.

A few days in, she realized the trash can was starting to smell. She was, too; it disgusted her, but she also liked it for some reason. Finally, the rotten stench around her matched the rottenness in her mind. One day when Quinn brought lunch, she had also placed a pretty yellow flower in a jaunty red vase on the tray. Davis put the vase on top of the folder that still sat untouched, save for the first time she glanced at it all those days ago. She scraped the food in the trash can, on top of the other junk, and wished she could crawl in there and cover herself with the waste.

Davis lost all track of time, but she thought maybe another two or three days had passed. She had finally had it with her stench. But she waited until it was very early in the morning. A bit past 2:00 a.m. by the clock on her table, she crept out as quietly as she could and took her trash can to the kitchen. She then took out the bag, tied it off, and threw it down the main trash chute that went to, she believed, an incinerator. Then she got a clean bag from the stock that was pointed out to her when she first settled in there. She then laughed to herself at the idea that she had ever been settling in there. Nothing could be further from her truth. When she was putting the bag in the can, she thought they felt weird. The bags were an odd texture, some kind of disposable, biodegradable bags that Ringo fashioned out of some of the byproducts from his garden. Davis decided she hated those bags.

After taking care of her trash, she washed her hands and then went back to her room and replaced the can. She then got the water pitcher that was in her room and refilled and replaced that. When she got back to the room again, she got her bath towels and a clean change of clothes and walked to the restroom. When she got in front of the mirror, she was horrified at how she looked. Large dark bags circled under her eyes. Her skin looked dry in patches, but her forehead and chin were so oily, and she had developed several acne spots, something she had never had trouble with before. Her hair was so oil-slicked that it almost seemed pasted to the top of her head. She looked ill and sickly. She was tired and felt disgusting, inside and out.

Davis took her time in the shower, not caring if she wasted every drop of water. She wanted to flow right down the drain with that hot water and those suds and never come back. She got back to the room and felt more exhausted than ever. Looking at the clock and seeing it was a little past 4 a.m., she felt surprised at how long she was gone. Realizing that she didn't care, she climbed into bed and found the cool sheets calming to her. Davis fell asleep quickly and solidly for the first time in several days.

When she awoke, Davis was surprised to see the time as a quarter past 2 a.m. She had slept almost an entire day. Or maybe two days; how was she supposed to know? And she still found she did not care. Rolling over, she fell asleep again. At eight o'clock in what Davis assumed was the morning, she started to hear a slight rapping at the door and someone saying, "Davis…Davis…are you okay?" Deciding to ignore it, she tried to close her eyes and shut out the sound. But, a few seconds later, it started again. So, she pulled herself out of bed and went to open the door.

When Davis opened the door, Quinn was standing there, and Buster ran inside. Davis stood there silently, staring at Quinn, who spoke first. "I'm sorry to bother you. I was just worried about you. You haven't taken a tray for a whole day."

"I'm okay, just sleeping. Thank you. Please excuse me now. I need to use the restroom." And with that, Davis walked out and down the hallway. Quinn stood there with her mouth agape; she had never heard her be so curt and short with her words.

Davis cleaned up a bit and then headed back to her room. Quinn had left. Davis felt like maybe she had been too blunt with her. But she was having trouble feeling connected to anyone right now. Even Buster, who was on her bed, stood up when she came in and started pacing around her bed, kneading the blankets at spots and purring. She walked over to him, and he butted his head up against her hand when she went to pet him. Buster then energetically allowed her to scratch behind his ears and under his chin, leaning and pressing into each scratch. She felt like she was just going through the motions, not enjoying the comfort of Buster's purrs and affection. Finally rested, she felt like there would be no more sleep for her. But she didn't want to get up, so she continued to lie there and snuggle and pet Buster despite the disconnect. At least his fur was incredibly soft and plush. Davis felt it comforted her a little bit, and finally, she let go and tried to sink her worries into his coat.

~

Over the next few days, Davis sunk into a routine. She was sleeping throughout the day, getting up once or twice to get the food left at her door or to use the restroom. She would tiptoe down the hallway, hoping nobody would see or hear her. She would eat and drink in her room; if she needed anything, it was a waiting game, only going very late at night or early in the morning. She did the same thing with her showers, going at midnight or well past, hoping not to run into anyone. And she didn't. Davis didn't realize that everyone was going to great lengths to give her all the space and time she needed.

Davis wasn't sure if it was three or four days later, but she was sitting up in bed, feeling very sorry for herself, when she decided she didn't want to feel sorry for herself anymore. She had just finished rereading *Little Women*, and she wished she was like the character Jo, so strong and willful. She also wished she had at least one sister to talk things over. She kept thinking of the quote from the book, "I could never love anyone as I love my sisters." She wished she knew what that felt like.

Well, she thought to herself, feeling a bit Jo-like, *if I want to get anywhere, I guess I need to start here*, and she grabbed the file that held the information about Ruby—her mom—in it. She opened it and stared at the picture. It was so odd to her, seeing her face in the face of Ruby. She finally turned to the next photo, which was in black and white, and it melted Davis's heart immediately. It looked as if someone had taken it in the hospital—Ruby in a bed, holding a wee baby in her arms.

Davis was touched and then confused. It didn't follow with what she had heard at all. Her whole life, authorities told her as an infant, they whisked her away to save her life and that her mom had died almost right after childbirth. In the photo, while Ruby looked anything but healthy, she certainly wasn't near death. Davis noticed that she looked healthy enough in the picture, too. She flipped to the next page and saw medical notes. They indicated that both Ruby Davis and baby Davis received the Marigold Injection to apparent success, with progress or declination closely monitored. Davis continued to read until she got to a part that stopped her breath. She picked up the jaunty red vase that now held a wilted and droopy yellow flower, and she tossed it across the room. The vase smashed into what seemed like a million pieces, and the flower lay still on the ground, an unwitting victim in a pool of stagnant, semi-mildew tainted water. Davis calmed herself and reread the paragraph to make sure she had read it correctly. According to the notes, she had spent six weeks with her mother until they had told Ruby Davis that baby Davis had died. Davis read the words over and over.

Davis put the files aside and curled up on the bed. She hoped that Buster would suddenly appear or if not the loving kitty, she wouldn't mind Brookshire coming by to hold her hand or stroke her hair. However, nobody entered the room, and she fell asleep, trails of tears streaked on her cheeks, and puffy eyes closed tightly.

She wasn't sure what the sound was at first, but Davis awoke with a start. Then she realized a light rapping on the door, followed by a quiet, almost whispery "Davis…?"

Davis got up and went over to the door and cracked it open. It was Quinn. "Davis, sorry to bother you or wake you. But we had some good news a bit ago, and I thought you might need some good news. Ringo's sister has rung the 'doorbell'—so to speak—and he's on his way to pick her up right now. We're going to get a little concert together. Tonight, at eight, after dinner. In the common room, next to the dining room. Ringo was in a band with Josie, and we thought they could play a few songs, and the kids will play a few songs they know. We wanted to invite you, but you know, no pressure." With that, Quinn smiled and gave Davis a quick pat on the shoulder before walking away.

SEPTEMBER 15, 2056 - REUNION

That evening, Davis went back and forth in her head, deciding whether she should go to the concert or not. She didn't feel up to seeing people or meeting the company or attending any event, but she wanted to support the children's music playing. She also had to come out of her room at some point and make an announcement about her decision. Finally, Davis decided to go, not feeling entirely sold on that choice but figuring, if anything, it wasn't the fault of the children. The kids were sweet, and she wanted to support them in the music they would play.

Davis did not attend dinner; Quinn was kind enough to bring it to her and take away the lunch tray and dirtied plate and utensils. When Quinn had come by, Davis told her that she would be there for the concert. She then ate, went to the washroom to freshen up, and then headed off to the show.

As Ringo introduced his "sister," Josie, to Davis, to say Davis was shocked would be the understatement of the year. And as she had been shocked to her core so many times these last few days, it was saying something that she was completely floored. She shook Josie's hand in greeting, trying not to look vacant. But confusion reigned. Like Ringo, Josie was tall, at least six feet, and slim but had striking features, long wavy black hair, dark brown eyes, and a deep taupe skin tone.

Luckily, Ringo picked up on her confusion and explained the difference in skin tone. "Josie is Black, as you've noticed. So, she's not actually my sister, as you may have guessed. At least, not biologically. But, emotionally, mentally, even spiritually, she is. You don't always need to be blood-related to someone for them to be family, you know?"

Davis did not know. But she nodded her head silently and told Josie it was a pleasure to meet her. Josie very kindly took Davis's hand in between both of her hands. They were warm, soft, and comforting. "So very nice to meet you; Ringo has told me a lot about you," she said with a friendly smile.

Everybody came into the room, giving Davis small pleasantries and smiles, and after she found a seat, Brookshire sat next to her on a softened sizeable brown leather couch that was in the shape of an L. Duffy and Hernandez, it turned out, were in the city and would not be there.

The children took the stage first. Olivia was on Ringo's drumkit, and Oliver had a guitar strapped around his shoulder. Both of the little kids had tambourines. Davis couldn't place any of the songs the kids were playing, and none of them sang. But Davis thought that especially Olivia on the drums certainly took after her father. Olivia was energetic and, you could tell, thrilled to be playing. It wasn't just good energy, though; she played well. Olivia's playing was smooth with a perfect groove. She was remarkably good at keeping the beat.

After the kids played a few songs, Ringo and Josie took the stage, announcing that it had been several years since they played together. Josie squinted merrily and said they would appreciate the patience as it would only be a short concert of just the ditties they knew best. All the songs were covers from the most popular band in the late 2020s, Complicated Justice. Davis had known this band, sort of a folksy pop-rock band with poetic and frequently political lyric writing. As Davis remembered the quartet, she realized that the band had gone away, inexplicably. She didn't know if they had been victims of the Lombardi Plague or "eliminated." Or maybe they just broke up and went their separate ways.

Ringo was, of course, on drums, and Josie was on keyboards and sang. Although they also originally had a guitar and bass players too, nobody had seen or heard from either James or Sakura in ages. The band started with "Sugared Quail," a fun yet risqué song about a sweet girl that stole men's hearts before running off. *Okay*, thought Davis, *maybe not as political and poetic as she remembered.* But then they broke into "Tomorrow's Legend." Davis remembered this song. There was the small war of 2023 that the former US had with Cuba. For years, stories of inhumane treatment and false imprisonments abounded in Cuba until the US conquered the Cuban government, changing Cuba from the Republic of Cuba to a US territory. The war was bloody, mostly for the Cubans. They were forced to fight but not given proper attire or weapons. Of course, the friendly relations that had been born since the war swiftly dissipated when the Lombardi Plague quickly spread there because of the open-door travel policy. Before that was the war of 2023, and Complicated Justice wrote "Tomorrow's Legend" to paint a picture of innocent Cubans suffering because of the war.

They say you can't win

But it's apparent

You'll be a legend,

A legend

You may have to wait until tomorrow

As the world turns in sorrow

But you'll be a legend,

A legend

Blood of the innocents fill the streets

As the government conquers again

But the people will be the legends

Legends

Legends of hope and pride

Legends as they abide their time

But they'll be legends,

Legends tomorrow...

Davis found herself singing in her head along with the words and was surprised she remembered them as well as she did.

The two bandmates finished off with probably Complicated Justice's two most famous radio songs, "Like a Heart" and "Shouting Through a Cackle of Hyenas," the latter quite a well-written satire how the voice of the people is often not heard through the ruckus the politicians create. However, "Tomorrow's Legend" was Davis's favorite. It always had been.

After the music ended, Josie and Ringo came and sat with Davis and Brookshire. Josie explained how when things got touchy; she had gone over the border to Canada and lived on Prince Edward Island, which was snappily known as P.E.I. Josie had been born there and, seeing the writing on the wall, she went back when things started going down. Josie's parents were already ailing, so she wanted to take care of them and not be kept from returning to Canada. They were already starting to crack down on border crossings when Josie went back. It was a little less tricky for her to cross as she had been born in Canada; her family had moved to the former United States when Josie was seven, right next door to Ringo's family. However, Josie's parents had gone back to Canada a few years before Josie, and when the plague started to hit, she had a desire to be closer to her parents. Josie was tempted to join Ringo in the bunker from the word go but couldn't abandon her parents. After both her parents passed away, she started thinking about her friend and "brother," Ringo and decided to attempt to come to see him and make sure he was okay.

Josie's next-door neighbor, Tara, owned a successful aerospace manufacturing company. Tara's husband, Michael, her dad, Bill, and Tara's daughter and son, Noah, and Sawyer, lived and operated their business out of P.E.I. Tara also ran an underground network of people that helped other people across the border. Many families had been torn apart and separated, just like what had happened with the Berlin Wall. So, Tara connected Josie to her network. There were two routes Josie could take after crossing the Confederation Bridge from P.E.I. and going into New Brunswick. From there, she would have a long drive to Windsor, Ontario, where she could cross the Detroit River alone, and into what was formerly known as Detroit, Michigan. With that route, Josie would join a long legacy of rum runners from the 1930s who brought bootleg liquor into the US from Canada. Then it was another long journey, using a combination of off the grid families and old vehicles provided by them that transported one from city to city until getting to the state formerly known as California and to Ringo's door-bell. The other option, the one that Josie opted for, was a little riskier in one way. She would be in Canada longer, which was safer. Still, crossing into the former US via an old border crossing in British Columbia into Washington state could be dangerous. The border crossing itself was closed with chains, red flags, and concrete pylons. Regardless, guards heavily monitored it. Security Patrols were both in the booths twenty-four-seven, and sentries patrolled the border on foot. Drone Scanners flew over the area regularly as well.

Tara had flown Josie to B.C., Canada, into Vancouver airport. From there, Tara handed Josie off to her brother, Chris. Tara then flew home, and Josie waited at Chris's house for two weeks. There was always more danger trying to cross the border after a private plane landed at Vancouver airport. It raised the hackles of the border patrol on both sides. So, it was prudent to make sure enough time had passed that fewer eyes were on the border.

Wow, thought Davis to herself as she heard Josie's tale. *That certainly is the mark of someone who would consider a person to be a close family member.* Davis could think of no one she would be willing to do this for, even now, with these new people she supposed would be considered her friends. Davis ended her silence with a smile. "That's impressive that you would risk so much to see your friend, Josie."

"Yes, well, Ringo has always been such an important part of my life. I missed him, and I was worried about him," she said with a smile toward Ringo. "He is just as much a part of my family as my family in Canada." At this, Ringo grabbed Josie's hand and raised it in the air, giving it sort of a shake and closing his fist over hers, holding it up as if in victory and triumph.

"How will you get back, or are you going back?" asked Quinn, who had recently come over and sat down with everyone else.

"I'm not sure if I will. At least, for a while. But, if and when I do, I'll go back the same way I came in. Unless life changes for you guys, then we'll see. I also have those connections to Tara and the aerospace industry. All I have to do is get back into Canada, and then I can get picked up by airplane if need be. As you know, we didn't lose our freedom as you guys unfortunately did."

"Well, now, how did you get past the border, exactly?" asked Brookshire.

"Well, Chris got me as close to the border as possible, and for two nights in a row, I watched shift changes and if there was a time that the Drone Scanners were more likely to fly over. I also found a pathway, I don't know how it got there, but it was a few miles east of the actual border. Tall trees pretty well covered it, and lots of bushes surrounded it, so it would be difficult for a Drone Scanner to penetrate to get a scan. More importantly, I noticed a big gap in guard coverage between 1 a.m. and 2 a.m. I waited until a little past one in the morning, and then I ran for it."

"Interesting," Brookshire said as he lightly scratched his chin as if he was trying to think about something simultaneously as he was talking. "At any rate, you made it; that's great. What did you do after the crossing?"

"Well, once I got into what was previously Washington, I traveled to a safe house. Then, I went to a wonderful place just outside what used to be Portland, Oregon. It's called Teeterville. It's a haven for people travel-ing—it's great. They have a pretty basic kind of circular bunker carved out into a huge mountainside. The dining hall and kitchen are in the middle, and all around the outside edge are about thirty old hollowed out VW Bug vans that have a mattress, blankets, pillows…those are the bedrooms. It affords privacy while maximizing space for as many beds as possible. The couple that run it, Mark and Tamara, brew their own beer, make wine, and hold concerts in the middle courtyard at least once a month. They have an amazing hydroponic garden too. I imagine if I hadn't wanted to come here so badly, I would have stayed there as long as they'd have me!"

Josie continued telling them that Mark and Tamara mostly catered to traveling guests, but their kids and grandkids lived there and a few neighbors who had lost the ability to stay on their own. Josie also told them how surprised they'd be by how many people were not following the "rules." They either live in bunkers or their old houses, even. There are even hidden caches filled with water, first aid kits, dehydrated foods, fishing poles—as long as you know what rocks to look for, you can know where to dig and get a quick supply fix if you need it.

"The rocks to look for?" Ringo looked confused, yet interested.

"Yes, it's a smart system. Since you're walking in rural areas, you look for the yellow and black "Deer Crossing" signs and then a large black rock about ten steps away from the road. Then you dig. They're not at every sign, but at enough of them, and it's supposed to be emergency supplies, right?"

Davis spoke up with curiosity on her face, "And you said something about sometimes people live in their old homes? Weren't privately owned houses outlawed? Even had all water, electricity, and services like trash, cut off?"

"Yes, they were," answered Josie. "But, a lot of them are self-sufficient as far as having gardens or well access that was never closed off. Many operate on a barter system. Maybe the house two miles away has a potato supply but no eggs, but their neighbor has chickens and eggs. And another neighbor has managed to keep up a strawberry and herb patch. And another person they know in the next neighborhood has a stream nearby that still provides fish. I guess they live somewhat of a pioneer life, but it works for them. Naturally, they've been outfitted with solar panels to provide electricity, and outhouses are back in vogue!"

"Don't they worry about getting caught?" asked Brookshire. "I mean, they are risking a lot, aren't they?"

"Yes, in one way, but they're all off the beaten path. These people were on the outskirts before anything ever happened. And they keep quiet, not calling attention to themselves; they don't hold anti-government rallies or anything. And, as you know, the Lombardi Plague decimated the population. While the Security Patrols and the Drone Scanners pick up some slack for the lack of Patrols—there just aren't enough people to enforce. So, if you keep quiet, they mostly let you be. If they are even aware of where you are, that is."

Davis was perplexed about this, the thought of people living on the outskirts, not following the rules, but getting away with it. It also occurred to her that these people were not scanning in at Pods and getting sent to medical for monthly vaccinations yet were not getting ill. They were living perfect everyday lives from what she understood from Josie. Or at least as routine as could be under the current circumstances. She was also intrigued by this place, Teeterville, that Josie had mentioned. It sounded like quite an exciting place, a refuge for tumultuous times.

SEPTEMBER 16, 2056 –
REVELATIONS

Davis decided the best way to sort out what was happening and what her next steps should be was to try and get back on a more regular schedule. She forced herself to get up at seven the following day, and after a quick rinse off in the bathroom, she went into the kitchen to help Quinn and Ana with the breakfast.

At the table that morning, everybody ate silently, in contrast to the lively conversation they had enjoyed the night before. Davis wondered if this would be the way things worked from now on. They would just go day by day, trying to be polite to each other, having a chit-chat now and then, but not really living any kind of life. While she did not have any close family or friends, she missed her acquaintances. Davis felt like she had more purpose outside; she might not always have the most exciting life, but it felt meaningful, at least. And in a short period, she had learned that all that meaning was most likely pointless. Davis let out a heavy sigh.

"What's up, Davis-girl?" Brookshire made Davis smile with his sweet comment.

"These vicissitudes of fortune, I feel I can't escape them, yet I can't adapt to them either. I've never really had to accept any kind of changes in my life, so these circumstances have made my life exceedingly difficult." Davis tiredly sighed again and looked down at her plate, where her fork was pushing roasted potatoes around.

"Wow! Ve-Sids-Te-Todos? What does that even mean?" Olivia was laughing a little bit as she asked.

"Ah, little one, try, Vuh-si-suh-tood," Davis answered very slowly, enunciating each syllable. "I don't know why I used that word. I've always just liked the way it sounds, I guess. But it just means a change of circumstances, one that typically is unwelcome. So, I was just saying, 'These changes of fortune,' I suppose." And yet another loud and heavy sigh.

"Oh!!" giggled Olivia. "That's a funny word. Mom! I can't deal with the"—here Olivia paused and said very slowly—"Vuh-Stis-Eh-Tudes of my chores, so I better not do them anymore." Olivia had said "vicissitudes" at such a slow and careful pace that she almost hit the nail on the proverbial head with the pronunciation. She also almost fell off the bench when she got into a giggling fit over her newfound favorite word.

Audrey squeezed her daughter's hand lightly and told her to settle down and finish her breakfast before school got underway.

Brookshire leaned into Davis's ear, getting very close, so close she could feel his warm breath playing on her skin and giving her goosebumps despite the warmth. Namaguchi caught Davis's eyes, flickering with joy. He nodded and asked, "All good?"

"Yes, Brookshire just let me know he has a copy of the book *The Great Gatsby* in his room. Reminded me it was my favorite and offered to let me borrow it," giggled Davis nervously, even though there was no reason to laugh. "So, yes, Brookshire, I'll borrow that book from you if I can."

Davis then asked the table collectively if they needed any help cleaning up after breakfast before she left. They all said "no," but Davis picked up hers and Brookshire's plates and took them to the kitchen anyhow. Namaguchi followed her in. He asked Brookshire to give him a minute and suggested that perhaps Brookshire could get the book while he quickly spoke to Davis alone. Brookshire obliged, and Namaguchi started, "Davis, I know things have been complicated for you. And we complicated them more. I want to make sure you understand whether you help us or not; I'm sorry for that. Even if you don't help us, Everett will propose to marry you. It's inevitable. It's too good of a story for him to resist. But the other thing you need to know is one of his many, many wives is your mom, Ruby."

Davis's mouth fell open with yet another shocking blow. "What, are you kidding me? I just can't believe one more insane thing!"

"No, I wish I was, but I'm not. It was always Everett's plan to marry you; that's why you've had no Inquiries of Interest. Everett considered you to be off-limits, always have been. Not to be indelicate, but he was going to marry you after Ruby died. He couldn't risk you running into her at the Palace, especially since you guys look so much alike."

Davis took a deep breath and stopped talking for a full minute as she mulled the new information over in her mind. "You know, Namaguchi, thank you for telling me. I appreciate it. But I just can't take one more thing. And I'm sorry, I need to go home. I can't help you guys, I'm sorry, but I've made up my mind. Can you let Brookshire know when he comes back with the book that I've gone back to my room, and I want to be alone?"

Namaguchi nodded; he had a small, downturned smile of sadness. "I understand."

"Well, I won't be completely alone," Davis said as she scooped up Buster, who had just walked in and was urgently rubbing her legs as if asking for petting. "He's the only one I can trust. I'm going to take him to my room so I can talk to someone who isn't absolutely crazy!" And with that, Davis stormed off, but before she exited the door, she turned back, stomped her foot, and said, "Another bonus for Buster? He's not asking me to commit murder!" Namaguchi saw salty tears budding in the corners of her eyes and starting to make their way down her cheeks. He felt terrible but didn't take offense. He knew Davis only said those things because of the stress and took Buster as she just needed to cuddle something warm, cozy, soft, and be with something that wasn't asking anything of her.

~

Davis spent the rest of the afternoon petting Buster in her room and letting him know what a beautiful, good cat he was. Buster agreed, and Davis found out that a soft coat on a docile cat was great for absorbing tears. She nodded off with one arm wrapped around the cat, Buster's head resting on her bicep. She awoke with what felt like only a few minutes later when Buster got up and went to the door. "Oh, you're leaving too, are you, turncoat?" Buster looked at her with all the sympathy a cat can muster. "I'm sorry, Buster, you're a good baby. Good kitty." And she went to let him out the door. When she opened the door, she saw *The Great Gatsby* lying there with a note attached:

Feel better, Old Sport. —b

Davis found the note odd. She hadn't said anything about feeling sick or unwell. Perhaps Namaguchi didn't want to say too much, and he kept it simple. Either way, Davis decided she would spend the rest of the day in her room reading, napping, and ignoring the world inside the bunker once more. She missed the lunch that Ana and Quinn served that day, although someone dropped off a tray at her door. All went untouched except the water. She didn't even bother to bring the tray in her room, just picked up the water glass, turned around, and went back into her room, closing the door behind her. Davis wasn't trying to be rude; she was just too tired to try and pretend she had any enthusiasm about anything right now.

Davis also skipped dinner and took a nap, sliding back into her old routine of late-night living. After she was sure everyone had gone to bed, she crept out to the kitchen to get some food and water to drink. To her surprise, Namaguchi was standing there and saw her before she had a chance to leave. "Hello, Davis, come on in."

"I'm sorry, I didn't mean to disturb you. I just want to get a drink of water."

"You're not disturbing me; come in. Help yourself to whatever you might want in here. By the way, I talked to Ringo about you leaving. It might take a couple of days to finalize logistics. While you're waiting, feel free to continue to eat your meals with us, if you want. It's up to you."

"Can I ask you a question, Namaguchi?"

"Yes, of course."

"How well do you know President Everett? Do you work with him one-on-one? How can you justify arranging for his murder?"

"Well, that's a few different questions. First, I know President Everett very well. I knew him before he even was President; I was a professor at the school he attended. He took a chemistry class of mine, and I thought he was bright and already well-educated. So, I offered to mentor him. We became friends, and from there, after the incident when the Lombardi Plague got created—well, he was my friend. His story checked out. It didn't occur to me then that he could be lying. When he wanted me to be an advisor after he got elected, I felt honored, maybe a bit puffed up over the title. But I also felt good about everything we were doing. I was on mind control for so many years. Afterward, I started to notice things, things he did that were cruel or manipulative. But I was scared, too. He was my friend and the President. So, I kept quiet; I had to fight it myself whenever I doubted him. But, soon enough, it became too much to overlook. Second, I don't work with him one-on-one. He is never without at least four or five Security Patrol Guards, so that would be impossible. But he's also intensely private and tends to pass laws and such on his own, without help. Lastly, you asked how I can turn on him and help plan his murder? Well, I just know, in my heart, he is an evil man. Take away the lying. The mass manipulation. The control of the people. Do you know how many deaths he directly caused? If he were a civilian, they'd call him a serial killer. Why should he be protected from justice just because he is President?"

"Has he killed people himself, killed people with his own hands?" asked Davis in shock.

"No, well—maybe. I'm honestly not sure about that. But what is the difference between ordering death and doing the deed yourself? In my mind, there is no difference."

"One thing I don't understand is you guys keep talking about this mind control and that our freedoms are gone. But we have libraries full of books and movies. We have 'family nights' where we play board games and sports with each other and mingle. All religions are allowed. Homosexuality is technically illegal, but they don't widely enforce the law. I don't understand where all the deficit in our freedoms is. As far as I know, except for the Pod living, assigned workforce, and plural marriage, much is the same as it ever was before the plague. And the changes were to protect us and help repopulate the earth."

"Well, that's both the evil and the genius in President Everett's plans. He took away your private homes and business, but he built these Pods that provide warm beds, a shower, medical exam, food, great libraries with all those movies and books. It's natural not to think about what is lacking when the government provides all your necessities. Especially when done under the guise that it's for your health and well-being." Namaguchi paused here and rolled his eyes up, looking at the ceiling, as if he were trying to gather his next thoughts. "Yes, you can go to church, too. The same church your family has gone to for generations or a new one altogether. But, the official religion of the United State is Everettisim. Does President Everett care if you believe he is the only one with direct communication with God and he is the final word here? Not really, because Everett still has the final word on what we do, say, eat—he doesn't need us to call him God because he knows people might rear up and kick like crazy mules if he takes their religion away. He also knows some people will believe he is the highest ordained and pass that thought to their family, friends, and children. So, Everett simply put his religion in and said, "Well, this is the government's religion, but you're still *free* to practice other religions." Things like that make people less aware. It feels like their religion is still protected. Not to mention the mind control drug routinely administered. That in itself takes away your right to free thought because it convinces you everything the government is doing is correct, whether it is or not. You lose the power to decide for yourself."

"I guess I see what you mean a little bit," mused Davis. "But I just still don't see all the evil in it that you do."

"That's because you see the big picture that Everett presents. Have you ever seen a completed intricate piece of artistic embroidery? It's a lot like that. Embroidery is a beautiful picture created on canvas with strings, yarn, or threads. It can be of a lake, sunrise, an animal—the options are endless. But the point is the finished picture is art. On the front side, you see a beautiful scene; that's the picture President Everett wants you to see. Now, if a real artisan made it; the back would look nearly as good as the front. But lots of people get lazy with the back or don't have the skill required. So, the backside gets all tangled and confused; back there, it's a jumbled mess. It doesn't form a clear image, like as seen on the front. President Everett is a master at making the front—the side everyone looks at—very beautiful. But, if you saw the back, it is a disaster. He simply became very adept at knowing which strings to pull to create the best picture on the front side."

"Well," Davis asked. "Then how did so many people get fooled? You remarked that the brain control element wasn't in the Marigold Injection at the very beginning. So, how did everyone all go along with it so easily?"

"People thought Everett was protecting them. They'd seen, if not all, almost all of their families and friends die a horrible death. Things were an absolute mess. They needed and wanted to hear they'd be protected."

"Well, I get that, of course. I've felt the need for protection since I got here—no insult to you guys. But I guess I just don't understand how it became such a big mess seemingly overnight."

"Oh, my dear," he said, "That's my point. A society never crumbles all at once. It is one piece at a time we march toward destruction."

SEPTEMBER 16, 2056 – PREPARING TO DEPART

Davis had gone back to her room after her conversation with Namaguchi and stayed awake a long time, thinking things over and trying to make sense of something, anything. She thought about when she got out of there; she would be expected to marry President Everett. The publicity of it was too good to pass up. She didn't want to inflate herself up with self-importance, but it made sense. She worked at the Everett Center and was always at every significant presidential event. Yes, President Everett kept her at a distance, but that made sense, knowing he wanted to keep Ruby a secret. It also explained to Davis why she had never had any Inquiries of Interest; she has always wondered. Davis was of a somewhat high position, not unattractive yet, well past her prime age to get married. And then there was Brookshire. Davis had always believed they would get married. That was not in her imagination. They had been fast friends, but they developed a love and affection for each other after some time passed. They had conversations about their love, so Davis knew it wasn't one-sided. Brookshire never told her that he was leaving. Just one day—the day after he held her hand at the Courting Dance—he was gone. No notice. No notes. No explanations. She had always felt like maybe she had said or done something wrong. Now she just knew she was a claimed property.

A little after 3 a.m., the nightmare Davis had become accustomed to awoke her. She was startled out of deep sleep and sat straight up in bed, swatting at the ghastly hands that still seemed to reach out to her, even though her eyes were now open. The phantom hands quickly dispersed, but she was now wide awake, her heart thumping in her chest. Davis got up to turn on the light and collect her thoughts. When she lay back down, she picked up *The Great Gatsby* to continue reading. Reading had always provided such a source of calm and peace for her. But now, she couldn't focus on the words. Her mind kept going to her inevitable marriage to President Everett, in reality, also her stepdad. She had to cope with the fact her mom was alive and married to the man Ringo and Namaguchi now expected her to marry. The whole thing made her sick, both physically and mentally. Eventually, complete exhaustion overtook her, and she fell back asleep; the book slipped to the floor, and the bright lights of the room shone down her.

When Davis awoke, she realized it was a little past lunchtime. After cleaning up, she went to the kitchen to find some food. Quinn and Ana were in there, cleaning up after the lunch they had served. Right away, Quinn went up to Davis and hugged her and saw that she had startled and surprised her with the affection. "I'm sorry, Davis. I've just been worried about you. I know you've been through a lot lately."

Davis didn't respond. She felt she might cry if she did, so Davis just gave Quinn a small smile and nod, hoping that would convey that all was good between her and Quinn. She decided to change the subject so that she could speak, if not about feelings, something else, at least. "Where are the kids at?"

"They're in school. Ringo and Josie are teaching them a music lesson."

"Oh, so do you guys need any help in here?"

Ana responded, "No, thank you. Can we get you something?"

"You know what? I'm starving! So, yes, I'd love something. But don't worry about it. I'll get it and clean up after myself."

Ana nodded and said if she needed anything else to let her know. When Davis replied she did not, Ana and Quinn continued cleaning while Davis prepared herself a snack. It made for an awkward silence. Davis, feeling very self-conscious about it, tried to hurry and finish up so she could get out of there. As that was going unsuccessfully, she quickly made up a lunch tray to take back to her room. Quinn expressed that she hoped that Davis would join them for dinner, but no pressure, of course.

~

Davis had every intention of joining them for dinner. However, on the way back to her room, Ringo stopped her. He told her that they had arranged to transport her back to the city the next morning, and they should perhaps go over a story for Davis to protect her best when she got back into the fold of things.

After Davis and Ringo had a conversation, they decided Audrey would drop Davis off near one of their revolving stops early in the morning and that she would be hooded. It was best for a Security Guard to find her that way and with her hands tied. Ringo assured her that he would fasten it lightly and regret it, but that he wanted her story believable. Davis had to sell the tale they kidnapped her but did not know why nor did she understand why she had been suddenly let go. Perhaps she could at some point surmise that people had taken her in a stance against the government, but they were uneducated fools, not knowing what to do with her once they had her, and she became too much trouble. Davis had to keep it vague and slim on details. Sooner than later, she would have a medical exam. It would prove they did not assault her in any way, and she would receive her Marigold Injection. Ringo told her that while the brain control chemical wouldn't be effective right away, it would only take a few injections until Davis was up to government requirements again. He also let her know that the transition back to the chemicals would not be nearly so difficult, and she shouldn't be sick or too ill, at least. He said there might be some confusion, dizziness, and general feelings of not being well. But, not a violent illness like before. He assured Davis she shouldn't worry about being scanned by a drone or any slips of the tongue. Those things could be explained as things she overheard, and perhaps, she had been a little brainwashed by her kidnappers, had a case of Stockholm syndrome, as it were. The government wouldn't expect she'd be entirely in her right mind after such an ordeal. All Davis had to do was keep saying how much she loved President Everett, and eventually, that would be the truth for her again.

Ringo then went onto a more sensitive subject. He parroted what Namaguchi had explained earlier. It would be too tempting for President Everett not to marry Davis. Davis needed to accept before she went back that she would be marrying the President, who was also her stepfather, and the reason her mother was vacant from her life. Davis couldn't help thinking that Ringo delivered this information almost a bit sternly. Not that anything Ringo said could be described as "stern." However, it was almost like he was trying to subconsciously implant the thought of *Is this REALLY what you're going to do...marry THAT charlatan?*

Davis thanked Ringo and then walked back to her room to finally eat her lunch. It was then she realized, though, her appetite was gone. Davis also realized she couldn't go to dinner with these people who had been nice to her and expect everything to feel ordinary. *No use in getting any closer to them*, Davis thought. It was easier to stay in her room until it was time to leave the next morning to go back to the city and her old life.

SEPTEMBER 16, 2056 –
DAVIS'S EVENING

Davis had every intention of not leaving her room again that night. But then, she got hungry. Very hungry. She ate everything she had brought in earlier on the lunch tray but was still ravenous. She looked at the clock and saw it was just after 10 p.m. and realized everybody should be asleep or at least in their rooms. After tonight, she also realized it would be nutrition biscuits for the rest of her life, so *why not enjoy one more salad*, she thought.

After Davis left her room and made her way to the kitchen, she figured she would clean up her lunch items quickly and then make another quick tray to take back to her room for the rest of the evening and a quick breakfast tomorrow. But Davis was surprised to see Quinn in the kitchen, eating. It was too late for her to turn around because Quinn saw her, also. But Quinn's bluntness shocked Davis. "Have you ever had wine?" asked Quinn with a smile. "I think you need a drink."

Alcohol was outlawed. *What could Quinn be talking about?* Davis thought. Quinn explained it was not seriously prohibited, only denied to "common folks." She told Davis that the upper echelon could get anything they wanted. It may take some phone calls, some money exchanging hands—and since money was only held by the governmental elite anymore, they were the only ones that got wine or other "forbidden" goods. There were ways in which the top folks had access to things—there were ways.

Namaguchi was a lead person, and he had got the wine for his wedding to Ana and kept the leftover bottles. When he started coming to the bunker, he brought the bottles, too. Quinn said he did not care if others drank them; there were plenty, and they were there for whoever wanted them. "I'll pour you some Riesling to try. It is very appealing. Almost everyone likes it."

Davis watched as Quinn pulled out a glass and poured in a golden-hued elixir. Davis took a sip of the cool, syrupy liquid. She flinched at first, jerked her head back, and squinted like she had no idea what was coming because she hadn't. But, after a second, she took another sip. Something was intriguing about it to her, something fascinating and inviting that Davis had never had before. It felt like it was warming her up from the inside out. She took another sip.

Before Davis knew it, they had moved to the dining table in the other room, and about an hour had passed. Davis too quickly had drunk two glasses of this wine, and now, Quinn was pouring her another. They were giggling; Davis, who had never really had any friends, felt a certain kinship with this young girl. Davis started to fight back the tears. She did not know what would make her cry, but she felt very emotional and worked up suddenly. "You know, um, you know…you are very nice, you know. What a nice young girl, you girl." Davis had meant the words to come out smoothly and be a nice compliment, but they seemed slurred and messed up. She wasn't even entirely sure where she had messed up the words but knew they were not right after saying them. Davis crossed her eyes, her face showing her confusion over her words.

Quinn looked surprised at first, and Davis felt sheepish and silly, glowing hot in the cheeks and wishing she hadn't said it. Davis started to apologize when Quinn, giggling, said, "That's very nice! By the way, when was the last time you ate? I think you may need some food in your stomach. Especially since you've never drunk alcohol before!"

"Um…luuuunch? Or…um, yes, I ate last at lunch!"

"Okay, I'm going to get some food; you wait here," said Quinn, giggling like crazy.

When Quinn came back, Cricket was next to her. "Hey-o!!!" Cricket gave a wave and called out to Davis before sitting down next to Quinn. Cricket explained she had been bored over in her bunker and was wandering about, exploring when she thought she'd pop over here and see if anyone else was still up. Quinn had mentioned the wine, and it didn't take Cricket a second of thought to agree. Before she knew it, Davis was drinking with two new friends—if you could call them friends. Davis had never really had any real girlfriends but assumed this was what it felt like as they were laughing, chatting, and giggling. *What an odd sensation*, Davis thought; she had always wondered how it would feel to have girlfriends. To sit, talk about something or nothing even. To connect and feel love and be loved, just for who you are, not doing anything specific. As Davis was pondering, Ana walked in. "Am I interrupting something?"

"NO!" said Quinn, and Davis noticed her cheeks blushed hotly. Quinn slid down the bench more, creating a space between her and Cricket and created a place for Ana to sit down. "I was just hanging out with the ladies. Having some wine and snacks."

"Oh, I came by your room to ask you something and was startled to see you were not there with it being so late," said Ana blushing. "I would love to join you guys if that's okay?"

Quinn was then pouring wine into a fourth glass, and before she knew it, Davis was drinking with three new friends. *If this is what friends are*, that nagging thought in the back of her head that she wasn't entirely sure persisted. Davis decided to test the water to see if this was indeed friendship and was glad that she had started slowing down drinking wine and was drinking more water. Davis had also been nibbling on the veggies and bread Quinn had put out. Davis assumed it was because of this she was feeling a bit more stable and less dizzy and silly. "So," she said, sounding sleepy, "Something has been bothering me, and I know my words are failing me a bit tonight, but I think I need you to know. Yes. I think."

"You can tell us whatever you want," Quinn replied kindly and delicately.

"I just need a few moments to compose my thoughts."

Davis took a good drink of water and popped a few nuts in her mouth. She was trying to think but also calm herself down as much as she could before speaking. Davis was aware that everyone was trying hard not to stare at her, making small looks and saying the occasional word to each other. As Davis continued to relax around everyone, she reached into a bowl on the table—Quinn called them chips, said they were sliced-thin potatoes and baked crisp. Davis found those were quite tasty. As eating and drinking water had made her feel better, eventually, she discovered she had kept doing it mindlessly. Finally, Davis realized that she had paused for a ridiculously long time before telling her story, so she started, "Well, um, this is difficult. But I have these nightmares. Um, scary stuff. A boy, reaching out, screaming from the dark. To me."

"Well, we all have bad dreams sometimes, as unsettling as it can be, everything is all right," offered Cricket helpfully. She also reached across the table and patted Davis's hand, which struck Davis oddly. The move felt motherly, and Cricket was anything but motherly.

"Yeah, I guess. But, hmmm, what to say. Well, the thing is, I know where the nightmare came from, and I'm responsible for it."

"What do you mean, 'responsible'?" asked Quinn.

"Well, I work at the Everett Center. And one day, they asked me to, I'm not sure what the right word is. Eh, to do something outside my regular job. Everyone else was busy, so they had me take a young boy; he was maybe eleven. He was terrified. I recall that. And then, you know?"

"I'm not sure what you mean. Can you tell us what you did with the boy or why he was so scared," Quinn asked, confusion knitted in her brow.

"Yes, I think. Wait, let me think." Here Davis paused for another long time, taking sips of water and looking as if she was trying to collect her thoughts. "Well, huh. I think they told me he was a transfer of some kind. I don't remember the whole story. Just remember the terror on his face. And at the time, I felt it was wrong. But it was, honestly, like something was controlling my moves, propelling me forward. For years in my dreams, it's haunted me. I think deep down, I knew something wasn't right. But, I did it anyhow. I took him down a long hallway, him crying and screaming the whole time. Being with me must have been better than what he expected to happen next because after I handed him over, he grabbed onto me. He didn't want to let go. But I forced him off. He kept grabbing for me, and I wasn't even brave enough to watch them drag him off. I just turned and walked away. Now, I get here and know they may have eliminated him." Davis gulped down a large breath of air and felt as if she was choking back tears. "It makes me sick. I knew…knew something was wrong and didn't do anything." Tears flooded Davis's eyes and poured down her cheeks. Her face got hot and sweaty, and she put her head down on her arm, noticing once again she had gripped her fingers into her palm so deep that blood was flowing from four crescent-shaped marks in her palm.

Quinn got up and sat next to Davis, lightly rubbing her back. "Davis, it's okay," she cooed.

"It isn't."

"It is. Really. We've all done things that haven't made us proud. Whether it was because of the mind control drug or just trying to survive in that crazy world, we've all made mistakes and performed with less than heroic behavior."

"And, if he was that young, and it was at the Everett Center, he likely went to reprogramming, not elimination," offered Ana in a light, delicate voice that indicated she was trying to be helpful.

"But," said Davis, "I knew it was wrong. Yes, I felt an almost per-sistent urge to do as they told me, and honestly, I'm not sure how I could have helped him anyhow. But I wanted to. Deep down, I wanted to, but I did nothing." Davis was now sobbing uncontrollably. She was also feeling self-conscious as she had shared more than she originally meant to.

"Crying and talking will help," chirped in Cricket. "I'm a champion crier! It helps to process things, and I'm glad you trusted us enough to tell us. I know it isn't easy, but try not to blame yourself. As you said, you were not in a position to help, and you didn't issue the order yourself to take the boy into custody."

Davis started to calm down a little, comforted by the ladies and having fatigued herself from such heavy crying. Then the tears suddenly started anew. "But I wasn't brave, and now, once again, I'm not brave enough to help you guys."

Quinn immediately and enthusiastically replied, "Oh, that's not a sign of being brave or not! We brought you here under our wishes; you had nothing to do with that. We gave you tons of overwhelming information, and you had to make the best decision for yourself. Nobody blames you for anything or has a second of thought that you are not brave."

"You know," added Ana, "You have been through so much lately. Try not to be hard on yourself. You're punishing yourself for things you can't control. The nightmares—you're punishing yourself even while you sleep! Oh, Davis! Thinking you're not brave, that's you punishing yourself for what? Thinking we might not like you anymore? Might be disappointed in you? I can assure you that's not the case. Not that I blame you for anything; none of us do. So please don't think that, but maybe tonight before you go to bed, just ask forgiveness from the boy. Pray if you do. Ask God and the boy to forgive you, then permit yourself to forgive yourself. Try to believe the best outcome possible happened to him. You are assuming he met a terrible fate. It's just as likely he's okay. Perhaps he was reprogrammed and is living a happy life, just as you did in the Pods. Or, perhaps he was rescued and is living in a supportive bunker. It's not necessarily bad." Here, Ana paused for a good beat. Tears were swelling up in her own eyes. "You know,

I had to forgive myself for something terrible too. So, I do know what it feels like."

Davis noticed Quinn giving Ana a look. It conveyed that Quinn was proud of Ana, which Davis thought was sweet and friendly. Quickly though, Davis saw that look turn into something akin to panic.

Ana ignored her look and started, "My mom, Camila, she kept us away from the Pods to take care of my father, Jose, who was sick and not allowed in any of the Class One or Two Pods and, therefore, could not get the proper care. We were starving, though, so my mom went to break into a storage unit to get us nutrition biscuits. Only ten years old, I was confused. My last injection had only been a few days before we fled into the woods. So, my mom took me to the edge of the woods to keep a watch out while she tried to get us food, and I saw a Security Patrol Sargent." Ana started to rub tears from her eyes and looked down, the first time she hadn't made eye contact as far as Quinn could remember. "I turned her in. I notified the Patrol Sargent because I thought they might help us. Instead, she got dragged into the town center and shot. I got my mom killed. And my father too. Because they took me to the Everett Center, and he was left alone in the woods."

The look of shock on Quinn's face told Davis that she had not known this story, or at least not all of it. But, as was Quinn's comforting way, she put her arm around Ana's shoulder and leaned her head against it. "It's okay; I'm sorry you had to deal with that. You were so young," she quietly said to Ana. Cricket and Davis nodded in agreement, both now crying. They all realized that sometimes there were just no words to offer comfort or fix a situation.

A mutual understanding seemed to be found by all the ladies, and slowly, silently, they sipped at the wine for a few minutes until the glasses started to empty. There was not much else to say this evening, so the party began to break up, and Quinn and Ana offered to clean up.

Davis started to feel tired but continued to sit there for a few minutes until—and she couldn't be sure—when she was so sleepy and couldn't tell if her eyes were open or closed anymore, she thought she saw Ana slip her hand off Quinn's arm and onto her leg under the table.

SEPTEMBER 16, 2056 –
QUINN'S EVENING

Quinn felt like she needed a drink of wine. She didn't drink much, and there were limited bottles in the bunker anyhow. They were for special occasions like birthdays, holidays, "freedom birthdays," what they called their anniversary of being in the bunker. But, *every once in a while, you just need a drink*, she thought. And nobody cared if you grabbed a few bottles for those occasions. She also thought it might help her bond with Davis a little if she brought her a glass. Even though she was leaving, she knew it had been a tumultuous time for Davis, and Quinn felt terrible for all she had gone through. Quinn thought it would be nice to put her at ease for her big day tomorrow, and of course, Ringo would let Davis know where the "doorbell" was, should she ever change her mind. A serendipitous event occurred when Davis entered the kitchen right as Quinn thought about bringing the wine to Davis's room. After acknowledging her, Quinn asked, "Have you ever had wine? I think you need a drink."

Quinn looked back at Davis's stunned expression and knew what she thought, that alcohol was outlawed. Quinn quickly explained that it was forbidden for most people. But, if related to President Everett or in the higher ranks of the government, you could pretty much get anything you wanted for exchange of goods, money, favors. Money in the United State was a weird thing. It had lost much of its value now that they were strictly socialist and the government provided all necessities. But some people liked it for the novelty of it, and in fact, Quinn had heard that in some places, the value was far higher than the number printed on it. "I'll pour you some Riesling to try. It is very appealing. Almost everyone likes it." Quinn said to Davis. She tried to say it with a smile, in a very casual way.

Quinn handed Davis a wine glass and watched her take her first sip ever of wine. Davis flinched back a little at first, squinted a bit, and looked like she was surprised and a little unnerved. In particular, this was a sweet Riesling that Quinn had poured. Long legs were streaming down the inside of the glass. Quinn watched her take another sip, then another, knowing they were going to be in for an unforgettable night, albeit a fun one. Before Quinn knew it, they were chit-chatting and giggling. She started to feel comfortable around Davis, who was older than her but reminded Quinn of her mother or what Quinn could remember of her mom. Then, without warning, Davis said, "You know, um, you know...you are very nice, you know. What a nice young girl, you girl."

Quinn suddenly felt warm all over and surprised as well, as she could tell Davis was embarrassed by what she has said. Quinn didn't want her to feel that way. Before Davis could say the apology that Quinn saw coming, she cut in, offering to get some food and water since Davis wasn't used to drinking and would need something besides wine in her stomach. Quinn acquired the giggles, which she hoped wasn't embarrassing to Davis, but it was a little bit funny to see Davis getting so tipsy so quickly.

Quinn went into the kitchen to gather a few snacks; she made up a quick vegetable plate, got a bowl of nuts, and a bowl of potato chips. She also got a large pitcher of water and some water glasses. Piling the whole smorgasbord on a large tray with some napkins, Quinn was just about to go back into the dining room when Cricket came in and asked her what was going on. It was so funny to Quinn that Cricket just asked like it was a regular thing to pop over to another bunker late at night and see what other people were doing. But Quinn thought Cricket seemed harmless enough, so she asked her if she wanted to join in the wine fun. *The more, the merrier*, she thought.

After Quinn and Cricket came back into the dining room, Quinn set the tray down in the middle of the table, and Davis quickly got some water and snacks. Quinn then sat and then patted the seat next to her on the bench, indicating Cricket should sit next to her. However, Quinn was startled when soon after Ana walked in with an indignant look and said, "Am I interrupting something?"

Quinn couldn't tell her she wasn't interrupting fast enough, and as she felt her cheeks blushing hotly, she attempted to quickly and simply explain she was hanging out with Davis and Cricket. Quinn wished she could somehow clarify that she was trying to bond with Davis, making her feel more comfortable and at ease. There was no way to explain in front of Davis, so Quinn quickly slid down, creating a space for Ana to sit down next to her.

As Ana went to sit down, she gave a quick explanation about how she had gone to Quinn's room to ask her something but was surprised to see Quinn was not there. Quinn noticed Ana was blushing, and her blush continued as she sat, making Quinn feel bad that she had created an awkward situation for Ana.

To recompense, Quinn started pouring the wine for Ana, then refilled the other glasses after. That's when Davis suddenly spoke up, sounding like there was something important to say. When Davis started speaking, it was not entirely clear what she was trying to get at, so Quinn wanted to encourage her. "You can tell us whatever you want," she said, looking directly at Davis.

Quinn watched Davis as she drank some water and nibbled on snacks, looking nervous, and as if she was trying to gather and control her thoughts. Quinn decided right then that no matter what Davis said, she would be as supportive as possible. But there was nothing that could have prepared her for what she heard. It started benign enough, about her nightmares, and Cricket said a generic yet kind platitude. Then it quickly went dark. Quinn was quite surprised to hear that Davis had been involved in transporting a terrified young boy to some kind of reprogramming center. While the details were not entirely clear, what was clear to Quinn was that this boy had been in a dangerous situation, and Davis had delivered him right into the hands of the enemy.

When Davis started to cry, although the shock had not worn off yet, Quinn jumped to one of the things she felt like she excelled at, comforting. She got up to sit next to Davis and rubbed her back. Quinn tried to put her hand on Davis lightly, not wanting to make her more nervous or put her off. She tried to say a few kind words, although this was a difficult situation. There was not much to say. And Quinn saw very quickly as Ana and Cricket also tried words of comfort that it was just one of those things that would take time. They could be as encouraging and friendly as they knew how—and they would be—but it would not be an easy road to navigate. Made evident by Davis, who was now sobbing.

Just when Davis started to calm down a little, she suddenly started crying hard again. Quinn felt so badly for her; clearly, she dealt with a lot of pain, confusion, and uncertainty. Quinn also realized Davis was worried and anxious about letting down everyone in the bunker group. Quinn felt torn; she very much wanted this plan to go forward and wanted Davis to help them. However, Quinn also wanted to be supportive and kind to Davis. She looked at Ana and lifted her eyebrows as if she was trying to ask her *what now?* Quickly, Quinn turned her attention back to trying to comfort Davis again. She barely said a few words when Ana jumped in with some surprising yet incredible words of comfort. Quinn found herself very proud of Ana, her wisdom, and the strength that her speech imparted. However, Quinn started to worry and shot Ana a look of panic as she continued her story. She was unsure Ana should share what Quinn was certain she was about to contribute to the conversation.

Quinn was stunned as Ana told her story and what had happened to her mom, Camila. Quinn had heard part of it but never the part about Ana talking to the guard and turning her mom in. Quinn felt the bottom of her stomach drop out. *What was Ana talking about?* she thought. Quinn decided to go back and sit with Ana. Quinn walked slowly back; it felt as if she was treading through molasses. Ana had told Quinn the basics of what happened, but understandably, she did not like to talk about it much and typically avoided the topic. In turn, Quinn avoided the issue and tried to protect Ana when and if the subject ever came up. Quinn was utterly taken aback and had no words when Ana started confessing that *she* had been the reason Camila got murdered. She wasn't mad, just very surprised by this revelation and so sad for Ana, and sympathized with how difficult that must have been. How painful that must have felt. And even if Ana had indeed forgiven herself, Quinn could see it in her face that the pain had not gone away. There was not much Quinn felt she could say in this circumstance. It was so beyond any words that could be helpful. So, Quinn just tried to be as comforting as possible and let Ana know that she still supported her.

The evening started to wind down after that. Quinn and Ana both offered to clean up, and Cricket departed with a kiss on the cheek for each of the other three ladies. Looking exhausted and beyond sleepy, with puffy eyes from crying, Davis sat there a few minutes until Ana slid her hand onto Quinn's knee. *That's a foolish move*, Quinn thought. *We can't get caught doing things like this.* She doubly figured they should be careful because she was pretty sure Davis saw the move Ana made and then took a quick departure upon seeing it.

Even crazier was when Ana looked Quinn in the eye—it felt to her like it was straight in the eye, but Quinn was a bit tipsy—and gave her a crooked smile and then planted a kiss right on her lips. Quinn, for a moment, returned the kiss but abruptly broke away, gasping. "We can't do this; what if someone sees us? This. Is. Not. A. Good. Idea." Quinn was fighting all her instincts to do what she wanted to do, which was kiss her back passionately.

"I don't care who sees!" exclaimed Ana.

"Well, I do," said Quinn, getting up from the table. "Please, I'm sorry, Ana."

"Please don't say anything else. Just go," Ana started to cry a little, breaking Quinn's heart with each tear that began to fall. Quinn reached out to put her hand on Ana's shoulder, but Ana had quickly put her head down on the table and nestled her head in the crook of her arm. Quinn thought better than saying anything at all and promptly left the room, apologizing again as she walked away, and her own tears started to sting her eyes.

SEPTEMBER 18, 2056 –
DAVIS RETURNS TO HER ROOM

When Davis finally returned to her room, there was something under her door. It was an envelope with a note clipped to it. Looking at it, Davis saw the letter was from Duffy. Davis glanced at the clock and noticed it was a little past 3 a.m. She was tired, her head hurt, and she wasn't quite sure she wanted to read it right then. However, remembering she was supposed to leave the bunker at about 7 a.m. today, she figured *no time like the present* and read the note.

Davis,

I know this will seem blunt, and I apologize for that, but I got back this evening and wanted to give this to you before you left. However, you were busy tonight—which is excellent; I hope you had a fun evening with the girls.

At any rate, your mom gave me this note a long time ago, after you were born, but before she had been told you died. I did read it, and I'm sorry. I just didn't know if we'd ever meet you or when. And, I wanted to make sure there was no valuable information we needed.

She had named you "Amelia," so that is how she addressed the letter. She wrote it after the cure for Lombardi Plague was introduced, but the brain control hadn't been introduced yet. That wasn't until a few more months down the line. Currently, your mom is very much under the power of the brain control drug. The person who wrote this letter would not write it now. You need to know that. I also think it's important for you to know that the Marigold Injection was initially called the Everett Cure. Early on, it was changed to the Marigold Injection, so that is all most people remember.

All my best,

Duffy

Davis reread the letter from Duffy before opening the envelope. Her hand was shaking as she opened it; her hand was trembling so much that she couldn't even get the letter out on her first try. Davis decided to sit on the bed while reading because there was dizziness in her brain. She took a deep breath before forcing her eyes open, although that wasn't too difficult as she was suddenly wide awake.

Dear Amelia:

My beautiful daughter! I am thrilled that I was able to stay healthy enough to bring you into the world. And now, we have both been cured of the Lombardi Plague! That cure opens so much possibility for you. I know already how smart you are—you're so alert when you look at me, and your little sticky-up tufts of golden hair look like sparks of brilliance to me. Regardless, now you have the chance to LIVE. Have a life to create a story that is remarkable and uniquely yours.

I never knew I could love someone so much as you; from the instant I saw you, you were my favorite person in the world. I do wish your father could have met you; I know he would have been crazy about you too. Honestly, I don't understand how anyone wouldn't be crazy about you. You're so cute, little, innocent, and sweet. I could stare at just your chubby, perfect little toes for hours.

There is something you must know, my dear. I do not fully trust Dr. Everett. I can't put my finger on it, but I feel there might be something malicious happening. Again, nothing specific, so maybe I shouldn't be so nitpicky. After all, he did save our lives! And for that, I'll always respect and admire him—he saved my baby daughter's life. But I've heard murmurs, grumblings, things that have made me uncomfortable. He seems to have a bad temper with the staff, which is never good, in my opinion. So, I have created a "password" for you, of sorts. In case something happens and we get separated somehow. I'm sure I'm worrying over nothing—new mom jitters—but just in case, this makes me feel better.

The password is "marigold." My father, your grandfather, used to call me his Little Marigold. Not because of the golden hair that adorns the women in our family, although he said that was a fun coincidence. He always said marigold flowers are associated with the brave and courageous lion. That he always knew I could be brave and courageous, knowing that I will have the support and love of my family. That I could accomplish anything that I set my mind to do. And I want to impart not just this "safety password" onto you but also that same strength, courage, hope, and love. You have courage, my daughter. Courage isn't doing something brave and strong—although I know you are brave and strong too—courage merely is doing the right thing, even if it isn't easy. And I can see in your eyes; you will always do the right thing. You will always have the love and support of your family. Even if we are not here when you need us, you will have a whole legion of people you can rely on to help you from the Heavens. You are my Little Marigold.

I love you, my dear one, always and forever.

Love, mom

~

Davis curled herself up into a fetal position, not crying, not even feeling anything but numb. Like her brain was dried out. She lay there, looking like a terrified child, hoping sleep would overtake her. She wanted to sleep for a few hours before departing and never look back. Her thought at that moment was that if the brain control could take back over, then she'd totally forget that letter and maybe even that Ruby was her mom. It would be so much easier. Davis just didn't want to worry about any of it anymore.

Much to Davis's dismay, sleep did not come; a half-hour later, she started to read the letter over and over. Trying to make sure what she was reading was also believable. She had never known her mother. She didn't think the few weeks before being separated counted since she had been too young to remember any of it. Davis *wanted* to believe it was true, but could she be positive? She decided that once again, she was not sure of anything that was happening.

The little of what remained of the wee hours of the morning found Davis exhausted, both physically and emotionally. Sitting on the bed, then pacing back and forth, even laying on the floor at one point. Sometimes, the letter in her hand, being held like a prized possession, sometimes it laying on the bed, and Davis just staring at it like it was carrying a virus and could not be touched.

Reading the letter several times over made her feel like she was sort of in a daze. Davis did not feel as if she was processing the words correctly. She read it so many times but was not even sure of what it really said. Finally, Davis realized to make any kind of real decision; she had to process the information correctly. Her brain hurt, she was tired and overwhelmed, but she had to find a way to reset herself.

Davis went to the restroom and took a quick shower to try and feel at least a little physically better. Then, she brushed her teeth and went by the kitchen to get water before returning to her room. When she got back to her room, she took a few sips of water, then lay down on the cool bed, trying to focus her mind on the warm, cozy covers and the soft pillow her head was on. She didn't think sleep would come, but pure exhaustion took over, and she did sleep a while, although anxiety eating away at her stomach soon woke her up. The words of the letter turned over and over in her mind.

Marigold.

Marigold.

You are my Little Marigold.

The words rolled around in her mouth, starting like a stone that was rough and bumpy and ended up polished and smooth.

Finally, when Davis could not push the thoughts from her mind any longer, no matter what she tried, she sat up in bed and turned on the light next to her. She then took the letter out of the drawer she had previously stuck it in and took a deep breath before rereading it. She took her time, reading it slowly, and focusing on each word. She did not know what it was, but some unknown force told her this *was* from her mother. Comfort gradually replaced unease and anxiety. But Davis still didn't know what to do about any of it.

Davis took periodic breaks of trying to take short naps, but mostly she lay in bed and alternated between trying to clear her mind, rest a little, and rereading the letter. Nothing felt secure to her, her mind feeling calm one moment and then a jumbled mess the next. And while she was able to get a few moments of sleep occasionally, it was broken and didn't feel like a respite.

Since she was not paying attention to the time, she wasn't even aware of the knocking on the door until Ringo had been at it a full five minutes. He finally broke her out of her reverie when he slightly opened the door and peeked in. "Davis, are you okay? It's past seven. If we're going to take you into the city, we need to go now."

A momentary pause stopped her as she walked toward the door. It was that pause that seemed to clear the fog from her mind. She said it before she could regret it. "Ringo, oh, I'm sorry for the trouble. Change of plans. I'll be helping you, after all."

SEPTEMBER 18, 2056 – SOME EXPLANATIONS

Ringo nodded and closed the door. Then he thought better of it and lightly rapped on the door again, once more opening it slightly ajar and putting only his head inside. "Sorry to bother you. Are you okay? Do you need anything?"

"No, I'm okay. Can you give me a few hours? I haven't slept at all. I need to rest a little. Then, if possible, I'd like to talk to Duffy. Is she around today?"

"Yes, she is—"

"Actually," interjected Davis, "Can I talk to Duffy now? Then I'll rest. I don't think I'll be able to sleep without talking to her. It's nothing bad, just need to resolve some things."

A few minutes later, Duffy was in her room, greeting her and asking Davis how she was doing. Then Duffy asked why Davis wanted to speak to her. Duffy said her words in a very calm and collected voice, tinged with kindness and compassion, making Davis feel at ease. "Thanks for coming in, Duffy. Can you please explain to me a little bit about how you knew my mom and what happened that caused her to write the letter and give it to you?"

"Yes. I was a young doctor specializing in obstetrics. I worked at a center with several doctors and OB/GYNs tasked with safely delivering and administering care to pregnant Lombardi Plague patients. To be honest, I had already delivered four babies and successfully administered the Everett Cure, as it was known then. That's not what they told people, though. You're recognized as the first, as you know. President Everett wasn't willing to risk your health, though, so there were tests before you were born."

"Why was I so important to President Everett?" asked Davis in confusion.

"No offense, but it wasn't you, specifically. It was your mom. He was quite infatuated with her; I think in love with her. Or more accurately, he confused his obsession with love. She was a medical assistant—and newly married to your father—when he met her. Your mom made friends with him, but there was nothing more than that for her. He wouldn't stop until he got her, though."

"Are you saying this whole plague, all these people gone, murdered and manipulated was because President Everett loved my mom?"

"I believe so. Well, not completely, only partly. Everett also wanted power and influence too. He wanted to be president and be respected by all. So, Everett hatched a plan. He needed one plan that all at once would eliminate your father, save you and your mom, and make him a hero to the world. Some of this is just speculation based on things I saw and heard over time. That's part of the problem, though. Everett is so dangerous because nothing seems crazy at the time that he's doing it. It's just this buildup over time, and finally, you look back, and you realize the whole thing it's all shams, deceptions, and sleight of hand trickery."

"Yes, I know he's evil. I got it. What I *really* want to know about is my mom."

Duffy looked startled at being snapped at, and Davis quickly remembered her manners. "I'm sorry. I didn't mean to be rude. I'm exhausted and overwhelmed. And anxious to know more about my mom."

Softening her look, Duffy said she understood. She then continued with her story. "It's okay. As I mentioned, I think a lot of the plan was to get your mom as well as have ultimate control and power. I made friends with your mom when I became her doctor at the birthing center when she was getting ready to go into labor with you. I suppose she trusted me, and we had many conversations. She never told me she didn't trust Everett straight out but one day mentioned a conversation she overheard outside her room. That's what prompted her to write the letter, but your mom never shared with me the details of what she heard. She only made me promise to hold it for you in case something happened. Naturally, she could not foresee all that would unfold, but I guess she saw enough to write the letter as a precaution. After they took you away and your mom and I were told you had died, she never mentioned the letter again."

Davis got a puzzled look on her face. "You know, just a question. If Everett was so smitten with my mom, but she still got extremely sick with the Lombardi Plague, right? Why didn't he save her from that?"

"Honestly, I don't know exactly. But I assume Everett couldn't control the virus as well as he thought he could. There are some theories that he had some control at first, targeting not only more men than women but also targeting women he found less attractive. But, as it is with viruses, they are not easily controlled. A lot of our people think Everett had the cure, all ready to go. That is why he never got it. Once he got the plague under control, he started working on the brain control element. Maybe he was just waiting for your mom to get it to start trials. That way, he could 'save' her. Her being pregnant wasn't likely a part of his original plan, but it made his savior story all the better." After a moment of thought, she added, "This is all just speculation. But, I do know for a fact that after your mom got pregnant and, then a few months later, got the Lombardi Plague, they admitted her to the top hospital, and she was taken care of when a lot of people could not get any help at all for their illness, pregnant or not. Then the trials started and, well, it was quick to the cure after they admitted her."

"Okay, you said you read the letter. So, you know, my mom called me her 'Little Marigold.' And the vaccination is called the Marigold Inoculation. I can't believe that is just a coincidence, right?"

"Well, no, probably not. More speculation, but we think that President Everett also saw that part of the letter; there were probably surveillance cameras in the hospital room. Or, it's possible he got her to confess after they were married and she was fully under the brain control drugs. He must have decided to use the word 'marigold' for the injection to make it more commonly used, less unique. That if, for some reason, you found out everything, 'marigold' wouldn't be as much of a password as it would be a very commonly used word by many, many people."

Davis didn't answer; she just slowly nodded her head in agreement and thanked Duffy for coming by. Her eyes were drooping and felt heavy. She almost felt as if she could fall asleep standing up. Davis asked Duffy to please let Ringo know she would be out later to discuss plans after she got some rest.

As Duffy was about to leave, she turned back around and faced Davis, walking up to her. She lightly placed her hand on her shoulder. "I want you to know the most important thing. Your mom is a good person. She is funny, smart, and she loved you more than words can tell you. And now, she is under the brain controlling drugs. It'll be okay, somehow, but it may not be easy."

"That's okay, Duffy. I'm finally learning that courage isn't doing the easy thing; it's just trying to do the right thing. And the right thing is to help you guys, and help and meet my mom, of course."

Duffy got a funny look on her face. "You sounded like her right now, when you just said that, about courage not doing the easy thing." Duffy then departed, leaving Davis with a warm feeling, as if healing was physically moving throughout her body. Davis lay down as soon as Duffy left. Finally feeling a little reassured and settled, she didn't even bother to get under the covers, just lay on top of the bed and, instead of drifting off to sleep, plummeted heavily.

Her sleep became restless after the first few hours. She tossed and turned and would occasionally grab the letter and clutch it to her chest in the still darkness of her room. It was almost as if she had to convince herself it was real and not a dream. Not only that the letter existed, but that it was in her hands. She didn't know if everything might be accurate. Davis assumed Ringo and his crew were also capable of lying to further their agenda. But, she realized, in a deep place in her heart, that this letter was from her mother. Davis couldn't explain it to herself better than that; she just knew she had a deep need to find and meet her mother.

SEPTEMBER 18, 2056 – PALACE EXPECTATIONS

The next few days flew by for Davis. It all felt like a whirlwind. She had many conversations with Quinn, Ringo, Namaguchi, and Brookshire about how everything would go down. They had decided they would stick to the original story they would have used if Davis simply went back. That she was kidnapped, but finding she was not very useful to the rebels' cause, they let her go. A new twist was that they decided Brookshire would go with her and "find" her after they dropped her off so that he could back up her story and support her. Brookshire would say that he found her wandering around outside the city center and bring her in. She would smuggle the bee venom in a secret compartment sewed into her knapsack. It was a given she'd be put in quarantine for fourteen days—more as a show than for any real reason, according to Ringo. As Duffy would be her doctor, Davis would be monitored by her. Fake reports for the Marigold Injection and a clean bill of health would be no problem.

Namaguchi started telling Davis about the harems at the Palace. He explained that President Everett had forty-six wives, from all different races and age groups. All the harems' rooms had a large living space with a living room, which included a large selection of lavish floor cushions, fine Persian rugs on expensive Italian marble floors. There were plenty of plush couches and chairs as well as a full book and movie libraries. Puzzles, games, cards, and a computer stereo with a complete "jukebox" program that had almost every song you could imagine on a karaoke system. The rooms had dining areas for the wives to eat together, and on a rotating basis, with their husband. They had unlimited access to filtered cold water and occasionally—very occasionally—some fruit. As the wives were expected to keep their weight under 145 pounds and weighed weekly to confirm they were, it was rare to get any food besides the nutrition biscuits. A combined sleeping chamber had between eight and ten beds, depending on the number of wives in that room. President Everett would choose a certain wife to sleep with him on occasion as he most certainly would do on Davis's wedding night. When that happened, President Everett escorted that wife to his private chamber.

Namaguchi also told her that Everett would give her a new name when she becomes engaged to him. It was unlikely Davis would have any influence over what that name would be. However, being called "Everett" was pointless because of the number of wives President Everett had, so the wives got first names to differentiate themselves. He then mentioned her mom Ruby had kept her name since, in the beginning, the threat of Davis ever finding out who she was, was negligible.

Here Ringo broke in and told Davis that it might not be as easy to meet her mother as she thought. He explained it was so because Everett kept the individual harems separate, beyond his reason wanting to keep Ruby and Davis separate. For instance, Caucasian women had a different room than Hispanic and South American women. The Asian women—be they Japanese, Chinese, Korean, or Thai, or anything in between—were all kept together, as were Black wives. Everyone was New American, so Everett based it on visible heritage, even if that heritage went back several generations. The only time the races were combined was when the wives reached over the age of fifty-five, which would be where Davis's mother was. Those wives, regardless of ancestry, made up the senior wife harem. He started to tell her about the zoo at the Palace and that President Everett assigned a different animal to each group of wives. President Everett thought it would give the women a sense of purpose and solidarity among themselves. The White women were in charge of the capuchin monkeys, and the primates would often have a free run in the harem room since they were relatively tame. The South American wives were in charge of the macaws, so they often had them in their room with them too. Asian wives handled dolphins, so obviously, they had an aquarium in part of the zoo. The Black wives took care of the koala bears, who had a eucalyptus patch made especially for them. And finally, the older wives took care of the tigers. The tigers had cages that had vast grasslands with sleeping caves and pools for them to swim in. He mentioned that Everett had an "animal," too, although he never paid attention to his crash of rhinoceroses; he used handlers.

"Oh," Namaguchi added, "there are so-called 'Den Moms.' Not wives, so they just have the customary last names; yours will be Cox. Be careful of her. Supportive of President Everett and the government, very much under brain control. You can't trust her nor count on her for any help." He continued to tell her that the Den Moms had a separate bedroom and a small bathroom within the harem room. Their apartment was not as nicely appointed as the area for the wives, and Den Moms were in charge of logging weight and ensuring each girl got enough water and food per day, was not complaining or starting fights, or spreading rumors. They kept calendars for medical appointments, public appearances, and dinners with President Everett. "Dillion is the Den Mom in the older wives' room. She may be more helpful; she's more sympathetic than Cox. However, she's still loyal to President Everett and under the brain control."

"There is one room where the wives might meet and run into each other—the gymnasium with every workout machine you could fathom. There are treadmills, weight balls, even a swimming pool, and an area to do dance and aerial arts, where instructors come in to give classes to the ladies." However, Namaguchi did not think that Ruby went there often. "Besides, President Everett will do whatever he can to keep you two apart. He doesn't want you to find Ruby or knowing the story of you two. Everett had only planned on marrying you after your mom passed, after all. That would have been the ultimate way to keep his secret. The circumstance we are creating will force it on him, but he's not going to hand it all to you on a silver platter."

Davis was focusing on meeting her mom and all that Ringo and Namaguchi told her. It was such a whirlwind, though. They inundated her with information, and they had given her so much data on varying topics so fast. As if they needed to shove the last twenty-nine years of information into Davis as quickly as possible. Therefore, she wasn't listening to Ringo or Namaguchi as closely as she should be. She hadn't meant to be rude, but this was a lot they were giving her. So, Davis didn't quite hear everything Namaguchi told her about the outfits that the wives wore. Something about them being more elaborate than Davis typically wore. She knew that the wives wore a dark cream tunic and jodhpurs in public and, in the back of her head, figured that was maybe what Namaguchi meant.

Ringo seemed to pick up that Davis was overwhelmed by the amount of information delivered so quickly. "Look, we don't expect you to remember this all. It's just to give you a reference point of where you're going and what to expect. You can't be upset there. Because when you get there, it will behoove us all that Everett gets poisoned quickly. Hopefully, before your wedding, even. He'll likely have dinner with you the night before; if you can slip it into his food or wine then, that will be perfect. Then you don't have to go through the process of marrying him, either."

"I understand. I just don't want to let anyone down. And I do want to meet my mom. That is important to me." Davis seemed close to tears.

"Absolutely," said Namaguchi. "I think that the best way to get to your mom will be to sneak out at night. I can draw you a map of how to get to the older wives' room. You'll have to figure out a way to wake up your mom without her screaming; that'll be the trick. But we can noodle that out together."

~

The next few days felt even more like a chaotic whirlwind to Davis. Coming up with all the plans to make sure she could meet her mom, that she snuck the bee pollen in without getting caught, and that everyone believed her story. She was glad she would get quarantined for two weeks before having to go to the Palace. She would have, as Namaguchi put it, "wife lessons." That would give her a little bit better idea of what to expect. And then, before she knew it, it was the night before departure and the start of yet another new chapter in her life.

SEPTEMBER 24, 2056 –
DEPARTURES

To say Davis awoke early was an understatement because, once again, she didn't sleep at all. She closed her eyes now and then, but tossing and turning had haunted her all night. So, when 5 a.m. rolled around, she wasn't exactly feeling rested but was anxious to get started and move onto the next step in this journey. Davis went down to the restroom and enjoyed one last hot shower. She didn't have time to make it as leisurely as she would have liked but made sure it was more than nine minutes because she knew it was back to timed showers again after this.

There wasn't much for Davis to pack. She pondered taking the copy of *The Great Gatsby*, but she didn't want to raise any flags and make it look like she had something she shouldn't. That made her think, and she checked the hidden pocket cleverly sewn into the seam and lining of her knapsack for the vial of bee venom. It was about the five hundredth time Davis had checked that pocket, and the vial was still there, as it had been the first time and every other time too. The darn thing made her nervous, though, and also, probably for the five hundredth time, she wished there was a different way to deal with all this. Something that didn't involve her murdering the President of the United State.

Davis smoothed down her tunic. It was the first time putting on her official clothing since taking it off early on at the bunker. It had been laundered, which was great; otherwise, it would be dirty and smelly. Davis now viewed it as an outfit of lies and not the Everett Center tunic and jodhpurs that once made her prideful. After going back to her room, she put the clothes she borrowed and the sheets from her bed folded up on the end of the mattress. Davis supposed there was no need to fold them if somebody was going to launder them. But, not wanting to be rude and not having time to clean everything herself, she assumed it was the best option. Never having had to deal with something like this before, it seemed to be the right thing.

After she straightened up the room, she headed to the dining hall to eat breakfast and say her goodbyes. Everything seemed so odd to her, as if she was walking in slow motion. Her stomach felt funny, and she felt light-headed. She stopped momentarily in the hallway before reaching the dining room to lean up against the wall and take a deep breath. Davis kept thinking about what it had said in the letter from her mom, *Even if we are not here when you need us, from the Heavens, you will have a whole legion of people you can rely on to help you. You are my Little Marigold.* She said a quick prayer, something she was only familiar with on occasion, as she forgot to do it a lot or sometimes didn't know what to say. But she asked God and her family to support her and give her strength. To look after her and help her get through this. Taking another deep breath and opening her eyes, she then carried on to the dining room.

Davis walked in, and everyone was there besides Duffy, Hernandez, and Namaguchi. She would see them on the other side as they had already gone into the city to report for their regular work duty and prepare things on their end. But even Cricket had come by to send her off. She felt love and friendship like she never had before. A choke rose in her throat, and she had to fight back the tears. Davis hadn't realized how difficult it would be to say goodbye.

As they sat to eat breakfast, there was minimal conversation. Not much eating, either. However, everyone was doing a great job of nibbling and pushing food around with forks. Davis tried hard to eat; she didn't relish the idea of going back to nutrition biscuits, and she didn't know if she would ever get a salad, potato, or strawberry again. But, a persistent lump in her throat prevented her from really eating anything.

After everyone finished, Davis started nervously to clear the table. Ana quickly stopped her and told her not to worry; they would take care of that later. What Ana hadn't realized was Davis needed to channel the nervous energy and delay the goodbyes. Time was growing short, and she had to repeat her silent prayer to keep her feet going.

Nothing could stop time, and finally, it was time to say goodbye. Davis hugged all the kids first and realized she hadn't gotten to know them well, which she now regretted. She supposed there had not been enough time, even though she had been there for quite a while. It all seemed like constant information overload. Olivia shook her hand after the hug and wished her good luck, which touched Davis's heart even more.

She then shook Ringo's hand, thanked him for everything, and gave Audrey a slight side hug and a quick thank you. She realized she hadn't gotten to know Audrey as well either, and again it saddened her. Davis thought perhaps she could suggest waiting a few more days to get more acquainted with everyone. She barely had time to think about it, though, because Cricket suddenly grabbed her and took her into a big bear hug, even lifting Davis's feet off the floor a little bit. "We're gonna miss you!" boomed Cricket.

Josie came up shyly, which surprised Davis since Josie didn't seem like the shy type. Davis quickly realized that Josie was another person she didn't know all that well. Davis assumed the shyness Josie exhibited was merely feeling as Davis did, that they were acquainted but not bonded like some of the others in the bunker.

Ana gave Davis a slight hug and then surprised her as Ana backed away and put both of her hands on the sides of Davis's face, then leaned in, lightly resting her forehead against Davis's. It made Davis feel loved and mothered like never before. Tears again began to spring in Davis's eyes, and she saw they had in Ana's too.

Even Buster came to say goodbye, weaving in and out of Davis's legs. Davis leaned down to give him a pet and few scratches behind the ear. Buster repaid her courtesy with an energetic bump of his head against her hand and a gentle mew followed by rumbling purrs.

Last was Quinn. She would be the hardest for Davis to say goodbye to. From the second this adventure had started; Quinn had been there. From day one. And while Davis had not always liked her, especially in the beginning, they had become friends, and Davis felt like she was the closest thing she would ever have to a sister. "Thank you, Quinn…for everything," she whispered as they hugged tightly and warmly. "I never had a sister, but I imagine if I had one, she would be like you." With that, Davis had to pull away and pat her eyes dry quickly; luckily, she had the forethought to bring a tissue with her to breakfast. Drying her eyes, she reflected a second on the craziness of it. As far as she could remember, she didn't think she had cried more than two times in her life before this. During her time in the bunker, it felt like she was always crying.

Davis stepped back from the group for a second and steadied herself. Knowing she had to speak quickly or she wouldn't get the words out, she rushed to talk. "I just want to thank you all for the food, conversations, help, information"—here she paused and gave a slight laugh—"and of course, the wine. I appreciate your friendship, and I will not fail you. I also know you pick your names here. It's moot at this point because I'm leaving, and I know I'll be known as Davis in the city until Everett gives me my new name. But, as far as I'm concerned, my name is Amelia."

~

Davis couldn't believe it when she found herself sitting next to Brookshire in the transport vehicle. She was nervous and sweating like crazy, even though it was cool that day. Brookshire leaned over and whispered in her ear, "Remember when we held hands that one time? I'm going to hold your hand the whole way there, so you know you're not alone." And with that, Ringo asked permission to put the black hoods on, and they were underway. Brookshire, lightly enfolding her hand into his, leaned over to whisper in her ear, "You can trust me."

It felt like hours to Davis, riding around in a car with a hood on her head. There were some big bumps in the road; from what Ringo said, they had to take back roads and rarely used passages. But Ringo said the whole ride should only take about forty-five minutes. Davis knew they couldn't have been in the car more than ten already, but anxiety and worry prevailed. That made the ride feel so drawn out, and she kept expecting something to go wrong, like a Security Patrol stopping them. Davis felt slightly comforted with Brookshire next to her, but she knew he had a hood on his head, too.

Eventually, they did stop. The first thing Davis saw was how bright the sun was when Ringo leaned back and pulled the hood off. Brookshire was already outside of the van, his hood off, and he was helping Davis out. He leaned into the transport to grab their knapsacks, and as he did, he said quickly, "We have to go, Amelia, now. Ringo can't get out and repeat his goodbye. He needs to go."

~

There was terror in Davis's eyes and urgency in Brookshire's as they set off. It had also startled her that Brookshire called her Amelia. She realized that even if she couldn't use that name, she wanted to start thinking of herself as Amelia. Feeling apprehension, nervousness, and anxiety, Amelia tried to focus on Brookshire's hand around hers and the kindness in his eyes to help her go forward. *Just one foot in front of the other, Amelia,* she thought to herself. And they set off into the chilly day, albeit the sun still blared brightly in the blue sky above them.

They were only walking for a few minutes, but Amelia was ready to be back inside. She was worried about the Drone Scanners. Although she could quickly explain any negative thoughts were only because of being kidnapped and the attempted brainwashing, she was terrified about being held motionless in the red beam until a Security Patrol picked her up. It then dawned on Amelia how absurd that was. That she wasn't even allowed to have a negative thought about the President or the government, she could see now how detrimental that could be to a society's populace.

It was hard to keep track of time for Amelia. It didn't help pass when Brookshire was quiet and just kept a determined look on his face. She guessed it was about fifteen minutes before a Security Patrol approached them. Brookshire quickly jumped into his role, waving his arms wildly and yelling, "Help! Help! I found Davis. The missing lady! She was wandering around out here, confused."

The Security Patrol came over and asked Davis about her ID Card. "Um, I gave it to him?" she replied, shrugging and putting her answer in the form of a question in the hopes it would help her seem confused. She added a few squints of the eye and simultaneously hoped it worked and thanked God she didn't have to act as a career. She felt like she was pretty terrible at it. "I don't know," she added inexplicably. Amelia then decided that maybe the less she spoke, the better. She blinked her eyes a few more times for good measure, then realized that she probably looked at worst, guilty, and, at best, like an oddball. Luckily for her, Amelia could look confused and crazy in this interaction because the role she was playing was that of someone muddled and perplexed.

The Security Patrol nodded and took her by the arm. Amelia was a little surprised, but he was not rough with her, so she decided the best thing to do would be to go with it and not put up any kind of resistance. Brookshire reached into his pocket, and at first, Amelia felt terrified. For a second, in her mind, she saw Brookshire pulling out a gun and getting into a shootout with the Security Patrol Guard. Of course, what actually happened was he pulled out her ID Card, giving it to the guard who looked it over quickly and scanned it; Amelia could see that her name—well, the name Davis—and a picture came up, along with her ID number and that she was missing and overdue for all medical exams. "Let's take you to the Palace Infirmary, then," he said. "That's what President Everett said to do when someone found you."

Amelia felt weak in the knees and tired. She was happy when they approached the Security Patrol Guard's vehicle. The guard set her down in the back and asked Amelia to put her hands out. "Sorry, Davis, I have to put these restraints on you. But, it's policy."

Amelia nodded as she stuck out her hands. After the guard secured them, she looked down at the thick silver cuffs that circled her wrists. They were sturdy and firm, the metal chilly. They had curved plates attached to the outside of each wrist restraint and forced her hands into somewhat of a praying position. They didn't exactly hurt, but it was odd to be restrained and have such limited movement of her hands and wrists. She definitely preferred Brookshire's hand around hers over the cold metal. It dawned on her as well that the guard had called her "Davis." It occurred to her this might get confusing, *Davis. Amelia. Amelia. Davis.* She also realized that President Everett would give her a new name when they were married too. It would be too confusing to go back and forth and try and remember her new name. With much chagrin, she decided to stick with Davis until everything else got sorted out.

SEPTEMBER 24, 2056 - INFIRMARY

The Security Patrol Guard escorted Davis into the infirmary door. He asked Brookshire to wait outside. When they walked in, Davis was somewhat comforted and somewhat unnerved by the presence of the blue light. She had forgotten about the ever-present ultraviolet rays that were everywhere, a never-ending beacon of death to bacteria and germs. Of course, it was also a reminder to the people that the government never stopped in the war against illness. They approached an older lady at a glass desk; she had tired brown eyes and gray hair in the ordinary bob. A thick glass partition entirely enclosed her desk. She had a tag on her mint green scrub tunic with her name, "Flynn."

The Security Patrol Guard spoke into the conversation speaker first. "Hello there, Flynn. I located Davis, the lady that has been missing. As you know, she hasn't received any medication or checkups since she disappeared. She needs to go into quarantine."

Davis laughed to herself at how easily the guard quickly took credit for "locating" her. It made her laugh even more when Flynn replied to the guard, "That's Great! You'll need to go to quarantine as well since you got exposed to her without protective gear."

Davis only had to wait a few minutes; however, Flynn had asked her not to move and stay exactly where she was. It was difficult because she was antsy and nervous. Luckily, it was reasonably quick that several orderlies came out in full hazmat suits. Two placed Davis in a rolling transport cubicle, enclosed in thick glass, a blue light situated on both sides of the door that locked once she was inside. There was a shelf on each side of the glass that held a communication tablet. The orderlies repeated the process with the guard, putting him in his own transportation cubicle. Then as they rolled Davis and the guard away, she noticed that three more orderlies in the hazmat suits locked the infirmary doors and now were cleaning and sanitizing the floor where she had walked in and had stood. They set up air purifiers, and Flynn had exited her cubicle out a back door not connected to the front office. *This is a bit much!* Davis thought to herself. She had to admit, though, that just about a month ago, all this would have made perfect sense to her. She wouldn't have even thought about it at all; it would have all been typical and much-needed actions to her.

The orderlies wheeled Davis into a room completely enclosed with the same thick glass walls. There were blue lights on each side of the door and in the middle of the room. The orderly that wheeled her in went up to the outer shelf and typed something on his keyboard. The message appeared on the screen inside for Davis to read. The statement said, "I'll unlock the doors, let me leave the room, then you can exit and get into the bed. Someone will be in shortly." Davis wasn't sure if she should type a reply, so she just nodded her head yes to acknowledge she had read the note. The orderly then punched some numbers on the door keypad, and Davis heard it unlock. She was tempted to step out early and freak him out but decided it wasn't worth it and not very nice. He would probably be terrified if she did.

After the orderly closed and locked the door to the room that Davis would call home for the next fourteen days, he nodded his head as a sign she could exit the rolling cubicle. Davis stepped out and took a deep breath. It smelled of antiseptic and eucalyptus. Davis had forgotten that they piped eucalyptus oil scent through the air ducts. President Everett had told everybody it was necessary to fight against germs as eucalyptus was a natural antibacterial, antiviral, and antifungal. It was also helpful in combating some of the effects of the flu, respiratory infections, sinus problems, and colds. Davis didn't doubt this might be true. She liked the smell of euca-lyptus, and to her, it smelled fresh and clean but also like it could do some damage to a virus. However, she did doubt that simply piping the scent through the air pipes would save someone from getting sick.

Davis situated herself on the gray bed and looked at the gray floors and the gray walls. She tried to acquaint herself with the fact that she was back in an almost colorless world again. When someone walked in, and Davis spied Duffy's kind eyes through her hazmat hood, it took all her power not to jump up and hug her. However, they had decided beforehand that they would act as if they didn't know each other. It was the only way to keep each other safe as well as the secret they now shared.

Duffy spoke first. "Hello, Davis, we are the people, and the people are we." It took Davis aback, but she realized she should start trying to say that again if she didn't want to alert suspicions. After she said it back, Duffy continued, "Nice to meet you. My name is Duffy, and I'll be your doctor. We're going to administer a basic physical and see where we are at with your health. Then we'll make sure we catch you up on all your injections."

Davis signed the intake form after verifying her name and ID num-ber, and a strong sense of déjà vu overtook her as she initialed. She'd ini-tialed before, of course; she knew she had, but now there was an odd sense from knowing something she shouldn't know.

Duffy ran through the procedures that Davis was familiar with after a lifetime of having them done to her. Starting with the dreaded female check, although it made her feel better that it was with Duffy. She always felt so uncomfortable when she got a male doctor for those. Next, she went into the adjoined bathroom with a cup. After that, breathe in, breathe out while Duffy listened with a stethoscope. The doctor did her job, looking in Davis's eyes, nose, and ears with a lit scope. Reflexes checked with a little rubber hammer. Then the questions: Had she felt ill at all? Where had she been kept? Davis and Duffy previously agreed on the answer: A room; she was unsure of the location or type of building. Davis explained they made her wear a hood in and out of the building. She added that they never let her outside, and she was always escorted to the restroom every time she needed to use it. Duffy said her lines with ease, "It's good you were kept for the most part inside, at all times. It limited your exposure to the outside world and, therefore, dangerous viruses and germs. We'll still keep you here for a few days since you interacted with these people who took you. But I think you'll be fine."

Duffy then had to administer the injections and a blood test; this was perhaps the only tricky part. She would give Davis a legitimate blood test and flu shot because they wouldn't harm her, and it would help prove that she was being taken care of properly. However, the Marigold Injection would be saline, and an excessive dose of beta-carotene only, no pharmaceuticals or brain control chemicals. The beta-carotene was to give Davis carotenemia, a harmless condition that turned the skin a light orange color. It wasn't the same gold hue that would generally be associated with the Marigold Injection, but it was all they had. Namaguchi, Brookshire, and Duffy had all received these beta-carotene shots in place of the Marigold Injection, and nobody had ever questioned it. But Duffy knew that a much tighter spotlight would be on Davis.

Davis was never fond of injections or blood tests in the first place. They always made her feel woozy. She asked if she could lie down, and of course, Duffy was okay with that. She lay down and tried to focus on other things. She was amazed that the uniformed hazmat orderlies were back in her room, sanitizing and cleaning the transport cubicle. She could tell they were trying to hurry so as not to be near Davis any longer than they had to be, which she thought was funny since there was no way for them to get infected by anything. "What happens after you leave this room, Duffy? I mean, the orderlies are so careful not to have any cross-contamination, but how do they manage after they leave? You always carry some kind of germs with you, don't you?" Davis chuckled to herself when she saw the look of horror on the faces of the orderlies. Duffy raised her eyebrow questioningly as if to say Davis should watch her words.

"Well," said Duffy. "There is a one-way door from your room to the offices of myself and the orderlies. When we walk out the door, we walk through an anti-bacterial and anti-viral gel that coats the shoes. Also, the hallway is flanked with blue lights in every direction. Then, we take a shower in the suit and then take another shower outside the suit. It's quite extensive to keep everyone safe."

"That is extensive. I can't imagine that anything would be carried back to your rooms, after all." Davis said, realizing the more she heard, the crazier some of these things seemed.

"All done, Davis, you good? Do you need anything?"

"I'm alright, thanks, Duffy," said Davis sitting up.

"Okay, great. I'm going to run your labs. You have an entertainment console in here you can use. It has some movies, music, books, art you can look at, and card games too. You have an unlimited water dispenser there, in the corner. And a kiosk to get nutrition biscuits from; you are limited to three a day, though."

Duffy looked around quickly, and when she saw the orderlies had left and nobody was around, she gave a quick, warm squeeze to Davis's hand. Then she departed the room as well.

Davis didn't do anything for a while. She just sort of lay on the bed and let her mind wander. She realized she would have several days just to think, so maybe she shouldn't waste all her thoughts right now.

As she started to drift off to sleep, she wondered if Brookshire turned himself in for quarantine. Since the guard that brought her in took credit for it, Brookshire would be off the hook for getting quarantined. As if the fates intervened, at that point, Duffy walked in. "Davis, I wanted to let you know, Brookshire turned himself in for quarantine right after we checked you in. They placed him in a room down the hall, but I requested they move him to the room next to you. I said it'd be easier to tend to you both if you're next to each other." Here, Duffy smiled and looked very pleased with herself. She then added, "You won't be able to talk. The glass is too thick.

But you can see each other, and you've both got drawing pads, pencils, and pens. You can write notes to each other, to hold up to the glass, at least."

~

Davis fell asleep to a happy dreamland. When she awoke, she saw Brookshire was already in the room next to her. He had fallen asleep; his entertainment console had dropped to his side. She tried to lean over to see if she could see what he was reading or watching, but with the screen at such an angle, she couldn't tell.

Davis looked at the lines of his face for a while. She mentally traced her finger around his jawline, somehow strong and soft at the same time. His long eyelashes looked so gently closed over his eyes. He started to stir, and she turned away to go back to her bed. She didn't want to get caught looking at him like a schoolgirl. She got a slight smile on her face when the thought popped into her head that perhaps he had watched her sleeping, too, when he came in earlier.

After Davis got back to her bed, she picked up her entertainment console and was going to look up something to read or watch. But suddenly, her little smile turned sad and dark. She realized it didn't matter how she felt about Brookshire or what he may think of her. She was going to be expected to marry President Everett. And if she weren't successful in her task, she *would be* married to President Everett. Her stepdad. The mere idea spun her head and churned her stomach. Equally disconcerting was the fact that if she were successful, she would be a murderess. For not the first time, she wondered if she could ever justify murder and if she could go through with it. Brookshire couldn't be with her if she were Everett's wife, and she didn't think he would want to be with her if she were a killer. And she had no desire to murder someone; it was as unsavory to her now as it had been the first time that she heard the plan. *A no-win situation,* she thought glumly.

As she lay there, Davis was figuring she should try to get some sleep. She didn't even know what time it was, but she didn't feel tired. It *felt* late, though. A sleepy feeling hung in the air; Davis thought it was just out of her reach, but she could sense it. It was dark and quiet in the hallways. She could barely see a nurses' station down the hall, but it was the only illumination in the section except for the hazy blue light that hung from the middle of each ceiling and at every doorway. It gave off an eerie feeling. Barely illuminated, everything swathed in a gauzy veil of blue light. Davis had a desk lamp, but she didn't want to draw the nurse's attention by turning it on, so she lay quietly in the blue-tinged room and tried to quiet her mind.

At some point, Davis drifted off. It was sort of a hazy, vague sleep, a rest reminiscent of that blue light that shone above her.

~

The first week that passed was largely uneventful. Davis tried to find amusing things on her entertainment console, which grew tiresome after a while even though she loved reading books and watching old movies. All the nurses and orderlies were kind enough but standoffish. The exception was Hernandez; he was funny and always had a joke and a few kind words for Davis. That was the fun part of Davis's day. The bright part of her day was when Duffy popped in, at least once or twice a day, to say hi, see how she was doing, or chat for a few minutes. Duffy could never stay long as she had other patients to attend to and, as she put it, "an endless mountain of paperwork that outweighed any patient roster." Then there were two days when she wasn't there because of her days off. The doctor on call when Duffy wasn't there, Abell, wasn't kind or courteous. She barely spoke to Davis at all and was curt when she did ask questions. Abell looked at Davis as if she expected her to spontaneously explode into a cloud of germs and viruses at any moment. Abell's harsh, angular features were not complemented by her dark eyes that looked full of malice or her hair in a bob style, which also had angular cuts due to how straight and thick her dark brown hair was.

Those were the fun and happy parts of Davis's day, minus Abell. But, the joyous part of her day, the thing that made even the fun and happy parts seem less than they were, was when she got to interact with Brookshire a little bit. He had a way of bringing in something she had never seen or experienced before. Every day, he would grab his writing pad and a pen and write out little notes saying hi and asking how she was, and they would have a conversation that way. Sometimes he would draw her a smiling face or flower. One day, he grabbed his paper pad and a marker and indicated she should do the same thing. Then he wrote, "Guess what I'm drawing?" First, he drew a typical stick figure girl in an outline of a dress and a stick boy next to her. Next, he drew the hand on the stick girl, out toward the boy. He put in a few music notes and some streamers in the corners and background of the picture. Last, he drew the arm of the stick boy and encircled the ends of the girl and boy's arms at the bottom. He had made them hold hands.

Of course, Davis knew right away Brookshire was drawing the dance where they held hands. But she let him finish before picking up her pad and writing, "The Courtship Event where we held hands?" Davis could not hide the smile that beamed across her face. Brookshire mocked a celebration dance to show she got it. He then held up his entertainment console showing the name of the song on his. Brookshire pointed to the song title and then to Davis to indicate she should put the same song on. Once she got it, he put down the console and then put his arms in a mimed dance position. Davis got the idea and mimed her dance position, and then they gently swayed and moved to the music, not really dancing but feeling almost like they were. Davis would generally feel a bit silly doing something like this, but Brookshire made it feel fun and like it was exactly what they should be doing.

And so, the days passed slowly for Davis. There were bright moments that flashed into an otherwise dreary world, but they mostly drew out long and tired, hampered further by her inability to sleep well. She imagined they were slow for Brookshire, Duffy, and Hernandez too. Everyone was just trying to pass the days until they could get to the next part. The big step. The only real step that mattered.

OCTOBER 1, 2056 - PROPOSAL

avis woke up to the sound of an orderly rapping on the window. After she acknowledged him, he pointed at a speaker in her room. She realized it must be 7 a.m. because the sound of church bells ringing and people chanting was being piped into her room. She had almost forgotten; it had been a long time since she had been in the vicinity of the Prayer Call. Regardless of denomination, churches rang their bells, mostly electronic but sounding as if they were coming from bell towers. Even churches without a bell tower had an electronic bell on the roof of their buildings. It was a call to the people to pray for the health and welfare of the President. The priests that belonged to the Everettisim Church filed down the streets, their hypnotic chanting echoing to the people. The people in the Pods would have gotten a wake-up bell at 6 a.m. A loud bell that nobody could sleep through. Davis imagined that they must not play the alarm in the infirmary because the ill patients might be startled awake. But the bells and chanting coming from the speaker were loud enough to wake her up, so she really didn't know why they skipped the call to arms. Davis thought about the priests that wore blood-red cloaks that had a hood for their heads and covered them head to toe. It was probably to bestow a sense of reverence in the people. But now, Davis thought it was odd and felt creepy, haunting. It felt bizarrely spellbinding. Davis started wondering if the chants held any subconscious thoughts; she had heard something once—she thought it was a vicious rumor at the time—reported by attendees of the reprogramming center. They had claimed the government played subconscious pro-Everett messages in the media center, the cafeterias, and even in the showers. Now it didn't seem like it could be a rumor but very plausible.

Davis drifted off to sleep, thinking about the Everettisim Priests after they had passed by, and a still Sunday morning quiet hung in the air once again. She didn't even know if females were allowed to be Priests. She didn't think so, but she wasn't sure. It wasn't illegal not to follow Everettisim, and to be honest; it hadn't really caught on. It was a bizarre religion by conventional standards. All at once, it claimed that President Everett was the only one who truly had God's ear. Simultaneously, other faiths were acceptable to follow because it was not to be a religion in the conventional sense of the word but more of a way of life. Everettisim celebrated Christmas and President Everett's birthday on June 17th, which was immediately followed by a three-day summer solstice celebration, regardless of whether the solstice actually fell on any of those three days. Halloween, a celebration Davis had read about in many books, was long ago eliminated in favor of a large fall festival ending in a two-day Dia de Los Muertos festival. There were so many festivals; it seemed Bacchus was the God who had President Everett's ear.

Even with alcohol and festive foods outlawed, Davis now knew those things were readily available to a select few. So, in all truth, a real party and feast were probably planned after the public festival for those deemed important enough. She wondered if she would see one of these festivals while she would be in the Palace. She had seen the regular ones; anyone could come into the town center and get a festival biscuit—a traditional nutrition biscuit but flavored with cardamom, cinnamon, and clove—given the nickname "Triple C Biscuit." And the water flowed freely. There were decorations, homages to President Everett; he stopped short of calling them shrines. There was live music and always a group of children who put on a play, usually about how the President saved them all from certain doom. Another group of children would come out after and demonstrate the yoga they had learned from their daily school rituals or recite a poem, short story, or another worded token of affection for Everett. One of the most significant tenets of Everettisim was that polygamy was not only allowed but encouraged. Almost everybody practiced it, even the non-believers, because there was the sticky task of repopulating the United State. And, the simple fact was there were far more women than men. For a chance for those women to have a husband and babies, President Everett had informed them all that God advised him to start a polygamous country. Most men jumped on board with that proclamation, even if they had no interest at all in Everettisim. Davis now imagined that President Everett just pulled whatever bits from different religions, cultures, and philosophies he thought sounded the best. It occurred to her that not that long ago, she never would have imagined that in a million years.

~

One day—and she could hardly tell one day from another—Davis got a new set of hospital clothing and a beautiful creamy rose-colored silk robe with lace edging. Duffy came in and told her that day, she would be introduced to President Everett. The robe was a gift from him, and he wished for her to wear it. Apparently, he felt as if the color would complement her honeyed-brown eyes and hair. Duffy whispered a reminder for her not to be surprised if Everett gave her an official marriage proposal. It would be an odd introduction in more than one way anyhow, taking place with thick glass isolation walls between them and only a communication tablet to talk. *What a lovely courtship* thought, Davis.

There was a conflict in Davis's mind. She had no desire to dress up like some odd hospital doll for President Everett so that he could give his proposal. However, she knew she had to play the game for a while longer, convince President Everett that she was all in, and her "kidnapping" had not changed her or her thoughts toward him or the government. And the robe was soft and lovely. *It wouldn't be too bad to wear while she played this unsavory game,* she thought.

There was a bigger surprise for Davis when Namaguchi walked into the hospital. Davis suddenly felt very self-conscious in that silly robe. He went to his side of the window, picked up the communication tablet, and motioned for her to do the same. Namaguchi typed out a hello and introduced himself, adding, "We are the people, and the people are we" at the end. Davis almost smiled and waved to him as she was still getting used to the unusual circumstances. She quickly remembered she shouldn't know who Namaguchi was, outside of the fact she had a general sense he was a government official. She typed back the standard greeting and introduced herself. Then Namaguchi typed out that the President was sorry he couldn't attend in person; his health and well-being was of utmost concern. Then Davis read the next message: "Despite President Everett not being here, he would like to extend a proposal to you to be his wife."

~

After Namaguchi left with Davis's consent for marriage, she lay down on the bed and sighed a deep and heavy sigh. It sounded as if she was letting out the troubles of the whole world with that sigh. Brookshire was trying to make silly faces on the other side of the glass, but she just wasn't in the mood. She went to the glass, tears in her eyes, and put her hand gently on her side of the glass. Brookshire stopped acting silly and put his hand upon his side of the glass, opposite of hers. For a moment, it was enough to have his hand opposite hers. Davis thought she saw a look in Brookshire's eye, a glint that she'd never seen before, but it vanished so quickly, she wasn't even sure it had been there at all.

A little while later, Duffy explained to Davis in hushed tones that Everett had sent Namaguchi at the last minute, and Namaguchi was sorry to have put Davis through that. Apparently, President Everett was working on making sure that Davis would never run into Ruby at the Everett Palace. Duffy then told her that another surprise was coming: she would meet the other wives in the group she was supposed to live with at the

Palace eventually. They were to arrive after dinner. The last thing Davis wanted to do was meet these women. She imagined them to be robotic-like drones to do Everett's bidding. Davis knew it was required to do it, though; it's not like she could leave the infirmary. "Do I have to wear the robe for them, too?" she asked Duffy sarcastically.

~

She must have dozed off because the next thing she knew, Duffy was shaking her awake and telling her that the wives were there. Duffy helped Davis quickly straighten her hair out, which was a bit wild and tangled from sleeping on it. Duffy brought her a washcloth to wipe her face and warned Davis before she lightly slapped her cheeks to give them a little blush and life. Davis was ready to meet the wives, whether she felt like it or not.

The wives filed in; they all wore the same outfit, the presidential wife cream-colored tunic and jodhpurs, seams done in golden thread, and pretty and sleek brown boots, far more stylish than the typical brown shoe given to everyone else. But, other than that, Davis was surprised. They looked friendly like in another life she could have been cozy pals with them. There was no trace of a hypnotic, vacant look in the eyes Davis expected she'd see. Each held up a notepad, the top sheet proclaiming their names.

Lisa was the shortest; she had brown hair with auburn highlights. A kind smile and friendly eyes looked over the pad where she had included the *"We are the people, and the people are we"* greeting under her name. Lisa had also written that they would communicate via paper pads since not all of them could use the communication tablet all at once. Rebecca had honeyed-blonde hair like Davis and welcoming blue eyes; she had included a picture of a carrot with a smiling face under her name. It was cute but struck Davis as odd. *How would Rebecca know what a carrot was?* She thought. As far as Davis knew, those shouldn't be something that was a part of Rebecca's life. Jessica had darker brown hair and a bit of a mischievous look in her eye. Tiffany surprised Davis the most because her hair was long, almost waist-long. It was smooth and brown, slightly curling, giving a bounce to it. Sunshine seemed to be the living embodiment of her name, like living sunshine could flow from her and bring others joy. Her fiery red hair almost looked as if it was aflame. Amanda, the tallest, had red hair too but not as bright and coppery as Sunshine's, and instead, it had blonde streaks through it. Davis had never seen a hair color quite like it. If someone had just described it to her and she had not seen it, she would not have realized how becoming it could look, especially with Amanda's green eyes.

Lisa, who seemed to be in charge, held up a communication tablet, showing that the two could now use those. Davis picked her tablet up, and there was already a message, saying it was nice to meet her and whether or not she had any questions. Davis just looked at Lisa and shrugged. She knew she should ask something, though. She typed out that it was nice to meet them, and she wasn't sure yet; she was just trying to figure everything out. Did the wives have any questions for her? Davis could tell that Lisa was not expecting to have this question. She guessed that it wasn't often that anyone asked them what they thought. Then she got a bright look on her face and asked about the only thing she could think to ask her. Cox, their "Den Mom." Lisa typed out the explanation that Cox was preparing the room to have Davis move in, getting the bed and bedside table located in the room. Putting Davis's bath towels, robe, and clothing in the closet, including the wedding dress Davis would wear. Reading that shocked Davis a little; she didn't even know how they knew her size. Lisa seemed to read her mind and typed out that the hospital rooms had scanners that took daily measurements, and Davis had weighed in daily. That made sense but didn't. She had no idea she was being scanned daily for her measurements. She tried to push that thought out of her head and typed out on her tablet: "Maybe not the most pressing question, but why is Tiffany's hair long?"

"Yes, it's an anomaly and a personal request from President Everett. He's asked she grow it long and trim it only for it to stay healthy. That is why Tiffany wears her hair up, in a bun, and under a hat when in public."

The answer struck Davis as so odd. According to President Everett, there were to be no differences in people. All individuality had supposedly been erased. There were to be no exceptions. The President had made it clear that all these things—the standard uniform, the same haircut for everyone, only having last names—were all supposedly for the country's betterment. The theory was if everybody had the same thing, nobody would be jealous. Nobody would be envious. It would help eliminate crime and, at the same time, give the reduced population a sense of solidarity and create a harmonious society to unify everybody. Here, Davis was face-to-face with proof that President Everett broke his own rules when it suited him. Until she had seen it for herself, she hadn't entirely accepted how deep his hypocrisy could go.

Lisa asked her if everything was okay, and Davis nodded her head, yes. She then typed a reply that she was just thinking about what Lisa had said and anything else that she should ask. Finally, at a loss for anything, she asked about what she should know about being President Everett's wife and life at the Palace. Lisa smiled as she handed the tablet to Rebecca, who typed out a reply. It wasn't very detailed; it just said, "All will come in time." *Great*, thought Davis. *So much for the "wife lessons" she was supposed to receive.*

OCTOBER 8, 2056 –
TO THE PALACE

It was unbelievable to Davis that she was leaving the infirmary today. She was waiting for her transport to pick her up and take her to the Everett Palace. Brookshire had been transported to his security headquarters at the Palace earlier that morning. He told her he would be there, although it may be hard to visit her right away or even frequently. She wasn't sure what would happen when she got there. Brookshire had only told Davis that she would be shown to her room and given an outfit that President Everett specifically picked out for her to change into. The ladies from her group and their Den Mom, Cox, would be in their room waiting for her.

After Davis had been waiting in the front office for about twenty minutes, Duffy came and got her and told her a transport bus was in the back to pick her up. She had no idea why they needed such a large vehicle for just her, but there you had it. Davis walked through the hospital and out the back. The driver had rusty blondish-brown hair, a color that looked like it gave up long ago what shade it was. Vibrant green eyes were her standout feature, and Davis noted the name tag, Fontanella, that she wore on her tunic.

"Hi, Fontanella, I'm Davis. We are the people, and the people are we," she said as a way of an introduction. She held out her hand for Fontanella to shake. Fontanella took it tentatively and shook it lightly like she wasn't sure if Davis had truly got a clean bill of health.

"Hi, Davis, we are the people, and the people are we."

Fontanella then helped Davis onto the empty transport bus, giving her the first seat diagonal from her, and then she took her place in the driver's seat before continuing to speak. "So, how are you today?"

"I'm fine. Thank you. And yourself?"

"Good, thanks."

"Not that I don't appreciate you picking me up, because I do, but I was wondering why did you pick me up in the back of the hospital with such a large vehicle just for me?"

"They want to throw off people who may try to come out and see you. We need to get you to the Palace quietly. You're big news these days, you know. Also, I mean, you *were* kidnapped! We have to make sure nothing happens to you."

Davis had known she was on the news alerts that ran on video consoles in the town squares and the Pod libraries. Duffy told her about all the stories they were doing regarding her kidnapping, heroic rescuing, and engagement to President Everett. As predicted by Ringo, the publicity was too good to pass up. The official government even gave daily updates on how she had been doing in quarantine, which was funny to her because nobody besides Duffy ever asked her how she was doing. So, that didn't surprise Davis when Fontanella brought it up. But what did perk her ears was how Fontanella had emphasized that Davis got kidnapped; it made her wonder if she was onto the plan. She started to feel a nervous sweat on top of her upper lip and around her hairline. She felt hot and uncomfortable. After a few minutes of silence, Fontanella chimed in again.

"I'm sorry if I upset you about the kidnapping thing. That must have been traumatic. I was just making conversation."

"No, it's okay, of course, I got a little nervous thinking about it, but I'm fine. Everything is okay."

Whew, Davis thought to herself. She decided that Fontanella hadn't some sixth sense of the plan; she was just cordial. The rest of the bus ride went smoothly, with Fontanella making polite conversation and Davis trying to keep her end of the banal exchange.

Before Davis knew it, they arrived at the back entrance to the Palace. She had seen the front in pictures, with its elaborate marble statues and fountains, but the back was more subtle. She could just see a peek of the stained-glass dome ceiling on top of the large white building that was flanked by green shrubbery on the sides of the long stone driveway. They passed a simple guard tower, and at an ornate golden gate in a filigree pattern, Fontanella had to swipe her ID and enter a passcode on a keypad. Then, to a second armed security tower where they took both Fontanella's and Davis's names. Finally, after a guard took a picture of both of them and the transport bus, they followed an armed vehicle up a long, curved marble driveway. After Davis got off the bus, Fontanella was thanked so quickly and dismissed by the guards that Davis didn't even have a second to thank her before she drove off. The guards then hastily escorted Davis into the Everett Palace.

At first glance, Davis was a little surprised. She was in a bare white foyer with clean gray walls that looked like they could be from a Pod. Very quickly, a tall woman joined her. She had dingy blonde hair and squinty eyes, her sharp features giving her an almost masculine look. "I'm Cox," she said by way of introduction, then added the common saying followed by, "I'll be helping you get dressed out of your civilian outfit before we reach the room. President Everett will be waiting for you in the Wives' Common Room Two. That's your group."

Davis didn't expect things to happen as quickly as they did, and Cox's harsh tone and look didn't give her much time to feel adjusted or welcomed. She couldn't even muster a greeting back to Cox. She just gave a slight smile and nodded her head, the whole time wondering why she would need help getting dressed.

~

Cox showed Davis into a side room; it must have been some sort of bedroom, maybe belonging to a maid or other Palace worker. Cox asked her if she needed to use the restroom first, and Davis shook her head no. She had no idea why this would be important but noticed a large dress bag hanging from a hook on the wall. There were multiple layers of fabric, and the overall effect was that the dress was quite voluminous.

"Is that my wedding dress?" Davis ventured to ask.

"No, this is your everyday dress. You'll get three for the week. Then you'll have three sets of official presidential wife tunics and jodhpurs as well as one causal dress and seven nightgowns. You get two sets of casual boots, one set of formal. You also get a set of winter clothing that comes in on November first, so soon. President Everett requests you always wear an everyday dress when he sees you. If he is not seeing you on any given day, you're free to wear a tunic or your casual dress. I have a calendar in your room to make sure you ladies always know what to wear on a given day."

Davis stood in shock and was quiet as Cox demanded sharply that she disrobe, and even though Davis's discomfort was at an all-time high, she felt like she had no choice but to comply. She peeled off the jodhpurs and tunic before dressing in her new outfit. Her brain swam with confusion, fatigue, and sadness as Cox tied a corset around her and tightened it to where Davis almost could not breathe. She had seen items like what she was wearing in books and old movies she had watched, but she never imagined having to wear them. After the corset, Cox had her put on a wide-skirted petticoat. Then a tight-fitting bustier and bodice laced up the back tightened her waist. Everything felt squeezed. Her breasts pushed up and almost out of the top of the dress. The skirt that went over the petticoat was layers and layers of beaded dark ivory tulle, masterfully detailed with cream-colored lace, emerald green embroidery, and luminescent pearls. It was beautiful, albeit heavy, and incredibly uncomfortable. Then, Davis's feet got shoved into high heels that felt two sizes too small. They were dainty and pretty, in a light blush rose color, and the fabric was a buttery soft satin. Unfortunately for Davis, they did not feel as buttery soft on her feet, pinching and squeezing her feet and creating a pain she had never before experienced. She began to try to walk, an uncomfortable and uneven wobble until she slowly and steadily found her feet. The walking experiment was the only time Cox seemed nice to Davis. Cox held out her hand for support, observing Davis, making sure she didn't fall and encouraging her to take it slow and take a break if needed. After Davis found a comfortable enough stride, she told Cox she was ready to go to the room. The friendly version of Cox was gone when she harshly replied, "Wives' Common Room Number Two, that's the official name. Before we go, we need to put on your jewelry."

Thankfully, Cox let Davis sit for the next part when her hair was trimmed, combed, and styled. A silver tiara adorned with tiny diamonds and emeralds finished her hairstyle. Then, Cox applied makeup, the first makeup Davis ever wore. And while it seemed like it wasn't much, only a little light blush color on her cheeks, eyelids, and lips, Davis felt like she didn't even recognize herself. Then, Cox slipped a diamond bracelet on Davis's left wrist, a dainty silver charm bracelet, the charms with initials *E* and *D*, on her right wrist, and a large diamond and emerald necklace around her neck. The diamond was a square cut, and if Davis had to guess, about two inches, all ways, length, width, and height. Around the entire diamond were emeralds. The necklace was so heavy, Davis felt like she couldn't even walk with her head held high. Lastly, Cox clipped diamond and emerald ear cuffs that lined her entire earlobe. Like all women, Davis had unpierced ears, ear piercings being an illegal procedure to have in the United State, along with tattoos or any other piercings. *That was one law easily upheld, considering the lack of personal businesses,* thought Davis as she became more and more aware of the absurdity of the items adorning her.

After a loud, audible sigh, Cox held out her hand to show she rather not be helping Davis dress or walk. Davis took it as a sign to get to her feet. It took her a few minutes to get accustomed to the pain and walk again, but Cox was impatient, telling her to hurry, and Davis felt rushed, so she said she was okay to go, even though she didn't feel that was true. After Davis left the room they were in, and they turned down the hall, they passed a bustling kitchen. That surprised Davis because she thought the nutrition biscuits were all made in factories. She wondered who the food they were preparing could be for but then realized she knew without a doubt who would be feasting that night.

After a short walk past the kitchen door, they went through another door into the Palace that Davis had expected. It was as if after passing through that door, they entered luxury that was beyond compare to anything Davis had ever seen. It was leaving Kansas and entering Oz. All the walls were spotless, clean white. The crown molding looked as if painted with real gold, and the embossing was an intricate pattern of flowers and vines. Davis thought she saw an *E* monogram within the flowers. There were beautiful fresco paintings on the ceilings; Davis couldn't take in all of the images as Cox was walking too fast and there was too much to see. However, at a quick glance, most looked like they were some type of homage to President Everett. Davis saw the dome ceiling's cap from the inside; the tip she previously saw while driving up did not do it any justice. It was a large modern stained-glass top. Large and small triangles in shades of blues, ranging from an icy almost-white to cobalt, formed an intricate geometric pattern. Large windows at the front of the house, which they now passed by to go up the grand staircase, let in plenty of light with their thick brocade curtains pulled back. Davis thought "curtains" seemed too modest of a word for those window coverings. They were more like art; she couldn't tell if they were black or dark blue but had exquisite gold thread that created patterns of flowers and vines reminiscent of the crown molding. And yes, Davis saw it well now. A large *E* monogram in the middle of the pattern looked as if everything began and ended with the President's initial.

Even though there was plenty of light, as they started up the center on the grand marble staircase, Davis noticed on the outside of every other step on each side was a little pedestal sticking off to the side. On that pedestal sat a tall candelabra, at least five feet tall, the base of which held what looked like a crane about to take flight. The birds' wing outstretched and held four long golden taper candles in hidden holders at the top.

"Those are beautiful candle holders," said Davis, trying to break the tension and venturing to speak for the first time since they left the room.

"Fake. Well, not the gold, that's real. The candles are; they're electric. Fire risk and all," Cox replied briskly.

Davis decided not to speak again and just took in the sights as they ascended the long staircase. The steps were marble, with hints of inky blue and black marbling through the light gray rock. Inlaid gold paint was at the edges of each step, and alternating with the steps holding candlesticks was the gold monogrammed *E* that was becoming more and more prevalent everywhere Davis looked. The Palace was beautiful, but it just oozed vanity, lust, and greed to Davis, although she wasn't sure if Everett's passion was for power or himself.

Finally, they entered the common room for the wives. Davis's first emotion was a shock. The outfits. Even with Davis's dress, she was unprepared to see a whole group of women without plain tunics and jodhpurs. Everyone was in a beautiful, intricate gown. Davis guessed hers was the most elaborate, but a sea of silk and tulle surrounded her in purples, pinks, blues, and greens—all royally appointed shades. Intricate lacework on some, embroidery in gold and silver on others. Large ballgowns, like hers, with large hoop skirts underneath. They were bustled and bowed intricately. Lavish diamonds, gems, gold, and platinum embellished the ladies. They were literally dripping in tiaras, necklaces, bracelets, and earrings. Although her mind had changed a lot on President Everett over the last few weeks, she could barely believe that President Everett, who talked of having a world where everyone had equality, was adorning his wives this way. Every one of them in old-fashioned, elaborate, and expensive dresses. The word "dresses" was distilling it down, "torture devices" seemed more accurate to Davis. This corset, heels, and fiercely-shaped bodices had thick wires and stiff fabric, holding things into a "perfect" shape.

Davis recognized Lisa, Rebecca, Jessica, Sunshine, Tiffany, and Amanda and just tried to focus on them so she could steady her thoughts and balance. Everyone hurriedly tried to get out the standard greeting of "We are the people, and the people are we." Because of that and the multitude of layers of fabric everywhere, Davis almost didn't see President Everett centered between the women. They were sitting and sort of forming a semi-circle around him, as he sat in the middle and back of the odd group. When it was apparent Davis realized he was there, they all turned their necks to look at him adoringly.

Everett spoke first in his relaxed, calm demeanor that could almost make an icy heart melt. "Welcome, Davis. We need to give you a new name." Davis noted to herself that Everett did not say, "We are the people, and the people are we," as everyone else had. But that's not why Davis interrupted him. However, when she did, she heard a gasp from Cox and noticed looks of shock on all the wives. "Can I request Amelia?"

Everett closed his eyes for a moment, then paused as if he spoke to a young child who did not understand something. "I'm sorry, that's not possible. I've already picked Delilah, and all of your monograms have been done in *D* already." The way he looked at Davis made her realize this was the final word. He continued, not letting her get a word in, "Delilah, I was planning on having dinner with you tonight. But it won't be possible now. I have to address some other issues. We will get married tomorrow; your dress, jewelry, and shoes are selected; your soon-to-be sister wives and Cox will help you get ready tomorrow."

He sounded determined but not cold and calculating. There was a strange warmness to him, and Davis had to admit he had a je ne sais quoi, a certain something that made him appealing. It went beyond his handsomeness; it seemed like when he looked at you with his chest-nut-brown eyes, he was looking into your heart and saying *I know you, and I care*. It felt like a peaceful, loving quality surrounded him, and Davis saw how people got so effortlessly snowed over by him. Even Davis quickly waved away the short-lived condemnation that she received from him when she had requested Amelia to be her name. She almost immediately found herself thinking it was a simple mistake or maybe even her fault. As he got up and walked out the door, he lightly touched Davis on the arm and, and even though she was ashamed of herself for it, it made her stomach do a little flip.

When Davis turned back to the room, several thoughts were going through her head all at the same time. Mainly that she was getting married tomorrow, so she would have to act quickly. She was promptly distracted when Tiffany turned around and picked up a little monkey that was hiding behind her skirt and had been tugging on the hem to get attention.

"This is one of our capuchin monkeys, Parker. He's very friendly."

Davis took a look at the diminutive monkey. His cute cream-colored face had a darker crown of fur on the top of his head. His beady little black eyes were not malicious but made him seem almost as if he had stepped out of a cartoon. A little pink nose twitched as if he were trying to figure out a difficult problem. Davis held out her finger to Parker, and he took it in his slender blackish-brown fingers. Davis felt comforted by the warm, subtle grip and went to pat the back of his head with her other hand. Parker gave off a short but sharp sounding squeak, which made Davis jump back slightly, but all Parker was trying to do was climb over to Davis's arms. He seemed disappointed that she had stepped away. As soon as she realized, she stepped back and again held her arm out. Parker tentatively took it and then clambered over to her with caution. However, once he was in her arms, Parker gave a friendly sounding little squeak and reached up, playing with the ends of Davis's hair for a minute.

She quickly realized she didn't know what to do with the monkey in her arms. Besides Parker being cute, there wasn't much she could do, nor was there anything to say to Parker. She decided to turn her attention back to the ladies. "So, it is nice to see you all again. Can you maybe show me where I'll be sleeping, and if it's okay, a little tour of our different rooms?"

"Of course," Lisa replied with a friendly smile.

Tiffany took Parker back and said she would put him in the zoo's capuchin cage and be back shortly. She then added, "On afterthought, I'll carry him with me through the tour. Then we can go have a little tour of the grounds and the zoo as well."

The entrance door Davis had come through a few moments before had led to a foyer, tiled in blue marble. They were standing just past that, in what looked like the entry into the library. And that is where the girls started. They showed Davis—well, they kept calling her Delilah, and Davis was trying to get used to it—the wall of books. Davis ran her finger over some of the spines, all very classic looking books with rich leather binding and gilt edges. The bookshelf reached from top to bottom and ran the entire length of the wall, maybe about forty feet long. At the end, there were large bay windows with cushioned window seats and royal blue window coverings with the monogrammed *E* in gold thread in the middle. Several large plush, comfy looking chairs were a light blush color and looked as if climbing into them would be the equivalent of climbing into a billowy cloud. They then pointed to a large table in the middle of the library; Davis had to stifle a laugh because there was a large inlaid golden *E* in the middle of the table. *Well, he is just everywhere, isn't he?* she thought.

Afterward, the ladies showed her where to get an entertainment console and how to pull up virtually any movie, book, or piece of music she wanted. Although Davis was familiar with it from the hospital stay, she kept quiet and let them teach her. They gave her a quick peek at the kitchen, so to speak. It was small and had glass-covered cabinets that held plates and cups. It was definitely not a kitchen to prep in; it had no stove or sink. Only a drinking water dispenser and some drawers labeled to show where they kept utensils, plates, cups, and napkins. Rebecca pointed to a silver box and told Davis that nutrition biscuits came up from the kitchen via the dumb waiter. Otherwise, the kitchen was unremarkable; yes, it was clean, tidy, and white. There was not a speck of dust seen; the only color and sound was the humming blue light above. To the right of the kitchen was a little hallway, painted a sunny yellow. Going from the white to the yellow made Davis feel overwhelmed by the differences between the Palace and the Pods. President Everett was allowed to live in luxury and a world of magnificent color. Everyone else lived in a dull world. *So much for equality,* Davis thought. She noticed toward the top of the ceiling, where the yellow wall met the blue light, it made a sickly-looking shade of green. Davis thought it was appropriate that at least one thing in Everett's world should look vomity. Laughing to herself, she wondered why she hadn't noticed this color in other rooms. Perhaps the more opulent colors absorbed the blue light better and, in many cases, covered it all together.

At the end of the hallway, to the left, was an immaculately clean white-tiled bathroom. The group only peeked in there, but one side had a row of sinks and a wall-length mirror. On the other side, a dark wooden brown tower held piles of fluffy white towels, and a rack held luxurious white bathrobes. At the back of the restroom, one side had a row of four showers, the doors covered with a thin opaque-white curtain. The other side had four toilet cubicles, the doors made of the same fine wood as the towel holder and robe rack.

To the right of the hallway was the bedroom she would share with the wives in her group. A rich burgundy color covered the wall in the room. There was a bed for each wife; all brown wooden beds, albeit small, were piled high with a sumptuous thick white comforter and several pillows. Davis realized right away many of those pillows would end up on the floor. She choked on her laugh when she saw the large *E* embroidered right in the center of her comforter. That wasn't the only laugh she had to hold back. On the other side of the room was an immensely large painting of

President Everett. Almost as large as the wall itself. It featured the President as a general of some sort. A black peaked cap was atop his head, and he wore what looked like a very traditional black, blue, and red general's outfit. Gold stripes ran down the length on each side of the pants, and golden epaulets capped his shoulders. Medals adorned the entire left breast of the jacket. In the top left corner of the painting, angelic creatures with trumpets looked down toward Everett with looks of reverence. In the top right was a golden shield, the emblem of the United State. The shield was divided into four sections. On the top left, a dove with wings outstretched and an olive branch flew. On the top right was the national flag, which had not changed since it was redone by President Everett about ten years prior. While the actual flag of the United State was a red background with a large blue star in the center and a smaller white star in its center, in the painting on the shield, everything was gold, with shading to show depth and layering. The lower left quadrant showed a bald eagle, an homage to the old United States. Lastly, in the lower right was the symbol "ॐ" representing om and the peace that was supposedly abundant in the United State, as well as representing President Everett's dedication to not only practicing yoga but teaching it to others.

The entire background of the painting, clearly a battlefield, was confusing to Davis. The battle was showing President Everett victorious and triumphant after combat. But, there never was such a battle; Everett became President because it was presumed that he rescued everyone from the Lombardi Plague. She didn't understand this scenery, but it's not what shook her to her core. What did was what lay at the feet of the President. There were all the wives, looking up to him in admiration and adoration. Davis spied Ruby leaning up against his right leg. All the wives were in various states of leaning against his legs or in a side bent sitting position. Regardless of position, they were all staring at him, not just with love but looks of obedience. Cox leaned over and, with a grin, whispered to Davis, "You're to be added to the portrait. The artist is amazing, he'll just find a place for you, and you'll cover up part of the battle background. You won't even be able to tell!" Davis thought that Cox almost sounded gleeful at this. But Davis wasn't laughing anymore. Now she just felt sick to her stomach.

~

After they showed Davis where her bed was, she was able to survey her little space. The area was only about ten feet by ten feet. Besides the bed, she had a little brown chair and a small brown bedside table with a drawer at the top of it. A fuzzy, cozy-looking burgundy blanket was draped over the chair back.

"Delilah. Delilah. DELILAH!" Jessica tried to get Davis's attention, trying several times until Davis finally remembered she was Delilah now.

"Oh, sorry. I forgot my name!"

"It's okay; it takes a while to get used to the new names. You'll get it. Tiffany had something to do, so I'm going to put Parker back in the monkey cage. Do you want to see the zoo? I'll show you our closet and dressing area on the way out so that you can change into a more comfortable outfit."

"Sure, sounds good, thank you."

"No problem, by the time we get back, it should be time for dinner. Then we usually sit around and chat for a bit or read before going to bed."

On the way out, they went through the bathroom. There was a door on the inside of the bathroom to the left of the towel rack. "It's kind of weird," Jessica said as they walked through it and into a supply closet. There was another door inside the closet that led to the dressing room. It was somewhat uninteresting; all the walls were white, and all the furniture was brown. A blue tinge from the light above bathed the room in a bluish glow. There were large closet spaces that had all the clothes hanging. Each closet space had a name above it, and Davis spotted a "Delilah" placard already above her area. A closet full of clothes that belonged to her but she had never worn before now hung there. Davis spied her knapsack, hanging there; someone had put it away in the closet for her. Davis wished she could check it for the bee venom vial again.

"Excuse me, but can I look in my knapsack? I want to see if I brought my comb."

"Oh, we have plenty of those here for you to use."

"I'd still like to check if it's okay."

"Oh, yes! Of course, please do."

Davis was glad her thin lie didn't raise suspicions. She quickly looked inside and felt the pocket to make sure her precious cargo was still there. The reassuring little bump comforted and caused her anxiety at the same time. She still couldn't believe she would have a hand in murdering someone. And the portal to that dark world sat in a secret pocket, hanging from a hook in a closet. Davis felt the location wasn't very secure, but at the same time, she had nowhere else to put it. She had to push it all out of her mind and carry on. To complete the act she was currently portraying; she confirmed she remembered her comb and then feigned interest in the rest of the room.

When they got into the dressing room, Jessica put Parker down, and the little monkey busied himself swinging from the edge of the bench that ran along the room's length up to the two privacy walls at the back of the room. Davis, at a loss for conversation, asked about them. Jessica answered, "We usually take turns behind the walls when we're getting dressed in our jodhpurs or nightclothes. But, when we are in the ball gowns, we need to help each other with corsets, zippers, buttons. Cox is usually here to help us too. Get your casual clothes and put them behind the privacy wall first. Then, I'll get the zipper at the back of your dress, and you get mine. I think you can manage, but let me know if you need help changing." Jessica also showed Davis where her jewelry chest was so that she could take off all her accompaniments. Then, Jessica had Davis turn around and hold the top front of her dress up. Jessica unzipped the back and said, "You have a corset, too; I think I can loosen it enough through the unzipped opening. Let me know if you need it loosened more after you go in to change." It proved to be enough, and Davis was happy to finally be out of the heavy gown and into a comfortable tunic, jodhpurs, and boots. Next, Davis returned the favor and unzipped Jessica's dress, and then she went to change as well. Once they were both changed, they continued their tour.

They walked through the changing room to yet another door on the other end. Davis had somewhat expected this after her conversation with Namaguchi. "This door leads to our exercise room." Davis took in the exercise room; it was spotless and very modern looking, especially compared to the luxury of most of the rest of the Palace. A gleaming dancer's bar sat on a wall covered in mirrors. Jessica pointed out the different aerial apparatuses that were hanging from the ceiling. "We have the gym every day from 5 a.m. to 9 a.m. They have aerial classes or dancing classes on most days. Other days, we use the equipment. And of course, we start our day following along to President Everett's yoga video." Davis looked around again. She didn't know much about exercise equipment, but there seemed to be several types of machines, floor mats, hand weights, and different ropes and bands hanging neatly on the wall. Davis also noticed the four other brown doors that were in the exercise room. In the center of the room, the exit to the main hallway had sizeable frosted glass doors. Davis wanted the second wood door to the left of that glass door; that's what Namaguchi had told her.

Finally, after leaving the exercise room, Davis and Jessica made their way out to the zoo area. First, they put Parker in with the other capuchin monkeys. There were seventeen monkeys in total. Davis was impressed with how large and spacious their cage was, how many things they had in their cage, and how many playthings they had. Different ladders to climb on and a rope course across the top of the cage. A large tree with lots of foliage and little sleeping bins they could pop into if they wanted to. Davis wondered to herself how someone could have evident compassion for animals and, at the same time, have such a mean streak toward humans.

After dropping Parker off, they went by the macaw cage, and again, Davis was stunned by the cleanliness of the aviary; the space was large and had several trees and bare branches for the birds to perch on. They even had a large rock waterfall flanked by gorgeous tropical plants and flowers. "Those flowers are beautiful," Davis said.

"They're fake," answered Jessica. "President Everett is allergic to bees, so there are no real flowers here. I wish we had a flower garden, but we can't. You won't even have flowers to decorate your wedding. He takes no chances."

Davis could have kicked herself for mentioning flowers; she had forgotten. She shouldn't risk in any way the plan getting discovered. Davis noticed Jessica sounded a bit disgruntled about the flowers. She decided to change the topic in hopes of leaving the talks of flowers behind. "Mmm hmmm...by the way, can I ask? You called him 'President Everett,' and it occurred to me that I don't know his first name. Does he have one? Do we ever use it?"

"It's Jack; you'll hear it at the wedding ceremony when they use his full name. But, probably never again. We never call him by it; we *always* say President Everett. Don't worry; after the marriage, you'll take classes, basically Everett 101. You'll learn everything. Usually, the classes take place before the wedding, but for some reason, yours isn't. And we can always help. We sister wives have to stick together."

Davis couldn't help but sense a little cynicism in Jessica's voice, but she didn't know if it was indeed there or she was just hoping it was there. She had a fleeting thought about if she should take a chance and see if Jessica could help her with her mission. Hastily, she realized there was no time to get to know Jessica or the other girls, so even if anybody could help her, there was no time to sort it out.

As they finished their zoo tour, Jessica told Davis about how their group took care of the monkeys, and the other wives took care of the other animals. But not to worry, it wasn't hard. She told her that there was a twenty-four-hour staff to feed, take care of, and clean up after the animals. Three veterinarians worked on a rotating schedule, with one always being present for a full day. The wives took publicity pictures with the animals or played with those tame enough to do so. Next, they went by the dolphin aquarium, again, beautiful, spotless, and huge. Davis believed they must have around the clock cleaning, especially as they saw more and more enclosures. The koala bears were more challenging to see, as they were hiding away in their large eucalyptus tree forest. Davis was most interested in the tigers. They looked so large and powerful. Jessica explained they were solitary animals, so even though there were five tigers, they each had their own enclosed space within the larger enclosure. Davis could only spot two as they walked by, and she wished they would slow down to look at them better. It looked as if each cage was quite large with a pool, a few trees and bushes, a swinging tire, and a mountain façade with a cave opening large enough for each tiger to lay in. The only tigers Davis could see was one lying on his side in the shade under a big tree, and the other was pawing at a fish carcass in his water, the only mark of anything not being ridiculously clean. Lastly, they went by the rhinoceroses' cage, where Davis felt tickled to see a large rhinoceros wading in a mud pool with a baby one. Jessica told her that the baby was about six months old.

Finally, they went back to their room, meeting the other wives who had changed into their casual clothes. Some were reading; others were lounging. After Davis and Jessica washed their hands, they came back out to find the wives and Cox at the dining table. Each place had a simple plate, napkin, and a glass of water. A nutrition biscuit sat on each plate. Cox directed Davis to sit on a chair that was between Lisa and Rebecca. Cox said grace, and then they started quietly chewing their biscuits and sipping their water. Davis had never realized how dry and bland the biscuits were. She found herself missing the food from the bunker. There was some polite, casual banter, but it seemed clear that nobody had much to say. There was a slight awkwardness that hung in the air. The awkwardness that told you it was in your best interest to get to know a person in your midst, yet that person felt like an interloper. Davis was just grateful that it helped pass the time, though, and kept her mind off her future task. There were no two ways about it, though; no matter how slowly they chewed and sipped, a nutrition biscuit and glass of water didn't last long. When they finished, Davis asked if she could help clear plates. They all looked at her like she was insane.

"No," Sunshine replied, "Cox takes care of cleaning up for us."

Davis nodded. "Oh, okay. Thank you, Cox. I guess I'll just take a shower and go to bed, then. I'm pretty tired after such a long day."

"We only take showers in the morning, after we exercise," said Amanda.

Cox stepped in, saying that Delilah indeed had a long day; a one-time evening shower was not a big deal, especially since she would have to get up early tomorrow and have a long day prepping for the wedding. She then told Davis that except for the morning yoga, she would not do the exercise class tomorrow as she'd have a long day of preparations. Davis guessed that hearing "thank you" was unusual for her. Maybe that's why she expressed a momentary kindness of allowing the evening shower and not talking to her in her usual harsh tone. Davis would have to get used to being called "Delilah," though. As if she didn't have anything to think about, she thought, now she had to focus on her new name, too.

After a quick timed shower, Davis lay down under the comforter and pretended to sleep. She didn't want to be bothered at all, but there was no way she could sleep. Her heart was pounding in her throat as one by one, the wives lay down, and the room went dark and silent.

OCTOBER 9, 2056 –
EARLY MORNING

After what felt like several hours, Davis slipped out of her bed as quietly as she possibly could. She had decided that if she got caught, she would say she had to use the restroom. That was plausible. A little clock at the end of the room read it was a little past 1 a.m. Once Davis got to the bathroom, she did use it as quickly as possible. For once, she was grateful for the blue light as it shed just enough light for her not to have to turn on the brighter lights. She then went through the supply closet door and into the dressing room, retracing her earlier steps. When Davis got to the exercise room, she thought again about the instructions Namaguchi had given her and silently confirmed to herself that it was second to the left of the frosted glass front doors that she wanted.

After Davis went through, she found herself doing a reverse of the way she came in. First, she was in a dressing room, identical to the one for her room except for the names above—it only took her a second to spot the name "Ruby." Davis didn't want to waste time ruminating over it, although it gave her sentimental feelings. Nothing could stop her from being startled in the supply closet she entered next when she ran smack-dab into a fake leg equipped with a shoe. It conked her head painfully, and she rubbed it and looked at the leg in startled curiosity. Namaguchi had warned her that Anabelle, one of the older wives, had a prosthetic leg, but it still didn't quite prepare her for the creepiness of it. Especially when she looked down the line and saw several prosthetic legs hanging from the ceiling, all with different types of shoes attached. After gathering her thoughts for a second, Davis continued until finding herself in the restroom of the older wives' harem. She then silently wondered to herself if that disrespectful moniker was actually their title, even though she had used it herself a few times now.

After making her way out of the restroom and into the sleeping quarters, Davis's heart started to beat harder than she knew possible. It sounded so loud to her; she worried the sound could wake someone up. Davis had to be very quiet and careful. She rechecked her mind for the information, and of course, her mom's bed was across the room and right in the middle. There was a blue light in the bedroom, but it was in a dim night mode. It gave off very little light as Davis inched her way to the bed where her mom slept.

It felt to Davis like every step took her several minutes. She wished she had planned out what she was going to do more thoroughly. She should have brought a pillow to hold over her mom's face until she could explain who she was and get her into the bathroom to talk to her. But that could have had obvious complications. Better yet, she had to find a way to quickly and quietly get her to the storage closet with all the creepy legs. That would give them more of a buffer to speak and not be heard. At one point, Davis had a sneeze coming on, and as she kept walking forward, she rubbed her nose to try and fight it off. The last thing she wanted to do was sneeze right now. Davis took slow, tentative steps, breathing slowly and taking in her surroundings. She was happy to see that in this room, they had thick curtain dividers between each bed. Anything that would help absorb the noise was a boon to her quest.

Finally, after what felt like forever, Davis got to the side of Ruby's bed and tried to lean in and look closely at Ruby sleeping, to confirm it really was her. When she was confident, she took a deep breath and said a silent prayer. Before she could overthink it, she quickly clamped her hand over her mom's mouth, trying to be as gentle but tight as possible. Ruby immediately sat in bed and started whimpering. The look of terror in her mom's eyes saddened and scared Davis, but she had to keep her quiet. She leaned close to Ruby's ear and whispered, "Quiet; I won't hurt you, please, be quiet."

Someone sleepily said, "Mmmm...everything okay...?"

Davis paused and listened as the other wives settled and rolled over in their sleep, and she just kept whispering as quietly as she could, "quiet, please," even though it appeared her mom was quite docile and willing to follow the instructions she had already given her. After maybe a minute, when it seemed like everyone had gone back to sleep, Davis said in a calm and hushed tone that she'd take Ruby to the supply closet and explain everything. To try and keep her mom's interest and stop her from making noise or trying to get away, she also leaned over and whispered, as quietly as she could, "I'm your Little Marigold."

Saying "marigold" seemed to have the intended effect, and her mother followed her quietly into the restroom, then the closet. Ruby spoke first before Davis had a chance to open her mouth. "Why did you say that to me? Where did you hear that?" she asked in a startled and indignant tone.

Davis took a step back and took a deep breath for what felt like the five hundredth time that evening. "Mom, it's me. It's Amelia. It's your Little Marigold."

~

It took a little bit of time for it to sink in and for Ruby to believe Davis. But, as Davis spoke, it dawned on Ruby that she looked exactly like her, just younger. And when Davis told her how she had met Duffy and that Duffy had given her Ruby's letter, it became irrefutable. Ruby took Davis into a big hug, and for the first time, Davis felt a warmness and love that she hadn't know existed. After what felt like only a few seconds, though, the hug ended abruptly, and as Davis pulled back, she saw confusion cloud her mom's face. "But they told me you were dead. They said you died," she said very slowly. Almost as if she was trying to noodle it out for herself, whether she had remembered that or whether she had made it up.

"I don't know, mom. I didn't…" Davis didn't know what to say. She knew her mom was under the influence of the mind-controlling drugs, and she wasn't sure how much of a jolt she should give her. Obviously, the meeting itself had already been quite a surprise and a shock. As if on cue, Ruby's eyes brightened up.

"I know," Ruby said, nodding and with all certainty, "It must have been some mistake. A simple mistake that grew as time went on. Maybe somebody put the wrong information in the computer. I'm sure Duffy found you and figured out who you were because you look so much like me." In the latter part of the speech, Ruby became gleeful and excited. Davis, not wanting to mar her jubilation, did not correct her "mistake." Ruby continued, "How lucky we were, oh my, I'm so glad Duffy found you!"

Ruby, of course, had questions. Much to Davis's delight, her mom warmly held her hand the entire time they were talking. Then, she wondered how her daughter had found herself in the Palace, and Davis explained to her that she was to be married to President Everett later that day, in a matter of a few hours.

"Well, that's wonderful!" her mother exclaimed. "We'll see each other all the time now!"

"I don't know, Mom. I think they might not want that." Davis didn't want to be deflating, but she didn't want her mom to be disappointed when they inevitably did not see each other after this. It was also hard to think straight, looking at her mom's eyes, holding her hand, and wanting more than anything to feel that love, connection, and support that could only come from a mother and daughter relationship. What made it even harder was that Davis could see it in Ruby's eyes, too; that was also what she wanted and felt.

Ruby was feeling sentimental; that was clear. Her eyes brightened, and she told Davis, "You know, the far too few nights I got to spend with you, in the hospital, I would sing to you every night...'Good night my lady, good night, my lady, I'll see you in the morn.'" Ruby's eyes darkened a bit, and then she added, "But then the morn came when I didn't see you again. Ever again. Until now."

Where Ruby was feeling confused, Davis was feeling saddened and overwhelmed with grief. Tears welled up in her eyes. She felt all the love bubbling up, yet at the same time, she was trying not to burst out with emotion and end up being too loud or saying something she shouldn't. The emotions made themselves present, though, and hot tears started to well up in her eyes.

"Oh! I didn't mean to make you cry. It's okay! We're together now and will be for a long time after, now." Again, Ruby paused, as if she was trying to figure something out, but her gears were rusty and slow. "Oh, my dear. President Everett told me earlier that I was going to move to his country home. It was supposed to happen today. But there was a problem with security, so it'll happen after the wedding. Isn't that something! If it had gone through today, you would have never found me! Oh my, the wedding! I had heard of it, of course, but never realized it was my darling long-lost daughter! At any rate, I didn't know why he decided to send me to the country. I thought I was getting punished for something..." her mom trailed off. "But that's not possible. There must be some mistake. He must not know yet that you are who you are. Why would he separate us?"

Ruby talked fast and nonstop, not really thinking through anything, just rambling onto the next thought that popped into her head. Davis wasn't upset with her, but it made her sad that her mom was so controlled and confused and determined to clear Everett of any wrongdoing.

Davis took yet another deep breath. "I don't know, Mom. Maybe Everett's afraid that we wouldn't like being married to the same man?"

"*President Everett*, dear. We must use proper titles and respect for our leader. And I don't know, maybe. But he's so kind and wonderful, you'll see. I just don't think he knows who you are! We just need to explain, and it'll get worked out." Her mom then stopped talking for a second. Her eyes were getting big with awareness and enlightenment. "You know what this means, though? *He saved us both!* President Everett saved our lives. Both mine and yours." Ruby was so delighted and thrilled at this prospect, but Davis couldn't help but point out an apparent discrepancy.

"Mom, didn't you ever see me at any of the events that I attended? You would have been at them too, although I used the name they gave me at the Children's Center, Davis."

"I don't go to any of them; President Everett always told me my best skills were sitting here, waiting for him to come back, and looking pretty." Ruby seemed pleased at this, while it made Davis cringe. "Besides, because of the mistake made all those years ago, I wouldn't have known to look for you or known you went by the name 'Davis.'" A light dawned behind Ruby's eyes. "That must be President Everett's problem in all this too! He didn't know they changed your name!" Ruby accentuated the last part of her statement as if she solved the entire mystery.

Davis quickly realized that there was nothing she could say or do to persuade her mom that President Everett was not the salt of the earth. She also concluded she should tell her mom her "new" name that Everett had given her, "Delilah," in case it caused her to get in trouble for accidentally calling her either Davis or Amelia.

Seemingly out of nowhere, in a moment of calm, Davis thought maybe a shadow of her mom's old self showed. Ruby looked at her daughter, deeply in the eyes, with love and simply and calmly said, "You are my daughter. My beautiful daughter, so courageous and strong."

"Thank you, mom. You are so strong too. Even when we don't always feel it, we have a whole legion of people in the Heavens we can rely on, right?" When she said this, Davis thought she saw a twinkle of something behind her mom's eyes, as if perhaps she recognized her old self, a recollection of a past fear she had about Everett. She seemed to shake it off, so Davis continued, "Look, mom. I better get back to my bed before someone notices I'm gone. I just wanted to see you as soon as I could. I'm sure I'll see you again soon, and we'll get this worked out. I love you, mom."

"I love you too, oh, my Little Marigold. My Amelia! Sorry, Delilah. It is so good to see you again." Then Ruby embraced her again and kissed her on the cheek. "Don't worry about anything. President Everett will help us. I'm certain." Then she let go and squeezed her hand as she walked away, glancing back once at the same time Davis happened to look back toward Ruby.

~

What Ruby thought was a glance back toward her was actually Davis looking behind and to the left of her mom. Davis did that because she thought she had heard a shuffling sound and saw movement in that direction. But, as her mom waved goodbye and started walking back, she decided it must be her nerves, so she turned back around to leave. Right after her mom had left and closed her door, she reached out to open her doorknob and thought she heard the noise again. Startled, Davis turned back around and tried to make her eyes focus. The blue light was present, but the storage closet was pretty sizeable, with several rows of shelving. It was impossible to see every corner, especially in the dim light. Her heart started to beat quickly, and she wanted to get back to her bed as soon as possible.

No sooner than she moved to the door again, she realized beyond any doubt she heard shuffling. She strained her ears because there seemed to be a very light and delicate humming sound. After a few seconds, she concluded there was humming, and more so, it was to the tune of the song her mom had sung her a few minutes ago. Davis paused for a second, wondering if she should figure out what was going on. Her stomach dropped to the floor when she realized that was precisely what she *shouldn't* do, and Davis started to rush into the exercise room.

A few seconds after she got into the exercise room, she heard the storage closet door open behind her and close again softly. Then the humming started anew, even louder. Undoubtedly, someone was behind her. The humming got louder. She couldn't help but turn around, and now there was enough light to see who it was.

~

Davis had a moment, one of those moments when her eyes knew what would happen before her brain knew. She saw Brookshire step toward her, and then in the glimmer of blue light; she saw the bee venom vial as it fell from Brookshire's hands and drop to the ground, his boot crushing it into the hard floor. "You *really* didn't think you could get away with it, did you?"

Davis's wheels started to turn as she realized: Brookshire had played her, played them all. The plan was falling apart quicker than an intricate embroidery having its strings pulled in the incorrect order. "Brookshire? I don't understand. What is happening?"

"Davis. Let's not be foolish. Did you think you could assassinate the President? I've already alerted him to the fact I think there is a security breach. But I've protected you, for now. I didn't divulge details, and I let you meet your mom. That was a charming reunion, by the way," he added sarcastically. "I've also protected Ringo and Audrey and everybody at the bunker. Even Namaguchi, Duffy, and Hernandez are safe. I don't have time for petty quarrels. But, if you don't do as I wish, I'll turn you all in. Even Josie was foolish enough to explain to me exactly how she snuck into the country and made her way down. All of it! The secret stops, Teeterville, everything!"

"Well, what do you want?"

"What does anyone want? Power, or to take power away. It's the tale for both of us. You want to take power away from Everett. I simply want more power. I don't need to be the top dog, so to speak, but I'm not content being a glorified Security Guard anymore either—"

"How does that fit into anything?"

"Uh uh…rude to interrupt. Weren't you taught *any* manners?" It was as if a dam broke, and he was channeling all the power he had seen used around him, but he had yet to use it himself. It had been out of his grasp until this moment.

Brookshire paused; he was enjoying this moment of power that he so clearly desired. Davis had no idea he was so capable of being so cruel. So deceitful. It seemed so unlike him. Davis felt this person was far away from who she knew as a child and got to know again as an adult. She wondered if Ringo or anybody else had any clue. She doubted they would. Otherwise, they wouldn't have sent her on a fool's errand. She didn't have much time to think. Davis stammered, "I just don't get it. You're nice, and you were always so kind. What happened?"

"Was I? Or did I just fit the perception of what a good mate would be? I am handsome, I must say." Brookshire chuckled after this egocentric comment. "I was nice to you and found you attractive. I couldn't help that you were 'off-limits.' That's one reason I wanted to increase my power. I should have been able to make you mine, but I was unable to."

"Where did you even get your hands on the vial? You went into the room, got into my private things?"

"You should be careful where you leave things, especially when there are ways to get to your things. You should know, I mean, how did you work your way to Ruby's room? So, beware of leaving your things lying around in the future. Anyhow, when you went to the zoo and the other ladies were preparing to get ready for dinner, it was easy to get the venom out of your knapsack. Even if I got caught, well, I'm security, easily dismissed. I'm untouchable, darling."

Davis felt queasy. She found the whole thing unbelievable, but she had no time to think things through or respond before Brookshire continued with his tirade.

"Have you ever heard the saying '*absolute power corrupts absolutely*'?" Davis nodded with hesitation and fear. "Well, what it leaves out is that for that power to corrupt correctly and thoroughly, it also needs absolute cooperation from the helpers of the person in power. Do you follow?" Brookshire did not wait for her to answer before continuing. "Yes, President Everett controls by keeping people in the Pods, having you all dress the same, and of course, the brain control drug in the Marigold Injection. Do you think he can do that all alone? There are plenty of people, like myself, who are immune to the brain control drug, yet, we crave power for ourselves, too. So, we cooperate. There are other people, like Duffy, who have chosen not to cooperate. But their voice is much smaller and quieter. That's why I'd rather just leave them alone but use you to get what I want."

Davis stammered, "I thought you cared for me, the others too. I still don't understand."

"Oh, Davis." He held his hand to his head as if just talking to her was exasperating. "I have absolutely nothing against you or the others. It's more about what is in it for me. So far, I have simply told President Everett I have uncovered some information you may not be as truthful as you seem. That there may be a plot implemented by the group that kidnapped you. If you agree to do as I say, then you, your mom, the bunker, it will all be safe. I'll say you got coerced, that you didn't want to participate in any of this, but they were trying to force you. You came to me for help, which is how I started to uncover the plot. They found out about Ruby being here, and they threatened that they would harm her. As I think of it more, Namaguchi may have to go down. I need an inside man to pin it all on."

Davis could not believe how cavalier Brookshire's attitude was about everything. "Well, what do you want me to do? What is to be my part?"

"Glad you asked. After I clear you, you marry President Everett. Act like the good, obedient wife he expects. You'll have a safe yet possibly mundane life here. But you'll be with your mom, and you'll make friends with the other wives. I guarantee it. You and I can even have a relationship on the side. It may be hard to believe right this second, but I do care for you. I just have my priorities, and becoming more successful trumps my relationship with you. President Everett will promote me to a high position in his cabinet since I not only broke up the plot but saved him and you. It also saves face for him. Because as I said, you participate, this gets minimized. He won't have an idea of how close he came to being killed. I'll probably get Namaguchi's position, come to think of it. But, I digress, back to our relationship. I'm still willing. Why not? Most of the wives have some kind of side thing going on with somebody here."

"You…want…to have a…relationship with *me?*"

"Well, whatever, that's not the important part. So, what do you say, ol' sport? You in or out?"

"Out. Most definitely out," Davis said with displeasure and loathing.

"Okay, you're going to be executed then. I will make sure President Everett knows this plan of yours. I'll keep it secret from everybody else at first so I can arrange for Ringo to 'meet' you. A Security Patrol will then trail us so the bunker can be found and destroyed; everyone there will also face execution. The trail between Canada and here will most certainly be closed. And your mom, Ruby, well, I'll say she was in on it too."

After a few minutes of thought and puzzling out her bleak options, Davis said, "Well, I suppose." Davis stammered as she tried to find the right words. "I mean, you haven't given me a real choice, have you?" The anger was rising in Davis's voice. "I'm under duress. I'm not happy about this. And, I hope you fail, even if it means I go down with you! But, to protect my mom and the others, I guess I'm in."

OCTOBER 9, 2056 –
LATE AFTERNOON

Davis didn't sleep after she got back to her bed. She crawled in and felt sick, then lay there all night trying to figure out how to get out of this predicament.

She got ready for her wedding in silent sorrow and regret. She took a shower, her allotted time, and then ate a few nibbles of her nutrition biscuit and took some small sips of water before the wives went to their exercise class. She thought for a moment that perhaps she could find Namaguchi and talk to him, but when she asked where he was, Cox told her that he was off. Brookshire had planned well.

"Why do you want him?" Cox said as she tightened the corset that would be under Davis's wedding dress.

"I was just wondering; he came to see me in the hospital. I wanted to ask him something about that day. It's not important."

As Cox attended to Davis to get her ready, depression hung on Davis more heavily than her large beaded white gown, the layers of fabric almost swallowing her up. She almost wished they would. She couldn't figure out how this could have gone so wrong, how Brookshire could have fooled everybody. She also couldn't figure out how to solve the problem. As the last step, Cox put very high-heeled high heeled shoes on her feet. Quickly realizing she wouldn't be able to walk in these, she asked Cox to please help her stand up and get the hang of it.

Cox was clearly not pleased to be asked this; she gave a gruff "humph" before extending her arm to help her up. Davis teetered and wobbled as she tried to find her footing. These were far tighter and more pointed than the heels she had the day before. It was almost as if someone was trying to punish her by shoes alone.

It was unfortunate that this was such a dismal day for Davis. Under normal circumstances, she would be fascinated by the beauty of her bridal preparation room. It had spotless white walls with a plush dove gray carpet. She had a beautiful chair covered in a soft pink fabric that she sat in while Cox applied makeup and styled her hair. The windows had thick, luxurious coverings the same color as the carpet. Of course, the curtains had a large golden *E* monogrammed in the middle, but they were still pretty. The beauty continued with an antique white mirror that Davis sat in front of while Cox attended to her. The candle holders, with their fake candles, were the same crane ones she had seen on the Palace stairwell when she first walked through. There was even a little golden capuchin monkey waiting for her when she came into the room. It was President Everett's wedding gift to her. *Too bad it's too small to bash him over the head with,* she thought.

A little bit before the ceremony started, Davis sat in this room on the side of the Palace church. Only Cox was with her, staring at her like she never hated anyone more. Right when she heard the music cue up, there was a soft knock at the door. Cox got up to open it, and Ruby was standing on the other side.

Ruby spoke first, "We are the people, and the people are we. Can I see Delilah for a moment?"

Davis held her breath, never thinking Cox would permit Ruby entrance. Luckily, Cox could not care less about her, the wedding, or anything to do with and of the wives. Davis hadn't realized it when she met Cox, but she must just be another one in the line of cooperators looking for a way to increase her power and position, in any way that she could. Or, for the safety of the secret, Davis presumed only the upper echelons knew that Ruby was Davis's mom. Cox must have assumed there was nothing wrong with letting a current wife talk to a future wife. It was natural to think Ruby would want to welcome Davis into the household and get her excited about her big day and the fantastic future that awaited her. However, even though Cox let Ruby into the room, she stayed put.

Ruby said somewhat harshly, "Alone, perhaps?"

Cox left, saying she would be right outside the door, and not to take long. Davis could tell she was suspicious of something but was trying to hedge her bet she'd do the right thing by granting this favor.

After she left, Ruby spoke quickly, "Dear. I remembered some things last night. Some things that made me uncomfortable. Years ago, when you were born, I trusted my gut. It led you to me after all these years. So, I am trusting my gut again. I don't know what is wrong, but I don't think you can trust Namaguchi."

Davis was surprised that her mom had a feeling something was off but pinpointed it on the wrong person. Davis almost wondered if Brookshire had said something to Ruby about Namaguchi since he planned to make Namaguchi the scapegoat. As if answering, Ruby reluctantly added that Brookshire had come to see her that morning and said that she should keep an eye on Namaguchi because Brookshire feared he was up to something.

Ruby then pulled out an oddly shaped knife, the blade shiny and almost two inches long, with a slight curve to the right at the tip. There were rubies embedded into the short, thin silver handle that curved slightly to the left at its end. "President Everett gave this to me on our wedding night. I doubt you'll need it. Brookshire doesn't know I'm giving you this; I'm sure he'd be appalled. But, in case you need to protect yourself from Namaguchi. If anyone finds it, just say I let you borrow it as a good luck gift for your wedding. As I said, I doubt you'll need it, but just in case, for protection."

Davis thought it was so sweet that her mom was trying to protect her. She was trusting her instincts that her daughter needed help. Perhaps she'd misplaced her help, but it was still kind of her mom to put herself at risk to protect her. Davis had only wished her mom could bring her a bee or two instead of a weird old knife.

Ruby quickly tucked the knife into the wide band on Davis's dress. She whispered, "Luckily, President Everett always likes these elaborate belted skirts, so it will hide well until you can get back to your room and find a place for safekeeping. And, on second thought, if you get caught with this, I could get in trouble; it's my knife..."

"Say no more, mom. I will say I found it and was holding it for safe-keeping until I located the owner. And mom, you know I love you. No matter what the situation, I'd always protect you and keep you safe. That's a promise."

After Ruby got the knife tucked in safely and securely, she gave Davis a quick hug and mentioned she should get going. And as if on cue, right after the hug, Cox annoyingly rapped on the door and called through it, "That's enough, I'm coming in."

Davis felt the knife hidden in the waistband belt. It was an odd belt, broad and made of a thick satin and studded with crystals. It tied into an elaborate bow at the back. The ends that hung down from the bow eventually became wider, then trailed onto the floor, creating a train four feet long. It was a lot of fabric to pull, and she would have never said she wanted more weight. She was happy to see that the knife made her feel lighter.

Cox and Davis sat in the room a while longer. Cox was looking disgruntled; Davis was pondering her fate. After about thirty minutes, the music Davis was supposed to walk down the aisle to began. She knew now that it was only a matter of seconds before she would have to walk down a long aisle and marry Everett.

The moment when Cox pulled her arm to get her up came too quickly. Davis clumsily got to her feet. Cox told her she would not go down the aisle with her, that when she got her to the door, they would open automatically, and she would depart. Then, Davis would be on her own. They walked out of the room, and Cox got her up to the doors. Then, as she mentioned, Cox stepped away, and the doors opened up.

~

Davis took a deep breath and started her walk down the aisle. She felt like she was in a dream and that it wasn't really happening. She walked so slowly to gather her thoughts and put off what was about to happen as long as she could. Even though she was trying to linger, she ignored her surroundings. She was vaguely aware the wives from her shared room were standing at the front, looking at her, and that people were sitting in the pews. More of the crane candleholders were at every other row of pews. There was some kind of showy tulle bow decorations in the blush color. No flowers, as predicted. Davis didn't even hold a bouquet. President Everett was not in the church yet. He would make his grand entrance when Davis was already up at the front; she didn't know what his grand entrance would be but heard they could be elaborate. Amanda had told her he rode in on a white horse with a long-braided tail and mane for their wedding.

It felt to Davis that it took her an hour to get to the front. But she was aware it was probably closer to two or three minutes. She heard a noise above her and looked up to see President Everett, seemingly diving from a ledge in the ceiling but wound up in the same kind of aerial fabric that was pointed out to her in the exercise room. He did some sort of complicated twist and descended in the material as it unfolded. *Please let him break his neck doing this*, thought Davis. But, before she knew it, he was down safely. Unbelievably, his tuxedo wasn't even wrinkled. She realized the other wives hadn't said his entrance would be "elaborate." That was her word. If she remembered correctly, they had said "beautiful" and "amazing."

Davis's knees were shaking. She felt like she could pass out at any moment. She felt the coolness of the hardened steel of the blade pressing against her skin. She felt comforted by it; her mom was right; it gave her a sense of security. It felt as if her mom was hugging her, almost.

After President Everett took his place at the front with Davis, he gave her a sly smirk and escorted her to the stair below where he stood. She was then looking up at him, and he towered over her by about five inches, even though they were close in height and she perched on stilts masquerading as shoes.

The Everettisim priest in his crimson cloak stepped in front of them. He looked at both of them with aged eyes; the only part Davis could see of him under the cloak's hood. His eyes were wrinkled at the edges and had dark bags underneath that gave them a droopy appearance. He then started in a monotonous voice about the solemnness of the occasion. It seemed as if they had designed everything to create a bit of confusion for Davis. Between the incredibly tight and uncomfortable outfit, and the priest, whose face was mostly covered by the cloak hood, slightly resembled Namaguchi. It wasn't him; she was sure. It wasn't as if he were a real doppelganger. However, there was enough of a resemblance to give her pause and make her feel uneasy. Unlike Namaguchi's kind voice, the priest's voice was droning and dull, almost lulling her into a sense of hypnosis. It suddenly occurred to Davis that she really couldn't trust Brookshire. *Of course, she couldn't, why did she ever think she could after what transpired! What was to stop him from still killing her and everyone else once the marriage was over? Why had she believed he'd protect them?* Davis's mind reeled as this fact settled in her mind like a heavy stone thrown into a deep lake.

Davis nearly turned around to look at the other wives, to try and settle her mind and try and get a second to think clearly. She was astonished to see they were all in large ball gowns in the same blush color as the decorative bows. All the dresses had elaborate lace patterns, gems, and dainty bows. The ladies themselves had assorted jewelry on, as before, but these pieces seemed even bigger and more dazzling. Every dress gave the ladies an hourglass shape and pushed up and accentuated the breasts. Davis didn't know why this astonished her. Her dress was similar, although her dress was white, and her gown and jewelry were even more extravagant and elegant. It just dawned on her fully, the absurd notion of these dresses.

The cost and labor involved in making them, but the populace never even saw them. And the wives and the people at the Palace never saw the problem. Or, if they did know the problem, they turned a blind eye to have their own desires met. Davis acknowledged the dresses and jewelry were the least of her problems while simultaneously being symbolic of all the issues. Clearly, the United State wasn't as united as it seemed. There was no same-same for everyone. And the depths to which it went were unfathomable.

"Delilah!" Davis was being called back to reality by Everett, harshly whispering her new name. "Pay attention," and at this instruction, Everett grabbed her elbow and jerked her back to looking at him and the priest.

The priest then went into how Davis was now going to be part of an exclusive group. Not just the wife of President Everett but an *obedient* wife and a servant to President Everett and the people of the United State as well. It was expected Davis would be not only a good wife but a great wife, indulging and eventually anticipating President Everett's every need and desire. "A woman must not simply do, but also want to do, with a grateful heart, all she can to ensure she meets the demands of her husband." He then finished by telling Davis that she must do this to not only preserve her emotional, mental, and spiritual balance but to help maintain the well-being of President Everett and the people of the United State as well.

This obscene diatribe woke up Davis. *Oh, hell no*, she thought. She knew she had to do something and that she had to do it quickly. But she hadn't thought much about the process of what she should do either. And after all, she had never attacked anyone before. Much less with a knife, at her wedding, in front of a church of followers of her intended victim.

~

Davis let the priest drone on a bit more while she tried to figure out what her next step would be. She knew she had to do something, but she just had not figured out the specifics yet. She knew she had to solve it quickly, though.

The priest went into some kind of prayer chant, and Davis should have been closing her eyes. She was glad she didn't, though, because she looked around a little and saw exactly where she was standing compared to Everett. She was suddenly pleased that he had taken place above her on the steps. It put her at the right angle to go for his neck when the time was right.

The priest then went into President Everett's expectations as a husband. The laughable difference floored Davis. "You are more than a President. You are a prominent human, you have the ear of God, and you saved humanity. There shall be no expectations placed on you as a husband because the expectations placed on you by God and humanity have been so high, there should be nothing asked of you from your wife. In reality, you owe nothing to humankind either, yet you selflessly offer more every day. It's even more of a reason for your wives to support you only and expect nothing in return. It should be their great honor to support you and never ponder a personal need they think they might have. You should only supply your wives with food, drink, healthcare, shelter, and clothing like you would do for any human in your charge."

Davis gave off an audible snort of disgust and disbelief. She quickly recognized her mistake when both the priest and Everett glared at her. "Sorry, itchy throat." They then returned the looks of disgust and disbelief she felt.

The priest continued, "Delilah Davis, with this knowledge and full understanding, do you commit yourself legally and spiritually to President Everett, never to fail in being an honorable, kind, honest and obedient wife?"

"No."

"I'm sorry, what did you say?" The priest gruffly said it, but the horror and shock on Everett's face made it obvious he was thinking the same things. Gasps came from the church congregation, and Davis felt like she could sense the collective populace holding their breath. It felt as if the air had got sucked out of the room.

Davis took every bit of strength she could from herself, her mom, and her friends. She tried to steel herself as much as possible and tried to make her body posture as intimidating as she could in layers of white tulle and a corset.

"I said no. And my name is Amelia!" The determination and forcefulness in her voice surprised even her. But it propelled her to her next step, and she pulled the knife from her belt and lunged toward Everett. The screams started to fill her ears as the knife plunged deeply and fiercely into the side of his neck.

Davis felt fulfilled and pleased as life started to drain from Everett's eyes. She was surprised how strange she felt, although she never expected she could kill someone. Her head rang, and there was a warm tingling in her body. She didn't think she was capable of standing anymore, so she sat on the steps. It started to surprise her that there was no blood. Davis began to worry she had missed her mark.

Davis tried to lift her head to assess the situation. Her ears were ringing, and her neck seemed like it had no strength, and she couldn't fully lift her head. She was grateful that she got her head up a little bit because she was genuinely pleased to see the guards coming toward her with guns drawn, thinking maybe if she surrendered, they would take her to the hospital. Something was wrong, beyond her having just committed murder. She felt almost as ill as she did when coming off the mind-control drug.

"Delilah! Are you okay?" Rebecca was kneeling by her side and lightly slapping her face. Duffy was rushing in the side door. "You got a weird look on your face a moment ago and sort of spaced out, like you were in a trance. You started breathing fast and hard, and then you sat down, and it looked like you fainted."

Rebecca helped support her neck as Duffy came up to Davis, asked her if she was okay, took her pulse, and checked her pupils. Cox came in with a cup of water for Davis and put a chilled cloth on her neck.

Davis looked up again at Everett, obviously incensed about the situation. He was fine. Davis saw nothing had transpired, except she had some kind of spell and fainted. There was more confusion than ever swimming in her head. As she sat there, still feeling faint and baffled, Everett said, "Enough. Do you accept your role as my wife?" Duffy tried to interject, saying Davis needed a few minutes, and even Rebecca looked startled at Everett's expeditious attitude. But Everett put up his hand to stop her. "Yes or no, Delilah?"

"Um, yes?"

"Great, I answer the affirm as well. Pronounce us as man and wife."

And then it was finished. Davis had made her vow and sealed her fate. She was Everett's wife.

~

Everett calmly escorted his new wife, Delilah, out of the church before going into the side room she had gotten dressed in. "What was the meaning of that?" Everett screamed at her. "You are acting ridiculous, like a child. Get yourself together. We're going outside to take a few photos in our wedding clothing; then, we'll switch to the jodhpurs for the formal pictures released to the public. Meet me outside in less than ten minutes."

Duffy asked to come in, and Everett granted it, telling her to make sure Delilah was ready for photos quickly and not looking pale and startled like she currently was. Duffy came up to Davis and asked her what had happened. She relayed her story to Duffy about the bee venom and how she thought she had stabbed Everett, but it was just a momentary dream of some sort.

Duffy spoke in calming and soothing words as she held her hand. "It's okay. You probably had a severe panic attack. Sometimes you can hallucinate during those. You've had a lot of stress and anxiety. It's okay, but I need you to pull yourself together. We'll figure out a plan later. It'll be fine. You have to go out there and put yourself together, though; if not, there will be more trouble for you. As you have seen, Everett is not patient or understanding. Take a few slow, deep breaths; have some more water."

"Duffy, I failed. I can't do this. I'm not a murderer. For a moment there, I thought I could do it. I *wanted* to when they said all these horrible things about what would be expected of me as Everett's wife. And, of course, already knowing what he's done and what he's capable of doing. But I can't. I let everyone down, and I'm defeated. I can't..." And Davis started to cry.

"It's okay, don't worry about that now, let's just get through today, and as I said, we'll figure out what to do next. Hope is not lost."

"Ok," said Davis, taking a deep breath. "I'm so confused, though; I knew Everett was evil behind the scenes. But I'm surprised he'd be so cruel to me today, barely knowing me and in front of everyone. Ruby kept telling me how nice he was!"

"He can be, I suppose. You have to remember, everyone in that church is fully dedicated to him. They don't televise the wedding because the public can't see the opulence. They'll just see the pictures of you in more casual clothing. You're a new wife, too. Everett wants to make sure you'll submit and know who is in charge. He asserts his power first; he's drawing a line in the sand right from the start. He'll be a little nicer as time goes on, I think. But he doesn't like being challenged or feeling like he's not in complete control of a situation, so he'll lash out against that. Don't forget, you're also not under the influence of the Marigold Injection, like almost everyone else here. Honestly, though, it's the last thing you should be worried about; let's get you ready to go out there, so this doesn't get worse for you."

Duffy dried the tears Davis was shedding and pat her hand. Cox came in and said they had to get Delilah ready immediately. Cox touched up her makeup and hair while telling her to calm down and pull herself together. "You're already late, Delilah. President Everett gave you ten minutes, and it's nearly been twenty. You can't keep him waiting. Get it together."

Davis said a quiet prayer to herself for strength to carry on. She asked for tenacity, hope, and determination. It propelled her forward, and she got further comfort as she decided Duffy was right. They would figure this out later. Duffy now had the information about Brookshire's double-cross and knew the bee venom was gone. There was always tomorrow to figure out what to do, and since she couldn't murder someone, no matter how much they might deserve it, there was no other choice but to carry on as if life was as orderly as Everett liked it to appear.

Davis walked out, determined to think of herself only as Davis or Amelia, despite them calling her "Delilah" so that she could hold onto a fragment of herself. She was also mad at herself for not having the strength to kill Everett when there had been a chance. Deciding to filter that anger into energy to get through the day, she slipped off her shoes before going outside. Just eliminating the pain helped her feel better and think more clearly. She did not care if Everett mentioned anything about her shoes. Her dress was long enough to cover her feet, and he was so self-centered, she doubted he'd notice anyhow.

As Davis walked outside, the sun made her squint. It seemed hot and harsh, bearing down on her without mercy. Everett came up to her, grabbing her hand and curtly saying, "Hurry up!"

They took a few photos; at some point, Everett noticed Davis was not wearing shoes, and he chastised her for that. She felt at her belt to feel the comfort of the knife. She was distressed to find it must have fallen out in the room. It was gone. Feeling dismayed, she realized it didn't matter anyhow. She didn't have the nerve to murder anyone.

Every photo felt the same. Everett's positioning was either in front of or above Davis. The photographer kept directing her to look at President Everett with "reverence and admiration." At one point, the photographer jubilantly said, "Look at him like all your dreams just came true because, of course, they have!" At the same time, the photographer's instruction to Everett was to "Look like he found a lost, injured puppy."

There were poses with the other wives, all of them lovingly arranged around President Everett, looking at him as a savior. Davis noticed Ruby wasn't in the photos and wasn't present, either. She hoped that Ruby didn't get in trouble for visiting her or that Brookshire hadn't mentioned to Everett that Davis and Ruby figured out their relationship. She hoped Everett had skirted Ruby safely away someplace, and that's all that it was.

Everett told Davis the photos would be quick, but they continued on and on, so she was more than pleased she took those shoes off. The photoshoot seemed to be more about stroking President Everett's ego and displaying as much admiration for him as possible. He relished his time, which was funny to Davis as he was always in the spotlight. She couldn't believe how ridiculous the whole thing was. Everyone else acted as if it were normal, though.

Finally, after about an hour, Everett pulled her arm to get her attention and said they would go up to an overlook above the garden for a few last photos before changing their clothing. He nearly pulled her up the stairs, making her trip and stub her toe on the way up.

Davis tried to find some humanity in Everett. "Please slow down. I'm hurt."

"You decided to take your shoes off. Deal with the consequences." He then calmed the tone of his voice and softened his face. "Look, Delilah, I can be a very nice and accommodating husband. I *want* to be. But I'm running a country and a household of wives here. I need you always to pay attention and keep up with me. I need complete cooperation and submission. When I ask you to be out of your room in ten minutes, I want to see your pretty face ready in eight."

When they got to the top of the stairs, Davis felt conquered, so she apologized for the trouble she caused and asked for a second to compose herself. Everett smugly told her, "That's what I like to hear," before propping himself up and sitting on the edge of the overlook's thick marble wall, looking inward toward Davis. The look on his face and the tone of his voice reached the epitome of vainglorious behavior. "Hey, Delilah, I have a great idea," a smirk spread across his face, which Davis realized was not as handsome as she once thought. "Get on your knees and look up at me adoringly." There was a light chuckle before he said, "Get used to being on your knees for me."

Davis fumed. She felt tired and overwhelmed, and so over the nonsense. Her dress and corset were hot and uncomfortable. It throbbed where she had stubbed her toe, and she was sure she was bleeding. It infuriated her Everett most likely talked to her mom in this rude, disgusting way, as well as all the other wives.

Davis walked over and put her hands on the marble wall encircling the small but beautiful balcony. The creamy pink color and the shape of the balcony made her think of an open clamshell. As she took in the garden's green shrubs and the beautiful stone tiled labyrinth beneath her, she started feeling unbelievable anger. For the first time in a long time, and the first time ever that it had nothing to do with her dream, she clenched her fists so hard her nails caused bloody crescents in her palms. All at once, she felt like she was a volcano bubbling over and Venus in Botticelli's painting. Davis was emerging into the open, newly born but fully grown. Standing in her perfect shell, she finally felt something settling in her mind, a round drop of clarity, pure and perfect as a pearl amid the grains of sand that coated her mind. But she had made a vow to Everett. She had to remind herself, though, that a vow was nothing more than a promise. And she had also made a vow to herself, to Ringo and Quinn, everybody at the bunker. And her mom, her mom, most of all.

Davis was finished getting pushed, so she pushed back. Literally. Everything happened so quickly; she didn't even realize what she'd done yet. From the look on Everett's face as he fell, he didn't understand what happened either. All Davis knew was that when she looked over the edge, there was a large pool of blood under his head, his face frozen in shock. And there was the horrified look on the faces of everyone below who witnessed what she'd done. There was that, too.

OCTOBER 10-22, 2056 - DAVIS

Brookshire roughly escorted Davis to a cell in the basement of the Palace. "You foolish, foolish girl," he sneered as he threw her in.

It was cold and damp and had none of the color and luxury the rest of the Palace had. Not that she expected that, but the cold hard gray stones that lined the walls, floor, and ceiling made the comparison between the two all the more depressing.

Nobody came to talk to her, and there was no way to keep track of the time. Davis had been in the cell a while when she found little pebbles in a crack between stones. But she didn't know how long she had been in there when she'd discovered the rocks, and as there was no view of the sun or moon, she had no real way to know how much time had passed. Davis tried to base it off the one nutrition biscuit she received a day, shoved through a small slot in the door by an unseen guard.

After Davis had moved two pebbles into the pile, guessing she had been there between three and four days, she realized she didn't even know if Everett had survived the attack or not. She knew nothing, and it put her into the depths of sorrow to grasp he might have been recovering nicely in the hospital, probably being tended to nonstop by her friends Duffy and Hernandez. *Of course, he would have the best medical care!* The flipside of the coin was, though, she could be a murderess. Although it was spontaneous, even the fact she attempted to kill someone was disgusting to her. No matter how she sliced it, it was an unsavory, regrettable thing to have in her soul. This was the mantra she beat herself over the head with, feeling defeated. *Would she have felt that way if she'd poisoned Everett?* she asked herself. She pondered over the fact that while poisoning was cleaner and less obvious than shoving someone off a balcony, it didn't matter at the end of the day; she had murdered, and she had to find a way to live with her sin. The price she was paying now in this cell felt like a small penance for her actions.

At one point, Davis felt foolish for another reason. She could not believe she had not thought it before, but how did she know she could trust Ringo, Namaguchi, et al.? What proof did she have that they were honest? How did Davis know they were not just in a power grab for themselves? Even if they were honorable, they never disclosed to her what the plan was for after Everett fell. *Did they even have a plan? Were their motives any better than Brookshire's?* She thought with shock. Even if they had a great idea, Brookshire, the turncoat, was still well, good, and off scot-free, as far as Davis knew.

After four pebbles, she stopped eating the one nutrition biscuit she was being given. She felt dirty and disgusting; her hair was oily and in mattes. She had not been allowed to shower and was even still in her wedding dress. Davis always felt cold and dirty; her hurt toe had not been tended to. She had torn off a few layers of the skirt and used the crinoline to make a bed and pillow of some sort, as the cell was without one.

There was a tear in her dress sleeve. Davis hadn't realized it at the time, but Everett must have pulled at the lace overlay as he went over, ripping the fabric. It bothered her emotionally, this reminder of her sin, of her ferocious attack. A jagged chasm between cloth and skin; she looked at it daily, and it settled into her soul. She had been able to clean her hands, arms, and face a little bit; her cell had a small bubbling fountain, intended to be both her shower and her drinking water. It tasted vile, though, and she only used it to drink when she felt parched and to clean what she could on her face and body.

When the fifth pebble got moved to the pile, Davis started to think of how she could kill herself. She could simply stop eating or drinking water. But she didn't know if she had the strength to do that. As thirst and hunger plagued her, she greedily ate without thought when her one meal a day arrived. The "bathroom" they provided her was simply a deep hole in the ground. It looked endless; Davis dropped a pebble to see if she could hear it fall, and she could not. Although it would be unpleasant to plunge herself down it, she imagined it would be quick; as soon as she hit bottom, that should be it. She felt like the opening was on the narrow side, though, and while the corset and bodice still pinched her waist, she didn't want to get stuck in the hole halfway down.

The cell didn't even have the benefit of blue light. It was dark and dimly lit with a few old broken crane candlesticks and electric candles, some no longer emitting light. Davis thought at one time those candle-holders were so beautiful; now they just looked like the twisted, broken mess that she felt like her life had become.

Davis was just about to put the sixth pebble in the pile when she was startled by the door opening suddenly. In walked her mom, Ruby.

~

"Oh, my dear…what did you do? What did you do?" Her mom rushed toward her. Thankfully, her mom had brought a bucket with water and a cloth. Ruby started cleaning Davis's face and hands, dunking the fabric until both the water and cloth were filthy, and there was no more progress to be accomplished. It hadn't made much of a difference, but her mom helped her, which made her feel better. Her mom brought a pair of jodhpurs and a tunic she could change into, and after Ruby loosened the back of the dress and the corset, that was what Davis did. She noticed they were not the fancy jodhpurs and tunic the presidential wives wore and that Ruby herself was now wearing. But they were clean, and she was grateful.

And so far, she didn't have a stunning record of being Everett's wife, so it made sense. Her mom had also brought her socks for her feet.

"I don't know, mom. I'm sorry. I never meant to do something so drastic or put you in this position. I don't want you to be implicated in this crime because you came to see me. Why did they allow you to see me?"

"I'm friendly with the jailer. He doesn't usually have anybody around, so he comes around and talks to all the ladies, but Amelia—" This startled Davis that this was the name her mom used, and she interrupted.

"Is he dead?"

Ruby paused, and a look of sadness washed over her face. "Yes, he died from his injuries," her mother said morosely. "Amelia, there is talk. Duffy and Namaguchi came in and said that President Everett was *brainwashing* us. With the Marigold Injection! I just don't know; it seems so absurd. They... Is it even possible? I don't think so. I've felt pretty ill for a few days; they're not giving the Marigold Injection anymore. And I was due the day after the wedding."

"Do you feel better now?"

"A little, but not much. It's not just me, though. Many people are sick."

"Has anyone died?"

"No, nobody besides President Everett."

"So, mom, I think it's true what Namaguchi and Duffy are saying. I don't have all the answers, but the government told me *you died* as I was growing up. And, you were told I died. I don't think Everett has been truthful." Davis then relayed all the information she had learned at the bunker. When she finished, she asked Ruby if she knew if she would be leaving jail or if she would be executed.

"Namaguchi is working on it. It seems as if he'll become the president. But you *did* assassinate the last president. It might be tricky."

"Can you send Namaguchi to see me? Please, I need to tell him something important."

"I'll try, but nobody is supposed to see you right now. The jailer will be kinder to you now, though, as he knows who you are. Can you tell me, in case I can't get Namaguchi down here?"

"Just tell him Brookshire was the one who destroyed our first plan, that any trust in him is misplaced."

"Oh dear…if what you say is true, we might have trouble. Namaguchi is proposing that Brookshire should be his second-in-command."

"Tell him, mom, please…tell him."

Before Ruby walked out, she hugged Amelia and left with the promise she would speak to Namaguchi.

The jailer came in soon after with an additional biscuit, clean glasses and a pitcher of drinking water, and a clean wash bucket and cloth.

~

Amelia did not have to wait much longer. She only moved three more pebbles into the pile when Namaguchi came to see her. He spoke first, "Davis, I'm sorry you were kept here, like this. I was trying my best to get you out. But, many of the officials were fighting for your execution. Now that everybody is pretty much off the brain control drug, and Ringo and his family, as well as everybody in the bunkers, have come out and started telling their stories, people are starting to see the truth."

"Did Ruby and Duffy tell you about Brookshire?" Amelia asked nervously.

"Yes, they did, I never imagined…" Namaguchi was nervous and sad. "I would have never put you in the position if I thought, for a minute, he was capable of what he did." Davis noticed a glistening in Namaguchi's eyes, and while she was too tired to appreciate it fully, she felt a stirring in her heart. "By the way, the reason I didn't come to see you earlier was that I was negotiating your release. It was part of the terms I couldn't see you until everything became finalized."

"It's okay, I understand."

"Everybody had to be off the brain control drug, too."

"Of course, I can sympathize with the detox; it doesn't put you in any position to make decisions."

"Look, also as part of the negotiation, we didn't have any proof of what Brookshire did. And he still has some supporters on the newly formed board. And while I didn't want him to be vice president, some of the new officials pushed it. And, well, I was trying to negotiate to get you out. So, I supported that position in the end."

"So, will he be…?"

"Yes, I had to give in to get you out. But we have an eye on him now, we know him, and I'll only have a short interim trial presidency and vice presidency. After a few months, when things are more sorted, we'll have a real election. If I run, he most certainly will not be my vice president selection. If I don't run, because I'm not sure at my age if I want this responsibility, I will not endorse him."

"What about everybody else?"

"It's tricky. We have to regain the trust of everyone. Being off the brain control will help, but it will take time and patience. We're trying to make the transition as easy as possible. Pods will remain open for a while until people decide where they want to live, what career they may want—time to reunite with family and friends. Also, private housing needs to have services restored so people can start moving back into their previous homes if they want. All the staff and wives in the Palace will be living here until we get the specifics worked out. Everett had many, many children too; some are adults now, and it needs to get sorted out. Nobody will be punished for the crimes of their father. Especially given the control he had."

"Ok. And not to be selfish, but what will happen to me?"

"That's the best part, Davis. After what you and Ruby went through, you'll be special advisors on a new board that we're setting up. You are welcome to stay at the Palace, too. And full transparency, it doesn't escape us that it is good publicity to have your mom and yourself on the board. But, because of what happened to you two, we're genuinely interested in your story and ideas, too, Davis."

"Thank you, Namaguchi, *thank you!* I don't even really know how to express my gratitude. Can we get out of here now, though?"

"Yes, Davis. With pleasure, and I'll escort you to the shower. You can clean up, and then, well, you're free."

"Just one more thing, Namaguchi."

"Yes?"

"My name is Amelia," she said with a smile and a glint in her eye.

OCTOBER 22, 2056 - BROOKSHIRE

Brookshire sat at his security desk, straightening up and packing a small box of his items. There was not much but a few things. The picture of President Everett and himself he'd toss out, *no reason to keep that,* he thought. He opened the box that came back with him from quarantine; on top was a picture of stick figures dancing. He crumbled it up and threw it in the trash bin. There was no reason to keep that; there was no time to be sentimental even if he wanted to be; the vice president's office was waiting for him.

As he packed, he kept an eye on a closed-circuit security television where he watched Davis and Namaguchi in the prison cell. *She played right into my hands!* he thought. True, he hadn't been sure she'd have enough grit to murder Everett, but when he convinced Ruby to give her the knife, he thought he'd made it simple enough. It surprised him a little that it didn't play out as he had imagined, but it didn't matter to him; Everett was dead, and his hands were clean. That was the goal. He smiled to himself at how easy it had been to convince Davis he was interested in having a relationship with her. He *would* have; maybe that's why the part was so easy to play. But that's not what the ultimate goal was. He hadn't disclosed that he wanted to be president in the gymnasium because it wouldn't have served him. But, of course, he wanted to be president, and now the pathway was clear. *Just to kill that old goat, Namaguchi, now,* Brookshire thought, feeling very proud of how his plan came together. *It all came together beautifully!*

He turned off the security screen and turned toward his computer. Taking one last look at his email, he noticed the screen glitched a little bit. He slapped the side of it and decided he didn't care if it broke or not; it wasn't his problem anymore. Brookshire resolved he would have someone come and get his property box tomorrow for him. *I needn't carry boxes anymore*, he thought.

As Brookshire walked outside, he took a moment before departing to stretch his back and congratulate himself one more time. He looked up at the full moon, pale behind gauzy clouds and hanging large and heavy in the sky. He thought it looked like a big white plum, ripe for his picking.

The gears turned slowly in Brookshire's head as if they were rusty and covered in a thick sludge. Finally, he realized, *Ringo! The computer glitch! He's hacking into my computer!* Brookshire rushed back into his office and sat at his desk. He checked over his emails and saw in the sent files emails delivered to all the newly formed senate and congress members and the newspaper created to inform the public. The email was seemingly from him. Opening the email on top, he saw it was a confession—*his confession*—to organizing President Everett's assassination and plans to assassinate Namaguchi and Davis next. His confession cited his immense guilt and refusal of the vice presidency. The letter was on Brookshire's letterhead and had his signature at the bottom. He was not sure how Ringo had created the forgery, but it looked perfect. While it might not be enough to put him in prison, it would be enough to ruin his immediate political aspirations and soil his name.

As the Security Patrols came in to arrest Brookshire, he realized sitting at the computer was the last thing he'd want to get caught doing right now. If he wanted to deny he sent the emails, sitting there would not assist his plea of innocence. But it was too late; he realized that. Then his face went as pale as the gauzy moonlight.

OCTOBER 22, 2056 - AMELIA

After her shower, Amelia put on clean clothing. It was still the jodhpurs and tunic, but she was okay with that. Mostly because afterward, she walked out of the Palace and felt the sun warm her face. Her mom was there, waiting to take her in a tight, long embrace. To her, the hug felt warmer than the sun that had just comforted her. Smiling, Amelia knew she now had time to get to know Ruby. *Who knew what the future would bring?* But the important thing was she would get to know her mother. She ached with a deep longing to love and protect her mom but also just to be Ruby's daughter. Loved. Looked after. Adored. Mothered.

EPILOGUE

"What about you, Quinn?" asked Ana as they were cleaning out the bunker and getting ready to move back into the row of suburban houses that had already been cleaned and had power and water supplied. "You never really got a chance to meet anyone; Namaguchi took you when you were just fifteen. Have you ever thought of getting married and having children?"

Quinn reflected and paused a few moments before answering. She realized it was the first time anyone had ever asked her what she felt about that. "I don't know if I want children, honestly." Quinn paused a moment to catch Ana's reaction to this. She noticed Ana silently rub her stomach, which was just starting to swell with her third child. "I mean, I like children, and I know it would be good to repopulate the world with honest and good people. But I just don't know if I would make a good mother."

Ana reached over and put her hand on top of Quinn's. Quinn couldn't help but feel the warmth that instantly comforted her and put butterflies in her stomach. Ana spoke slowly and with a determined look on her face. "You," she said very sincerely, "would be a great mother. I can't believe how different my life would be if you had not been here with me. You help me with my kids, plus your friendship is invaluable to me." Ana stopped talking and looked down and over at their hands. There was an uncomfortable pause, and Quinn started to fidget. As she did, she pulled her hand away.

All Quinn managed to say was "Well..." before her mind ran out of things to say. Ana replaced her hand over Quinn's more firmly so she couldn't pull it away. Very quietly, almost in a whisper, Ana said, "Your love too. That has been more than invaluable to me." Quinn felt her cheeks get red.

"I want you to know," said Ana, "that I talked to Namaguchi. Between Ringo and his research, they found your family. The government relocated them to the east coast after Namaguchi took you."

Ana paused for Quinn to process the information. "They're on cross-country transport to come here, and they will be here in a few days. They have detoxed and know what happened to you and why. Your sister is married, and you have a nephew." Ana paused again, not entirely sure how to proceed, but it was clear she was happy for Quinn. "I know this is a lot to process, but I am here for you, and I will be with you when they get here if you want."

"I would like that," Quinn barely mumbled out. She put her head down in the hopes that Ana couldn't see she was blushing deeply. "I only know one other thing I want, but I don't think I can have it," Quinn said, thinking her heart was about to jump out of her chest as the pounding reached her ears.

Ana interjected, feeling protective of her dear Quinn. "That's the other thing I wanted to talk to you about, something I also discussed with Namaguchi," Ana said delicately. "He knows how close we are, and he also knows times are changing. Multiple wives may not be allowed anymore, and even if they keep it in place, he has other wives that he is fond of and loves. He did say I was his *favorite*, but because of that, he only wishes me—us—to be happy. He'll, of course, always be a friend and part of our children's lives, but he knows I don't love him as I should. I'm fond of him; he's been good to me, but it's not right. I'm so much younger than him too. And I don't know how else to tell you this, but I love you. I have loved you since I first met you. I think I know you love Cricket, but—"

"NO! I do not love Cricket. I mean, she's nice, a friend and pretty, but you, well, you're *YOU*. You're beautiful and amazing, and…"—very softly, almost inaudibly—"I love you too." Quinn then did the only thing she could think of, which was to pull Ana into an embrace and kiss her with warm love and tenderness. After the kiss, Quinn rested her head down on Ana's shoulder and nuzzled into her soft hair. She inhaled the scent and let it out with a deep sigh. It could be magic or destiny, Quinn wasn't sure why sometimes two people just click, but Ana and herself, she knew it was pure kismet.

#End#

THANK YOU AND ACKNOWLEDGMENTS

First, thank you to all the readers out there. I appreciate those who decided to buy and read my book, and I hope you enjoyed it. Your support is vital to me, and I encourage your feedback and constructive criticism. You can reach me via email at hmmwriting@gmail.com.

Thank you to my husband, Todd, for all the rough drafts you read, all the editing you helped me with, and the ideas you contributed to this book. Thank you also for your support and encouragement as I endeavored to write this.

Thank you to my family and friends! To my dad (who said to me one day when I announced I was writing a book, "I always wondered why you never wrote a book"), my mom, sister, niece, nephew, brother, and my families in Oregon (Crazy Cousin Crew), New York, Utah, Arizona, Florida, Alaska, and Canada. I especially want to send a "thank you" to Heaven. My grandparents were amazing and wonderful people who encouraged me to write, and they read everything I sent them. They are missed every day and never forgotten.

Thank you to my girl crew, who I love. Thank you for laughing with me, crying with me, and enhancing my life as my un-biological sisters (This is in order of how long I've known you, not reflective of my love for you)! Tamara, Audrey, Lisa, Rebecca, Chris, Jessica, Amanda, Sunshine, and Tiffany. And my best guy friends, I didn't forget about you (How could I?) Mikey-pants and Matt.

Thank you to the Capotosta's – a special family that has always treated me as one of their own.

Thank you to Mary, who I first told I wanted to write a book based on a dream I had. She gave me a ton of support and information, even when my original idea didn't come to fruition, and I completely changed the book (the book we initially talked about is coming next)!

Thank you to my fellow bus drivers and the students who have ridden with me. You inspire and support me every day.

Thank you to Mr. Stover, who first introduced me to the world of Creative Writing. Thank you to the teachers who put up with me in my morose years, and for those who didn't put up with me, I can't say I entirely blame you!

Thank you to Dr. Sun, Dr. Wheaton, Dr. Babbit, Dr. Jacobs, Luminous Glow Skincare, The Hair Shack, Caroline Jordan Fitness, and Up to the Beat Fitness by Gina B. Thank you for keeping healthy and well.

Thank you to all my early readers, Todd, Vicki, Tamara, and Tiffany. The feedback, edits, help, and advice were invaluable.

I will not thank those who bullied me because there is never a reason for a child to feel tortured every day at school. But I will tell all those who are suffering through being bullied; those people do not define you; they do not have control of you or what you are capable of achieving. And you are capable of achieving so much. You will overcome it. Ryan, you were the one popular kids who didn't torment me. I never said thank you for that, but I do now.

Thank you to BookBaby, Frank, and the BookBaby editors.

There is a multitude of people who helped and supported me through this book. I'm grateful for every one of you, and any omission is due only to my mistake and not a reflection of my appreciation for you.

Last, but importantly, thank you to God. The day I was in despair, and I asked you what I should do, clearly, in my head, I heard, "Write." That was the start of this and the others to come.